Things We Left Unsaid

ZOYA PIRZAD

Translated by Franklin Lewis

ONEWORLD

Oneworld Fiction

First published in English by Oneworld Publications 2012
This edition published by Oneworld Publications in 2013

First published by Nashr-e-Markaz as
Čerâġ-hâ râ man xâmush mi-konam, 2002

English translation rights arranged through
agreement with Zulma, France

ISBN 978-1-85168-967-5
ebook ISBN 978-1-78074-084-3

Printed in Great Britain by CPI Group (UK) Ltd, Croydon, CR0 4YY

Oneworld Publications
10 Bloomsbury Street
London W C1B 3SR
England

Stay up to date with the latest books,
special offers, and exclusive content from
Oneworld with our monthly newsletter

Sign up on our website
www.oneworld-publications.com

Things We Left Unsaid

1

The sound of the school bus braking...the squeaking of the metal gate swinging open...the footsteps running up the narrow path across the front yard. I did not need to look at the kitchen clock. It was 4:15 p.m.

As the front door opened, I wiped my hands on my apron and called out, 'School uniforms, off; hands and faces, washed! And we don't dump our satchels in the middle of the hallway.' I slid the tissue box to the middle of the table and turned around to get the milk from the fridge, which is when I saw that there were four people standing in the kitchen doorway.

'Hello,' I said. 'You didn't tell me we have a guest. Go get changed out of your uniforms, and when you get back I'll have a snack ready for your friend.' I thanked my lucky stars they had only brought one guest home and looked at the girl standing between Armineh and Arsineh, shifting from one foot to the other. She was taller than the twins, but sandwiched between their chubby pink and white faces, she seemed pale and thin. Armen was standing a few steps behind them, chewing gum, and looking at the girl's blond locks. His white shirt had come untucked, and the three top buttons were undone. He must have got into a scuffle with someone, as usual. I set out a fourth glass and plate on the table, thinking, I hope I won't get summoned to the school again.

Armineh stood on tiptoes and placed her hand on the girl's shoulder. 'We met Emily on the bus.'

Arsineh stroked Emily's hair. 'They just moved to G-4.'

I took another roll out of the breadbox. How could I have missed the move-in? G-4 was the house across the street, just opposite us.

Armineh broke my train of thought. 'They moved in yesterday.'

Arsineh continued, 'While we were at the Club.'

Both of them twirled around to the girl. Armineh's pocket was torn at the corner for the umpteenth time. 'Sophie used to live in G-4.'

Without even looking, I knew the seam of Arsineh's pocket was torn, too. 'Sophie's mother is Auntie Nina.'

Armineh's white collar strings were untied. 'Uncle Garnik, Sophie's dad…'

Arsineh also undid her collar strings. 'Gosh, he's funny! Isn't he, Armineh?'

Armineh nodded quickly. 'He makes us crack up so much, we almost die laughing.'

I undid both of their collars and eyed the new girl, whose attention was not wholly focused on the twins. She stood, hands clasped behind her, looking furtively all around. Her lips were flushed pink, as though she had lipstick on. I split the fourth roll in half and said, 'Wash your hands…AND faces.'

When they left the room, my pessimistic streak began gnawing away at me as usual. What was the girl staring at so intently? Had she spotted any dirt? Maybe she thought the kitchen old-fashioned or cluttered? My optimistic streak came to my defense: Your kitchen may be a bit cramped, but it is never dirty. Anyway, who cares what somebody's little girl thinks? I spread some cheese over the butter and put the sandwich on the fourth plate.

I looked around the kitchen, at the dried flowers, the clay jugs on top of the cupboards, the strings of red chili peppers and garlic hanging on the wall. My optimistic streak was comforting: other women may not decorate their kitchens this way, but it looks beautiful to you. So even if your mother and sister laugh, or your friends and acquaintances make remarks about how Clarice's kitchen reminds them of the witch's hut in *Hansel and Gretel*, you shouldn't change your taste to accommodate theirs. You shouldn't let what people say offend you, and you shouldn't... The flower box on the window ledge caught my eye. I should have changed the soil.

Armen came back to the kitchen before the girls, hands and face all washed. He had wet his hair and combed it back at the sides, leaving the bangs hanging down into his eyes. He was wearing his favorite black shirt, sporting a picture of a huge bighorn ram's head. Maybe the daily nagging was having an effect little by little, and my fifteen-year-old son was finally learning to keep clean and neat. I wished my mother were there to see it.

I poured some milk in to a glass. 'I wish Nana were here to see it.'

3

He picked up the glass. 'See what?'

I sat down across the table and gazed at him, chin propped in my hand. 'That her grandson doesn't only comb his hair and put on clean clothes for the Club or for a party. That he listens now, and keeps himself clean and neat even around the house.' I reached out to caress his cheek, but he yanked his head back.

'Don't! You'll mess up my hair.' My hand hung in the air for a second. I picked up the salt shaker, though I had no need for it.

Arsineh and Armineh were holding Emily's hands, leading her into the kitchen. 'Come along. Don't be shy. Come!'

Emily looked at me, her big eyes like shiny black marbles. I smiled at her. 'Come on in, Emily.' Armen got up from the table and pulled out a chair for her. I was dumbfounded – this was not one of the items on my list of daily reminders for him.

Armineh and Arsineh fired off their usual alternating barrage of words:

'Emily has come to Abadan with her grandmother and father.'

'I wish we had straight hair, just like Emily's.'

'Emily is three years older than us.'

'Emily used to go to school in Masjed-Soleiman.'

'She's been to school in London, too.'

'She's been to school in Caklutta, too.'

Armen broke out laughing. 'Not Caklutta, you dimwit. Calcutta.'

The twins tuned him out. 'Mom, see how white Emily's hands are!?'

'Just like Rapunzel's.'

Armen, who was surreptitiously eyeing Emily, burst out laughing again. This time the twins bristled. Before they began bickering, I broke in to explain: 'Rapunzel is Arsineh's doll.'

Armineh said, 'We already told her on the bus.' She downed the last of her milk and held the empty glass out to me.

Arsineh took a bite out of her sandwich and said, mouth full, 'That's why she came over...'

Armineh continued '...to see Rapunzel for just a sec and run back home. Milk, please.'

I poured some milk for Armineh and told Arsineh, 'We don't talk with our mouths full.'

Armineh took a sip of milk. 'Otherwise, Emily doesn't have permission to go over to anybody's house.'

Arsineh said, 'Her grandmother will scold...'

Together they shouted, 'Oh no!' And they stared at Emily. Armineh had a milk moustache.

I pulled a Kleenex from the tissue box and gave it to Armineh. 'Around the lips.' Then I turned to the girl. 'Did you tell your grandmother that—' Just then the doorbell rang.

Emily jumped up. I had made it to the middle of the hallway when it rang a second time. I stepped over the satchels dumped on the hall floor and opened the door. I did not see anyone in front of me at eye-level and had to lower my gaze a long way down before I saw her. She was short. Very short. About up to my elbow. She had on a kind of flower-patterned smock and a knitted black shawl, which she had tied around her waist. She wore a pearl necklace, three strands wide. A frog croaked in the grass and the short woman practically yelled, 'Is Emily here?'

I was agitated. 'These kids! They never do what you tell them.'

She clutched at her necklace. 'She's not here?'

She turned around to go, so I blurted out, 'She is here! I've only just found out that she came without telling anyone. You must have been worried.'

She let go of the necklace and closed her eyes. 'Thoughtless child!'

'I know exactly how you feel. If it were me, I would have been worried, too. Do come in.'

She opened her eyes and looked up, as if she had only just noticed me. She stared at my face and then quickly smoothed her hair, which was tied in a bun at the back. 'Forgive me. That brainless child made me forget myself.' Her hair was all white. She stretched out her hand, 'I am Elmira Simonian. Emily's grandmother.'

The unseen frog croaked again, and this time it was answered by a louder croak from another frog. I was flustered. Maybe it was because of her short stature, or the pearl necklace at four in the afternoon, or her woolen shawl in this heat, or her very formal manner. Or maybe it was those damned frogs; despite living so many years in Abadan, I had never gotten used to the sight and sound of them. I wiped my hand on my apron and offered it to her. 'I am Clarice… Ayvazian.' And why did I find myself mimicking the tiny creature in front of me?

She squeezed my hand so hard, my wedding ring dug into my fingers. She squinted at me. 'The Ayvazians from Julfa?' The wrinkles around her eyes were symmetrical in size and shape, as if someone had meticulously etched them in. I could hear my mother's voice in my ear: 'Why don't you wear your wedding band on your left hand, like every other woman?'

I explained that Ayvazian was my husband's surname. 'The Ayvazians of Tabriz. My mother was born in Isfahan. Arshalus Voskanian. Do you know her?' My sister would have sneered, 'But then how would people know that Miss Clarice is not like every other woman?'

She smoothed her hair again. 'If I knew her family nickname I might recognize her. It's been a long time since I was in Julfa.'

I hemmed and hawed. The nicknames the Armenians of the Julfa district in Isfahan gave one another were not chosen with a particular eye for kindness. They used to call my mother's grandfather 'Missak the Blabbermouth,' which I, of course, had no particular desire for everyone to know. Fortunately my tiny new neighbor did not seem to expect a reply. She shifted from one foot to the other. 'Could you call Emily, please? I have a lot to do.'

I stepped aside. 'Do please come in. She's having an after-school snack with the children.'

She clutched at her necklace again. 'Snack?'

There was no croaking of the frogs now, but I was still flustered. 'Cheese sandwiches with milk.' Why was I explaining this?

She lowered her gaze to the little cross around my neck and stared. 'She doesn't like cheese. And she absolutely has to have her milk warmed up. With two teaspoons of honey.' She was yelling again.

It felt as though I had administered the wrong medicine to a patient. Before I could say another word, she barged in, hopped three times over the scattered satchels, and found the kitchen. I kicked the satchels aside and followed.

Emily was pressed up against the wall. The pressure of her slim body was tearing the etching of Sayat Nova, whose silhouette was facing Emily. It crossed my mind that the beloved 'Gozal' whom Sayat Nova addressed in his poems must have looked very much like Emily.

This time the grandmother really did shout. 'If I had not seen you come in here from our window, I suppose I would have had to search for you all over town?'

The twins stared at her, open-mouthed. From the look on Armen's face as he watched this short woman, I was convinced he was about to burst out laughing any second. In order both to distract him and to steer the conversation in another direction, I asked, 'Emily, why didn't you tell me you don't like cheese and cold milk?' All eyes turned to her empty plate and glass. Mortified, I looked at the grandmother. 'When kids get together, you know...'

Paying no attention to me, she turned to Emily and roared, 'Get going!' The girl scampered out of the kitchen like a rabbit on the run.

I closed the front door and watched them through the lace curtain of the window panel. At the end of the front path, near the spot where we had planted the larkspurs, the grandmother raised her hand and gave the granddaughter a hard smack on the back of the neck. I straightened out the pleats of the lace curtain and headed back down the hallway, hoping the children had not been at the kitchen window to see the beating their friend had just received.

Armineh was standing on the chair in the kitchen, her stomach thrust forward. Facing Arsineh, she shouted, 'Get going!' The three of them cracked up. I tried hard not to laugh, but could not help myself. Armineh was almost as tall as Mrs. Simonian and had a brilliant knack for mimicking people.

2

The twins' bedroom had its old familiar smell. A sweet smell, the kind of smell that could lull a person to sleep. Artoush called it 'the rice pudding smell.' Armen's room had lost that smell long ago.

I found Armineh's teddy bear, Ishy – God only knows how it got that name – under the piano lid and placed him in her arms. She would not go to sleep at night without Ishy cradled in her arms, but every other night, Ishy would mysteriously disappear. I straightened out the long, thin arms and legs of Rapunzel the Blond, a doll named after the heroine in *The Little Blond Princess*, and handed her to Arsineh. On my way to close the curtains, my foot knocked into something on the rug. I bent over and picked up a wooden yo-yo. I told the twins, both of them chanting 'Story, story!', that I was too tired and not up to telling them one. To make up for it, I told them that in the morning they could pick flowers from the garden for Miss Manya, their favorite teacher – so long as they promised not to trample over all the other flowers in the process.

I put the yo-yo in the toy chest, drew the curtains, kissed the twins, said good night and went to Armen's room. He was in bed, reading a magazine. I picked his navy blue trousers and white school shirt off the floor and hung them up in the wardrobe. I went over to tidy up his writing desk, making him frown. I sat on the edge of his bed and looked at the large color poster of Alain Delon and Romy Schneider that he had thumbtacked to the wall. Written in thick Persian calligraphy at the bottom of the picture was:

Betrothed for Eternity
A Norouz gift from *Tehran Illustrated*

Romy Schneider had grey eyes and a cold smile. I felt like reaching up and pushing back the hair falling over Alain Delon's eyes. I remembered, 'You'll mess up my hair.'

Then, for the thousandth time, I gave Armen an earful – it isn't funny at all to hide the twins' toys, and furthermore, you do not call your sister the town idiot in front of other people. I kept at it until he pulled the sheet over his head and said, 'Alright, alright, alright already.'

The moment I shut Armen's door, the twins called out, 'Mommmmmyyyy!' I looked in on them. They were sitting cross-legged on their beds in their red and yellow plaid pyjamas, which I had bought from the Kuwaiti Bazaar a few weeks before.

Armineh asked, 'Why is Emily's grandmother...' and here she held Ishy in front of her face.

Arsineh finished her sister's sentence. 'Why is she so short?'

Every night they found some excuse to stay awake longer. 'Tomorrow night,' I said. 'I'll explain tomorrow night. Now it's time for night-night.'

Armineh lowered Ishy so I could see her face. 'Then at least tell us a story.'

My hand was on the light switch. 'Didn't I tell you I was tired? Tomorrow night.'

Arsineh cocked her head. 'Just one little story?'

Armineh also cocked her head. 'Just one teeny tiny story?'

I looked at them. In their twin beds with the identical sheets, pillowcases, and pyjamas, they were like Xerox copies of one another. As usual, I gave in. I frowned in fun, and said, 'A teeny, tiny one. Okay?'

They squealed in tandem, 'Goody!' and crawled under the covers, waiting excitedly.

I began. 'Once upon a time there were two sisters. Everything about them looked exactly the same. Their eyes and eyebrows, their nose and mouth, their school satchels, their recess snacks. One day, these two sisters...'

The twins loved to hear stories that I made up myself, featuring them as the heroines. I was still sprinkling fairy dust when their eyelids began to droop. I closed with the usual fairytale ending: 'Three apples dropped from the sky...'

Armineh said drowsily, 'One for the teller of the tale.'

Arsineh added with a yawn, 'One for the hearer of the tale.'

I kissed them and said, 'And one for...' All three of us chimed in together, '...all the good little children of the world!'

I turned off the light and left the room. In the hallway, I smoothed out the cloth doily on the telephone stand. I knew that in another year or two the twins would exempt me from nightly story-telling duty, just like Armen, who lost interest in stories years ago. Then I will finally have time for the things I want to do, I thought. My critical streak started in, 'Like what things?' I opened the door to the living room and answered, 'I don't know.' It was a depressing thought.

The television was showing a documentary about the Abadan oil refinery. Artoush was on the sofa, feet stretched out on the coffee table, reading the newspaper. I sat next to him and for a few minutes watched the pipes, the observation deck, and the workers in their hardhats. The pages of the newspaper turned, and a section that had already been read fell to the floor. I bent over, picked it up, and asked, 'You're not watching? They're showing your work.'

'I get to see my work in person from dawn to dusk,' he muttered.

I read the bold print of the headlines: Ambassador of the Soviet Union to Tour Abadan in Coming Days. The Majles Elections and the Six Reform Bills. Construction of Homes for Factory Workers in Pirouzabad. New Swimming Pool Opened in the Segoush Neighborhood of Braim.

I folded the section. What was it in all this boring news that Artoush found so interesting? My ever-present critical streak chided, 'First of all, it's related to his job. Second, you knew about this from the beginning.' I recalled the period of our engagement, in Tehran. At Artoush's insistence I had gone to several meetings of the Iran–Soviet Society, or as everyone called it, VOKS. Each time I was bored.

I got up, turned off the television and went over to the window. I looked out at the boxwood hedge under the moonlight, bordering the yard in straight, orderly lines. Mr. Morteza had trimmed it the day before. After he mowed the lawn, I took him a sour cherry sherbet. He thanked me and then moaned that although it had been six months since he qualified for a scheduled promotion, the Oil Company's personnel division had still not awarded it. He asked me to have Artoush put in a recommendation for him. 'If nothing else, the Doc is *Senior Grade*. What we workers say carries no clout.'

Then came the same old question. 'Why doesn't the Doc get a house in Braim? Mr. Hakopian, who is *Junior Grade*, got a house in Braim.' I repeated the explanation I had been giving to everyone for years – to my mother, my sister, my friends and acquaintances, and even to Mr. Morteza himself – that *Senior* and *Junior Grade* does not mean anything, and that one neighborhood is the same as another neighborhood, and that we are comfortable in this house, and that... Mr. Morteza just listened, as he did each time, then shook his head and wiped the blades of his garden shears on his oversize, baggy pants.

I ran my hand over the drapes and tried to remember the last time I had washed them. Then I remembered to tell Artoush, 'Mr. Morteza asked that...'

The pages of the newspaper turned. 'He deserves it. He works much harder than most *Senior Grades* in the Company.'

As usual, he pronounced *Senior* thickly and derisively. 'Remind me tomorrow to tell Mrs. Nurollahi to remind me to call Personnel.'

I turned back to the window and said to myself, 'Our master had a valet and the valet had a servant...' Mrs. Nurollahi was Artoush's secretary.

Across the street, the light in one of the rooms of G-4 was on. It was too far away to see clearly, but since all the homes of north Bawarda were alike, I knew it was the living room. The similarity of the houses aside, I had been to G-4 on many occasions, when Nina and her husband Garnik had been living there. Artoush did not like Garnik that much – not surprising, since there was almost no one that Artoush did like. The strange thing was that on this one issue, my mother was in agreement with her son-in-law.

The first time that Artoush and Garnik argued politics they went on for a full two hours. After Garnik left, Artoush said, 'The Armenian Revolutionary Federation was once a powerful political party. Now times have changed. Why does Garnik still pound his chest for the Federation? I just don't understand.'

Mother had replied, 'I, for one, understand perfectly. Garnik's father and uncle were infamous throughout Julfa for their tomfoolery. They called his uncle Arshak the Cackler.'

If Artoush was surprised by this irrelevant line of reasoning, he did not let on. After Mother left, I explained that many years ago my father had a friend who was a member of the Armenian Revolutionary Federation, and he was always joking and kidding around. My mother did not like this friend of my father's, which was not very surprising, because Mother did not like any of Father's friends.

I looked over at the window of G-4. Nina and Garnik were still living there just six months ago, and I used to pop over some mornings to see Nina, or she would come to see me. We would have coffee and chat.

Someone came and stood in their window. I only saw a shadow, but I could guess from its height that it was not Emily. It was certainly not her grandmother. It must be her father.

I remembered the night in that very living room when Nina set out what she called a ready-made dinner. Mother said, 'It's not healthy to eat cold cuts, sausage and scraps all the time.'

Garnik laughed. 'Is there really such a thing as healthy or unhealthy food, Mrs. Voskanian? A smiling face and good intentions are all that's needed! The way my wife serves up our food, why, even bread and cheese taste like Chelow Kebab. Where there's a smiling face and pure intentions, vitamins will make their way through the body!' With a guffaw, he put his arm around Nina's beefy shoulders, and she went weak at the knees from laughter. Mother had frowned and the next day said, 'Idiotic clowns! God's matched them perfectly, snug as a door and its jamb.'

It did not matter to me at all if Garnik was a supporter of the Armenian nationalists (or as Artoush put it when he got over-excited, 'He doesn't realize that what's best for the Armenians, as for the rest of the world, is joining the down-trodden masses.'). And it did not matter if Nina was messy (or as Mother put it, that 'a whole camel caravan could get lost in her house.'). What was important was that Nina and Garnik were good together, always happy. I had never seen them angry with each other.

Once, over coffee, the subject of Artoush and Garnik's arguments came up and Nina said, 'You heard it from me, the both of them are talking nonsense. But I always tell Garnik, "You are right, my love." And you must always tell Artoush, "Of course you are right, my love."' She roared with laughter, took a sip of coffee and leaned back in her chair. 'Men think that if they don't discuss politics, they are not real men.'

I leaned on the window frame and thought how much I missed Nina's laughter. I should call her up tomorrow, I thought, to ask how she's doing. The light in the living room of G-4 went out. I thought of the afternoon again, and Emily's frightened, delicate face appeared before my eyes. The girl had not said a word the entire time.

Facing the window, I said, 'Some new neighbors have moved into Nina and Garnik's place.'

The newspaper rustled. 'Hmmm.'

I considered going out to water the lawn and the flowers, then remembered that the yard lights were not working. I decided against it, for fear of stepping on a frog or a lizard. I should have called the Company Housing Services to send someone out to fix the lights. I closed the drapes and sat back down next to Artoush. 'The Simonians. Do you know them?'

The newspaper replied: 'Emile Simonian?'

I pulled out a dirty old sock from under one of the sofa cushions. It was Armen's. 'I don't know his first name.' Then

I remembered. 'Yes, that might be him. His daughter's name is Emily.'

The newspaper pages turned. 'He's been transferred to our division from Masjed-Soleiman. He's a widower. He lives with his mother and daughter. I'm sure he's all we'll need to replace Garnik and make our world an oh-so-much brighter place.'

I looked at the newspaper, waiting for him to continue, but when no more news came out, I went over by the window to sit in the green leather easy chair, sock still in hand. I listened to the monotonous hum of the air conditioners for a while, then, from the bookcase by the window I took out the book that Mr. Davtian, the owner of the Arax bookstore, had sent from Tehran the day before. It was a novel by Sardo. Like all books published in Armenia, the colors and the print on the cover were very poor quality. A man with a goatee and a black cape had his back turned on a woman, who was kneeling on the ground. The sock in my hand got in my way. I tucked it in the pocket of my apron.

My hand rested motionless in the pocket, still holding the sock. I remembered the day I told my mother and my sister Alice, 'I hate women who wear an apron from morning to night just so that people will think they are good homemakers. A woman is more than just a homemaker [thinking of Mother] and she should not dress up just to please others [thinking of Alice]. A woman should above all be neat and nicely dressed to please herself.' I was, I suppose, hinting to both of them. Mother, though it had been years since Father died, was still wearing black and did not bother to dye her hair. And my sister was without equal when it came to messiness and clutter.

Mother had cocked her eyebrow. 'So that's how it is, is it? So a woman should just live her life and do everything for herself?' She scoffed, 'So why do your lips quiver with disappointment when Artoush doesn't notice you are wearing a new dress, or that you've gone to the hairdresser, or put flowers on the table? If I'm lying, go right ahead and say so.'

Alice had joined in. 'Well, where has it gotten you – you who are always supposedly so neat and tidy?' After Mother and Alice left, I had repeated the question to myself: 'Where has it gotten you?' I had to answer, 'I don't know.'

I drew my hand out of the apron pocket and set the book back on the shelf. I was tired and did not feel like reading. Artoush tossed the newspaper on the coffee table and stood up. He stretched and yawned. 'Will you get the lights, or shall I?' The newspaper slid onto the floor. I looked at him. He had gained twenty kilos over the past seventeen years and his formerly thick black hair was now limp and thinning. Everyone called him Doc, because of his standing as an engineer, but because of his goatee, which was no longer so black, Alice called him Professor behind his back. He has changed so much, I thought. I must have changed too, but his voice cut off my thoughts. 'I asked whether you'll get the lights or—'

I cut in, 'I will.' I picked up the newspaper and stood there, untying my apron. I headed for the door and turned off the living room light.

3

Mother drank the last drop of Turkish coffee and turned her cup upside down on the saucer. Then, staring into space, she squinted and pressed her lips together, making her small eyes and thin lips appear even smaller and thinner. She was thinking. 'Did you say she was very short? Was she pretty?'

I cut a piece of salted Gata and put it on her plate. 'Pretty? I told you, she was at least seventy years old!'

Her chin tilted upward and she frowned. 'Meaning what? Anyway, if it is really her, she must be over seventy. I was still wearing bobby socks when madame, with her wide-brimmed picture hats and frippery...'

I saw the spot. 'Mother, your nose.'

My mother had a long nose, and when she drank coffee, the rim of the cup would leave a spot on the tip of it. She quickly wiped it off. '...and her seven-strand pearl necklaces hanging from her neck, cruising up and down Nazar Avenue in a convertible.'

'She drove herself!?'

She bristled. 'Go right ahead and interrupt me at every turn. No. She had a driver.'

I looked at the flower box on the window ledge and wished I had asked Mr. Morteza to change the soil. Gazing at the flowers, I remembered Mrs. Simonian's face. 'Yes, she must have been pretty in her youth. High cheekbones, big dark eyes and...' silently I added to myself: a small elegant nose. In Mother and Father's wedding photo, in the silver frame on the piano, Mother's nose did not look long at all.

Mother put a piece of Gata in her mouth. 'Delicious!' she said.

I watched her, my chin resting in my palm.

Along with the books that Mr. Davtian sent from Tehran, he always included some salted Gata. One day Artoush had asked, 'How does he know that you like salted Gata?'

Before I could think of an answer, Mother said, 'He doesn't send them for Clarice, he sends them for me. When we were in Tehran for the holidays, I went with Clarice to the book-store. He was kind enough to offer us some coffee and Gata. I said that I don't have time to scratch my head, much less to read books, but I just love salted Gata. Since then, whenever he sends books for Clarice, he sends some Gata for me.' As she said this last part, she laughed loudly. Artoush looked over at Mother in surprise, and I looked down. Was it Mother's exaggerated laughter that annoyed me, or the fact that I could not get my tongue to mouth the words: 'Mr. Davtian always treats me to coffee, and he has known for a long time that I like salted Gata.'

Mother wetted her fingertip with her tongue, gathered the little crumbs of Gata left on her plate and ate them. Then she drew a Kleenex from the tissue box, folded it twice, and pressed the upside-down coffee cup onto it a couple of times. The rim left brown rings on the tissue. 'It's her, alright. Elmira Haroutunian. Daughter of Haroutunian the Merchant. She married Vartan Simonian, who owned a trade entrepôt in India. She had inherited a fairly substantial sum from her father, and the husband's money made her really flush. She was known in Julfa as Elmira the Jinxer.'

I burst out laughing.

Mother frowned. 'It's no laughing matter. It's not for nothing she got the name. Her mother died giving birth to her. A few years later, her nursemaid threw herself out of a window into the garden below.'

I wanted to clear the coffee cups, but she brushed my hand away. 'Wait. I haven't read my coffee cup yet.' She stared out the window into the distance. 'On the night of her wedding, her father got food poisoning and a few days later, he died. They said it was from the wedding cake. But why did only the father die? Everyone ate some of that cake...'

'There go those Julfa Armenians again, churning the rumor mill,' I said. 'So maybe the cake wasn't what killed him. Maybe he had a heart attack, or...'

Mother turned my coffee cup over on the tissue and blotted it three or four times. 'She went to India with her husband and a few years later came back to Julfa with her son. The husband had been killed. They said the deed was done by one of their Indian servants. Then she disappeared for a few years – they said she had gone to Europe. When she showed her face again in Julfa, her son was all grown up. She was looking for a wife for him. Word went around in Julfa that the son had an incurable disease – otherwise, how was it he hadn't married while in Europe? Much later, I heard the son had married an Armenian girl from Tabriz. Those Tabrizi Armenians are so easily taken in.'

She picked up her own cup and stared at the intertwined patterns left by the coffee. She said 'Hmm' a few times, 'Ahh' a few times, shook her head several times, and then set the coffee cup back down on the table. 'Mine doesn't say squat.' She picked up my cup.

I thanked God that Artoush wasn't there to hear the bit about the Tabrizi Armenians. The day I told Mother I wanted to marry Artoush, the first thing she asked was, 'He's Armenian, but from where?' The instant I told her, she screamed, 'What?! Who do these Tabrizis think they are?!' If not for the intercession of my father – for whom it made no difference whether his son-in-law was an Armenian from Julfa, Tabriz or the planet Mars – our marriage would not have been so easy to pull off.

I looked at my own cup in Mother's bony hands. A white cup, with tiny pink flowers. My mother's hands were wrinkled, etched with protruding blue veins. 'Well, what happened then?' I asked.

She looked up. 'I heard her daughter-in-law went crazy after a few years and wound up in Namagerd. That's where she died. Look! There's a cypress in your coffee cup.' It depressed me to think of Namagerd.

Mother set the cup down on the table and stood up. 'A cypress means change and development. Maybe the Doc has magnanimously decided to oblige the Oil Company and accept one of the homes in Braim! Your Arab woman will eventually wind up in Braim, while you all continue to stew right here in Bawarda.'

I began clearing the coffee cups. 'My Arab woman?'

She shook what must have been crumbs of Gata from her black skirt. 'That dark tawny woman who, every time Mr. Morteza finishes mowing the grass and trimming the hedge, turns up to gather all the clippings into a bag and haul them away. She just materializes, presto! As if by magic.'

'Do you mean Youma?' Youma obviously lived in the Arab quarter, and the thought of her with a house in Braim made me chuckle.

'Yeah, Youma. What kind of a name is that! I told you a hundred times, don't let her in the house. You yourself told me the kids are afraid of her. With those crooked teeth and that tattooed face, you can't blame them. She's always wearing black, worse than me.'

She was right about that. Youma was always dressed in black, because she was always mourning the death of someone or other. I put the cups and plates in the sink. 'They're not afraid of her. It's just that Armen once said he saw her eat a live sparrow, which was nonsense.'

Mother slung the black strap of her purse over her shoulder. 'I wouldn't be surprised.'

How long had she had this purse? How many times had the strap broken, and Mother had sewn it back on? How many times had I suggested, 'Isn't it time to get a new purse?' How many times had she replied, 'If I had wanted to buy new bags and new shoes all the time like all those bimbo ladies, neither you nor Alice would have gotten your Bachelors.' I had repeatedly explained to Mother that the certificate in English language I got from the Oil Company was not called a Bachelors. And although Alice had gotten her Bachelors – in England, as an Operating Room Charge Nurse – the Oil Company had paid for her education.

In the hallway, Mother swiped a finger over the telephone table. 'Haven't you dusted?'

Looking at her black purse, I replied, 'Sure, I have. Eight times the day before yesterday. Sixteen times yesterday. Thirty-two times today.' I looked up, stared into her eyes, and made a face.

'Don't get smart with me.' She took hold of the door handle. 'In this Godforsaken town if you dust ten times a day, it's still not enough. I'm going to the Company Store; they have some new imported chocolates.' She must have noticed the surprise in my expression, because she quickly added, 'I know. Call me an ass. But…' She drew a deep sigh, let go of the handle and busied herself with tidying up the pleats of the lace curtain. 'Alice is out of sorts. You know that…' She let go of the lace curtain and spun round to face me. 'On the soul of your father, be careful not to say anything that will start a fight. Do you need anything from the Company Store?'

I said I did not need anything and asked, 'Please do not buy chocolate for the children.'

As the door opened, hot air rushed in along with the smell of red clover. Mother said, 'Don't come out. It's hotter than God's own hell out there.' She opened the screen door and set off.

I held the screen door open and leaned against the door frame, watching her. In the middle of the path she stopped, bent over and picked a flower. Then, with some difficulty, she straightened up, smelled the flower and walked on. She opened the metal gate, closed it behind her and turned in the direction of the bus stop. How quick Mother's step used to be, the summer we went to Namagerd.

4

I sat down on the front step and drank in the view of the flower beds that bordered the path – the carnations, the verbena, the snapdragons, the larkspurs and petunias that Mr. Morteza had planted in bunches on either side of the path. Then there was the willow tree overhanging the metal swing seat. We also had three ornamental trees on the lawn. Youma called them Persian Turpentine trees. Mrs. Rahimi, our next door neighbour, used to call them ash trees. But Alice said that was nonsense; the real name was Judas trees. The twins, oblivious to these conflicting views, called the first one Armineh's Tree and the second one Arsineh's Tree. The third one was smaller than the other two, and despite all Mr. Morteza's pruning and fertilizing, it gave fewer flowers.

The name of the third little tree depended upon the twins' best friend of the moment. When Nina and Garnik were our neighbors, it was called Sophie's Tree, after their daughter. Then Sophie broke the twins' Sing-o-ring transistor radio and they stopped talking to each other. The tree remained nameless for a few days, until Sophie's brother, Tigran, fixed the radio, whereupon it was renamed Tigran's Tree. Before

Sophie and Tigran, there was Elise, the daughter of Mother and Alice's neighbor. And then there was Tannaz, who lived two streets over and had taught the twins how to tell fortunes using larkspur petals. The day Tannaz moved away to Tehran, Arsineh and Armineh cried. For several days they augured with larkspur petals, foretelling the date their friend would come back to them. A few days ago the third little tree had been re-christened Emily's Tree.

'*Alice is out of sorts. You know that...*'

Of course I was aware that Alice was out of sorts. I knew why, too. The week before, one of the Armenian nurses working under my sister's supervision at the Oil Company Hospital – whom Alice thought to be 'the ugliest, dumbest, hickest girl God ever created' – had married the Armenian doctor whom Alice – gazing off into the distance with a half-smile on her lips – had often called 'the most handsome, most considerate man I have ever seen.' The fact that Alice took every wedding as a direct personal insult was beside the point; the heart of the matter was that for some time my sister had been murmuring, 'I think Doctor Artamian likes me,' and just when she was sure the handsome and considerate doctor was thinking of asking her out to dinner, the invitation to his wedding had arrived.

'*Be careful not to say anything that will start a fight.*'

A bougainvillea bush clambers up the front of our house, and when a bright pink blossom fell onto the doorstep beside me, I remembered.

I was ten, maybe twelve years old. Alice wanted to play with the stones I had been collecting for the game of jacks, and I wouldn't let her. She was screaming and crying. Mother shouted at me, 'The poor child's nearly fainted from crying. Give her the stupid stones. You are older and have to cooperate.' But I wouldn't cooperate, so Mother shouted at Father, 'Say something, for once! I have had it with these two and their fighting.' Father looked at me for a moment, then at Mother, then at Alice. Then he calmly folded the newspaper, got up, took the stones that I had spent months hunting and collecting, gave them all to Alice and told me I had to go to bed without dinner. He sat back down and picked up his paper. Alice made taunting faces at me, Mother resumed knitting the shawl she was working on, and I cried myself to sleep that night.

A few days later, when I asked Alice for the stones, she just shrugged, by way of saying, 'I lost them.' It was a month later, maybe, that Mother found the stones Alice had scattered here and there around the house, and put them on the nightstand next to my bed. And maybe a few days after that, early one morning before leaving for work, Father dipped his hand into the pocket of his raincoat, took out five smooth stones of the same size and shape, and quietly put them in my hand.

I set my old stones in front of Alice. 'You can have these. Father has collected some new stones for me.'

Alice shot me a dirty look. 'Only babies play with jacks. I'm collecting movie star photos.'

'*On the soul of your father...*'

I picked up the pink bougainvillea blossom and jiggled it around in my hand. Why did Mother swear on the soul of my father? How did she know?

I remembered the anniversary of Father's death, in Abadan. We had just come home from the church. Mother and Alice were sitting at the kitchen table arguing, and I was passing through on my way to the backyard to collect the clothes off the line. I was still dizzy from the smell of frankincense and candles, and numb from crying. Mother told Alice, 'It wasn't anybody's fault. Don't go accusing people for no reason. It was probably not meant to be.'

Alice shouted angrily, 'It wasn't anybody's fault!? What about his slutty little sister, who appeared like the Grim Reaper out of nowhere – rushing all the way down from Tehran to get her brother to change his mind!' Standing with the empty clothes basket in my hands, I remembered the red rose bush I had planted at the head of Father's grave in Tehran the year before. Had the cemetery attendants remembered to water it?

Still thinking of the red roses on Father's grave, it just slipped out of my mouth: 'It wouldn't hurt to consider our own faults and shortcomings, too. Expecting a three-carat diamond ring...'

Alice did not let me finish. 'And just what faults and short-comings do I have that I should not have a diamond ring? I don't come from a good family? I do! I'm not educated? I am! Just because I'm not all skin and bones like you, but have a little meat on me, should I settle for whatever grouchy loser happens along, like his Excellency the Professor? Should I sell myself short, like you, and wind up with a crummy little gold wedding band not worth a red cent instead of an engagement ring?! No way, sister! I'm worth quite a bit more than that. The thing is, you've been jealous of me ever since we were kids. You still are. Well, you know what? If I had wanted to settle for a husband like yours, I could have been married twenty times by now.'

I set the basket down and wheeled round to face my sister. I don't know whether I turned pale or flushed, or there was something in my expression. But it made Alice look first at me, then at the basket, and then turn to Mother and say, 'What is it? I didn't say anything wrong.' I left Mother and Alice in the kitchen and went to the backyard with the empty basket.

Every time we went to Tehran I planted a red rose bush at the head of Father's grave, and every time I made the cemetery attendants promise to water the rose bush, but they never did. So each time I went, I would plant a new rose bush. In the backyard, I looked at the laundry on the clothesline. My son's socks, the twins' slips in identical size and style, Artoush's shirts, the sheets and the pillowcases. I took them all off the line, folded them one by one and put them in the basket. I gazed at the empty clothesline I had stretched between the jujube tree and the backyard wall. The branches of the tree rustled and a few ripe jujubes fell to the ground. Why hadn't I reminded Alice what a tempest she had raised over my marriage to Artoush?

How red the jujubes are, I thought.

Why hadn't I pointed out to Alice that she had tortured me for months after my marriage, hinting here and there behind my back, and even to my face, that 'Artoush first wanted to marry me, then Clarice shoehorned in between us like a dirty spoon.'

Instead of a red rose bush that no one remembers to water, it would have been better to plant a jujube sapling over Father's head. The next time Mr. Morteza comes, I told myself, I should ask him where I can buy one. Maybe jujube trees grow wild? Maybe they don't thrive in Tehran's climate. I had never seen a jujube tree before coming to Abadan.

Alice and Mother argued right up until it was time to leave. After I put the kids to bed that night, did the dishes, and cleaned the kitchen, I sat in the green leather chair. I ate those red jujubes one by one and remembered how Father would say, 'Don't argue with anyone and don't criticize them. Whatever anyone tells you, just say "you are right" and let it go. When people ask your opinion about something, they are not really interested in what you believe. They want you to agree with them. Arguing with people is pointless.'

I ate a jujube and said to myself, 'You were right about that, Father. Arguing with people is pointless.' I promised Father that no matter what Alice said, I would just tell her 'you are right,' and that I would approve of whatever she did. I ate the last jujube and thought, 'I wish Father were here; I bet he would have liked the taste of jujubes.'

Now, sitting on the front step, I noticed the bougainvillea flower lying crumpled in my hand. A fat frog hopped out of the flowerbed, came to rest directly in front of me, and stared into my eyes. I got up, went inside, closed the door behind me and said out loud: 'Yes, I know I have to be quiet, and just listen. And you, Mother, you know that for at least a week you must not nag Alice for over-eating or being overweight.'

When Mother nagged my sister about over-eating, if Alice was feeling good, she would tell a joke, make light of it, and somehow change the subject. If, as of late, she was not in a good mood, she would yell and scream: 'Why can't you let me be! What joy do I have in life? Yeah, I'm fat. But exactly who'm I supposed to keep myself thin for, anyway? My boyfriend? My husband? My kids?' And Mother would have to give in and bring out the Cadbury chocolate bars Alice was always buying and Mother was always hiding, and lay them in front of Alice. Or, when the situation got really grave, as it had been for the last few days, Mother would say, 'Call me an ass,' and then traipse off to buy chocolate for my sister herself. I ran my hand over the telephone table. Mother was right. If you left the door open for two minutes, the house filled up with dust.

I tied on my apron and before turning on the faucet over the dishes in the sink, I looked inside my coffee cup. There was no sign of anything whatsoever that resembled the shape of a cypress tree.

5

I drew the curtains in the twins' room and straightened their bedspreads. Mother had stitched the quilts for them out of swatches of cloth she had been collecting over the years. On the day she finished, after months of hand-sewing, the twins counted the patches in both bedspreads to make sure they were equal in number. At the foot of each bed was a pair of plastic house slippers, both red with yellow tassels. In a room where everything came in identical pairs, only the dolls were not lookalikes. Once I asked them, 'Why do you like all your things to look the same?'

They pow-wowed together before answering. Armineh said, 'This way, it seems like…'

Arsineh finished the sentence, '…it seems like we are never alone.' And she put her arm around her sister's shoulder.

When I asked, 'How come the dolls aren't lookalikes, then?' They looked at each other, then at me, and said, 'We don't know.'

I tidied up the room, thinking about the close rapport between my daughters, and hoping they would remain close friends as adults. I folded Arsineh's pyjamas and put them under her pillow, thinking about me and Alice when we were kids. Which one of us was to blame for how things turned out? I put Ishy on Armineh's bed and thought, well, there were also times I was mean to Alice. I picked the black doll, whose name was Tom, off the bed. The twins were more careful of Tom than of their other dolls. 'We don't want the poor thing to think we like him less because of the color of his skin.' I remembered the day when, out of spite, I taught Alice the multiplication tables all wrong. And there were a few times when she asked me to write her composition assignments for her, and I had not done it. I put Tom in the dolls' crib. As the little cradle rocked, I recalled yet again the promise I had made Father, and repeated it to myself: 'Whatever Alice says, I will say she is right.' The doorbell rang.

I opened the door and, again, did not see anyone at the expected height. This time I lowered my head more swiftly than the day before.

She had on a white blouse with buttoned-up collar, and a black skirt. Yesterday's pearl necklace dangled over her blouse. She was wearing nylon stockings – it made me hot just looking at them. When I saw her black patent-leather high-heeled shoes, I thought her shoe size must be a 30, the same size as the twins. She held out a box in my direction. 'It's sour cherry cake. Home-made.'

I suggested that we go to the living room. She held up the palm of her left hand and looked downward. 'No. This is not a formal call. I've actually come to apologize.' Her eyes gazed up at mine. 'For my behavior yesterday.' She put the box in my hand and headed for the kitchen.

By the time I could close the door and follow after her, she was already sitting at the kitchen table. She had on two rings today, one with a green stone and the other with a big, colourless stone, which I presumed must be a diamond. If Alice were there, she would have known for sure. My sister loved jewelry almost, or maybe even just as much, as chocolate and sweets.

My short-statured neighbor was looking around. 'What a pretty kitchen. How *originale*!'

I couldn't see, but I was sure her feet did not reach the floor.

I took a cake plate down from one of the kitchen cupboards, a round china dish Alice had brought back as a souvenir from her last trip to England. I opened the box and slid the cake off its cardboard disc onto the serving dish. I left the box and the cardboard disc on the counter and took the cake plate over to the table. 'What a pretty cake! Why did you go to all this trouble?'

She gave a half-smile. 'Bravo!'

Seeing my confused look, she explained, 'Every other Armenian lady I've brought cake for just sets it on the table on the cardboard platter.' She preferred tea to coffee. She poured milk in her tea and started to stir.

The sour cherry cake looked better than it tasted. 'What a tasty cake,' I hurried to reassure her.

'It's not tasty,' she said. 'I had no vanilla.' She was still stirring her tea.

I tried to find a conversation topic. I started with the heat and humidity of Abadan, which seemed to my neighbor to be nothing compared to the heat of India. The sound of her spoon clinking against the sides of the cup was beginning to get on my nerves.

What could I say that would interest her? My eyes fell on the small basket on the table, which still held a few left-over Easter eggs. 'Take a colored egg for Emily,' I said, offering the basket.

She finally set down the spoon next to her cup. She picked up one of the eggs and, turning it over in her hand, asked, 'Colored them yourself?'

'Yes,' I said. 'No. I mean, with the children…'

She returned the egg to the basket. 'Emily doesn't like such things.'

'Oh, but children love colored eggs,' I suggested.

It was as though she had heard something offensive. 'Emily is no child. She does do some strange things now and then, but – she is not a typical child. She has her own ways.'

I made a conscious decision not to speak about anything else, at which point she drank her tea and started talking away. She began every other sentence with 'When I was in Paris…' or 'The year I was living in London…' or 'My house in Calcutta…' In spite of this, I can't say why, I did not feel she was posing, like Alice. Talking about herself was my sister's forté.

She got up suddenly, thanked me for my 'kind hospitality,' and headed for the door, saying over her shoulder, 'We are expecting you Thursday evening for dinner. The children will play together, you and your husband will meet my son Emile.'

She did not even bother to ask whether we had any plans for Thursday night.

6

Artoush had been grumbling and grouching about it for several days, and he repeated it all in front of Mother and Alice. 'It's the first and the last time! *Puleez* don't start a social circle; I've got no patience for it, at all. And I won't put on a tie.'

Alice took out a chocolate square from her large straw purse and opened the gold-foil wrapper. She popped the chocolate in her mouth and tossed the gold foil on the kitchen table, saying with bulging cheeks, 'Was the ring stone an emerald? She probably got it in India.'

Mother scraped back her chair and stood up. 'I agree you should keep the socializing to a minimum.' She picked up the gold foil and tossed it in the garbage pail. 'This woman did not have a sterling reputation in Julfa.'

'So the mother didn't have a sterling reputation,' said Alice. 'What's that got to do with her son?'

My eyes met Mother's. I knew what was going through her mind: 'Not another bachelor prospect.'

Arsineh burst into the kitchen. 'Rapunzel's red dress is gone!' She turned to Mother. 'You know, the pleated dress you sewed for her.' She stomped her foot on the floor. 'If it's lost, Rapunzel is not coming to the party. If Rapunzel doesn't come, me and Armineh aren't coming either.' She stared straight at Armen, hands on her hips.

Armen was ready an hour ahead of time. He wore his bighorn ram shirt with the worn and faded jeans that I had tried to toss out several times. Every time, he raised a ruckus to stop me. Now he wiped his shoes, first with spit and the kitchen dust cloth, and after I shouted at him, with water and the shoeshine cloth. I said, 'It's not a bad idea. If Rapunzel's dress doesn't turn up, Armen will stay home, too.' We were all staring at Armen.

Armen looked first at me and then at Arsineh. He seemed unsure whether to keep up his prank or not. He took a few grudging steps, opened the tea tin on the counter and produced the doll's dress. Arsineh huffed loudly, snatched up the dress and ran out.

I knew Mother and Alice would now burst out laughing at Armen's antics, and my son would therefore completely ignore the brow-beating I was about to give him. 'Go to our bedroom,' I told him. 'Your father left his tie there.'

Artoush was tying his shoelace. 'I said I would not wear a tie.'

With a silent nod, I sent Armen to fetch it.

As soon as Armen stepped out of the room, Mother remarked, 'He carries it off so magnificently! I wonder who my boy takes after with all his charm?'

Alice laughed. 'After his aunt.' Then she looked at Artoush. 'What did you say her son does?'

Artoush said, 'Structural engineer,' and chocolate number two dropped in Alice's mouth.

'Structural engineer. Hmm.' And she stared at the flower box on the ledge.

Mother couldn't hold her tongue: 'Now she's popping chocolates again like they were peanuts.'

This time I cleared the gold-foil wrapper off the table, surprised at my sister. Since when did she show *interest* (it was Alice who used the English word) in a previously married man who already had a child? Mother returned to the theme of Mrs. Simonian's not-so-sterling reputation in Julfa. I hoped she was not about to launch into a repeat of the whole saga she had told me just a few days ago.

Artoush was shining his shoes with the cloth I used to polish the kitchen floor. I put the shoeshine cloth in his hand. He grabbed the cloth and said, 'It's not about what the folks of Julfa were saying then, or what they say now. I just have no patience for social obligations and neighborly entanglements.'

Alice, chin propped in her hand, was still staring at the flowers on the ledge. 'India's famous for its emeralds.' She took some gum out of her purse.

In the hallway I looked at myself in the mirror one last time, unable to make up my mind if my sleeveless dress was too low cut. And wasn't it too tight around my hips?

Alice and Mother headed for the door. Mother looked me over. 'We're going. Why don't you put on a shawl or something over your shoulders?'

'Do you want Artoush to take you home?' I asked.

Alice blew a bubble with her gum and popped it. 'No, we'll walk. We're not far away, at least not for another four or five months. But when I get my promotion...' She looked at Artoush fussing with his tie in front of the mirror. 'When I get my promotion, I'll have to trouble my dear brother-in-law to take me home in his latest-model car.' She laughed uproariously and looked at me. 'One can't go from Bawarda to Braim on foot! Bye. By the way, that dress swallows you up – makes you look scrawny. Bye, kids.'

I closed the door behind them and drew a deep breath.

7

It was Emily who opened the door. She was wearing a white dress with puffy sleeves, and white socks and shoes. Her pigtails were tied with broad white ribbons. She looked like a white feather that might suddenly float up in the air.

Armineh said, 'Wow! Emily...!'

Arsineh said, 'You look just like an angel.'

Arsineh put Rapunzel into Emily's hand. The doll's red dress seemed to help tether Emily's feet to the ground. Artoush whispered in my ear, 'What a sweet girl.'

While waiting for the actual hosts to appear, I looked around. Their hallway was a replica of ours, but seemed a little bigger to my eyes. Maybe because there was no furniture in it, other than the telephone table. I was thinking they couldn't have had a chance to set up their furniture yet, when Mrs. Simonian and her son stepped into the hallway.

Her short stature was not the only thing that made us stare at Mrs. Simonian. She wore a black silk dress that was so long, it trailed on the floor. She had on a big brooch and pendant earrings, and her long, multi-strand pearl necklace hung all the way down to her thick gold belt. Armineh said,

'Just like a Christmas tree!' When I elbowed her, she and her sister stifled their laughter.

Mrs. Simonian reached out with her small hand and shook Artoush's. 'Elmira Haroutunian-Simonian. Welcome!' Still facing us, she pointed behind her. 'May I introduce my son, Emile Simonian.' I had only ever seen such formal introductions in the movies.

Emile Simonian was the same height as me, which was unusual, because I was taller than almost all the men I knew. Except for Artoush, who was the same height as me – but only when I was wearing flats. I don't know if I avoided high heels to keep from looking taller than my husband, or if flats really were more comfortable for me. I held out my hand to Emile Simonian. Good thing I had forced Artoush to wear a tie.

Emile Simonian, with his green eyes, in his navy blue suit and grey tie, smiled. As I stretched my hand out, he stretched out his. But instead of shaking my hand, he bowed and kissed it. Artoush gave a little cough and the twins stared at my hand and the back of Emile Simonian's head, with its thick, straight, neatly combed and shiny hair. I couldn't tell which of the twins said, 'How cute.' The other one chimed in, 'Just like in the movies.'

I hoped the sweat under my arms had not left a perspiration stain on my dress. Armen wasn't paying attention. I had no time to figure out what was on his mind.

As Emile Simonian stood upright again, Armen shook Emily's hand. Artoush looked at me and raised his eyebrows. I always told Armen, 'You're grown up now and should act

43

like a gentleman. Shake hands with people.' But he'd shrug his shoulders and go right on not shaking hands with anyone.

Arsineh told Emily, 'Rapunzel missed you very much.'

Armineh said, 'Very, very much!'

I gave the little bouquet of red roses to Mrs. Simonian.

I had planted the rose bush in the front yard myself. Despite all Mr. Morteza's pessimism – every time he came he would say, 'Mrs. Doc, it's not my place to say so, ma'am, but I don't believe them roses will take' – the bush had been awash with roses for a week.

Mrs. Simonian smelled the roses. She did not thank us, but gave a crooked smile and with a wave of her hand ushered us into the living room.

The living room also seemed to be bigger than ours. On one side of the room were the easy chairs with metal armrests, and across from that, the dining room table with its six chairs. This was the furniture provided by the Oil Company to all the houses in Bawarda. Most families preferred, like ours, to buy a somewhat better dining room set, sofa, and easy chairs. The windows had no drapes and there were a few wires sticking out of the empty slots for the wall fixtures. The twins said with one voice, 'We're going to Emily's room.'

I felt Armen wanted to go too; he was shifting from one foot to the other. I knew that if I told him to stay, he would go. 'You stay with us,' I said. He shook his head emphatically and went off with the girls. God, don't let him pick a fight for at least half an hour, I thought.

Mrs. Simonian smelled the roses again and headed for the large cabinet filling at least half the wall. It was made from a dark wood, with two mirror-mosaic doors. Between the doors was a niche, like a recessed shelf, on which stood two candelabras, each boasting two white candles. The heavy cabinet did not go with the rest of the furniture in the room; they must have brought it from India. Mrs. Simonian opened one of its doors and took out a crystal vase. The mirror mosaic on the doors was etched all around with fine designs of flowers and birds. Emile Simonian politely invited us to sit down.

From this side of the room, which seemed unrelated to the other half, I watched Mrs. Simonian. She put the crystal vase back in the cabinet, picked up a red china vase, closed the door and turned around to face me.

'This vase will complement the colors of the flowers better than that one.' I don't know what she saw in my look that made her smile. 'Do you like the cabinet? It's made in England, late eighteenth-century.' Then she extended the hand holding the vase. 'Emile!'

Her son got up, took the vase and went through a door that I knew opened to the kitchen. 'Complement' the colors better? It had been a while since I had heard this formal Armenian vocabulary. Had it been me, I would probably have said, 'it matches better' or 'goes better.' The black silk dress and jewels certainly went better with the cabinet – 'complemented the cabinet better' – than the rest of the furniture.

In another corner stood a black piano, dominating the room, its open fallboard revealing yellowing keys. There were a few pages of sheet music on the music shelf. I was too far from the piano to make out the name of the piece.

Mrs. Simonian held the roses in front of her. She was still looking at me with that crooked half-smile. 'What a pretty ribbon you wrapped the flowers with.' From the corner of my eye I could see Artoush shifting in his seat.

That afternoon I had tied and untied the red ribbon around the roses several times, looping it again and again until I was finally pleased with the bow. Whenever I wrapped a present for someone, I had to tie the ribbon just right. If Artoush was watching, he would say, 'What a perfectionist! Who's going to notice the ribbon?' This was the first time anyone had noticed the ribbon.

Emile Simonian returned with the vase full of water. His mother set the vase on the dining table and put the roses in one by one.

Artoush and Emile were talking about the heat as I watched Mrs. Simonian's hands. The vase was exactly the same color as the roses, and the only light in the room came from a bare bulb dangling from a long wire next to the ceiling fan. My neighbor wound the ribbon around the vase and straightened out the loops in the bow. She went and sat on the sofa, beckoning me to sit next to her. I went over to her and sat down. The springs creaked. She patted my knee several times with her little hand, then said, 'Emile!'

Emile went out again through the door leading to the kitchen.

Sitting on the edge of the sofa, Mrs. Simonian's feet just reached the floor. She had on black satin shoes, high-heeled and open-backed, embroidered with rhinestone moths. She turned to Artoush. 'Your wife is among the limited number of Armenian ladies of culture I have been honored to meet over the many years I've lived in the far-flung corners of the globe. You are a fortunate man.'

Artoush blinked several times. Then he nodded and loosened the knot of his tie. The room was quite warm and our short neighbor's long sentences contained words Artoush and I had not heard in years.

Emile came back into the room, a small silver tray in his hands. A white doily embroidered with flowers decorated the tray, and on the doily stood a pitcher of orange juice with four glasses.

I swallowed the bitter, lukewarm juice and listened to Mrs. Simonian compare the heat of Abadan to the heat of India. She explained that 'the chill breeze of air conditioners causes irreparable harm to those suffering from back problems.' I would have said, 'It's not good at all for back problems.' My critical streak grew weary of this game and chided: 'Stop it! There is no need to relentlessly translate your neighbor's formal Armenian vocabulary to colloquial.' My positive streak chuckled at that: 'There you go, speaking formally yourself.'

I was trying not to look at Artoush. The demeanor and stiff behavior of both mother and son, the forced conversation, the bitter lukewarm orange juice, the heat and the bad lighting of the room – it was all unbearable for me. Not more than ten minutes had passed before Mrs. Simonian stood up. 'We eat dinner early.'

Artoush volunteered 'We do, too,' with such haste that I felt sorry for him. Why had I forced him to come? Why had

I accepted this invitation in the first place? Probably because the twins had been talking non-stop about Emily for several days and because, well, we were neighbors, after all.

This time when Mrs. Simonian barked, 'Emile!' I got up. 'Please allow me to help,' I said. Emile, half standing, looked at me, smiled, and sat back down.

The kids' menu was steamed rice with boiled chicken, which they were to eat at the kitchen table. Whenever we were invited somewhere new for a meal, I would feed my kids something in advance. It was a good thing I had given all three of them sandwiches before we came over, because steamed rice and boiled chicken was the diet Mother imposed on them when they were sick, and they would never eat it.

The adults were served rice with an okra and tomato stew. The table was set before we got there, with a white cotton tablecloth and matching napkins. The china plates decorated with orange flowers must have been old and were certainly expensive, though my plate was chipped in two spots. Mrs. Simonian sat at the head of the table and told Artoush and me where to sit. I remembered the twins' quip – 'Just like in the movies.' The hostess opened her napkin, dropped it in her lap and, motioning to the wooden cabinet, said, 'Emile!'

Emile brought the candelabras from the cabinet, set them in the center of the table and lit the candles. Artoush stole a glance at me. Mrs. Simonian waited, still and silent, for the final candle to be lit, as if anticipating the conclusion of a ceremony. When her son sat down and opened his napkin, she said, 'Please begin.' In the candlelight, the white tablecloth looked yellowish. There were faded stains in several places, and a cigarette burn.

I put the first spoonful in my mouth and tried not to look at Artoush. The stew was so spicy that even I, who liked spicy food, was on fire. Artoush hated spicy food.

Mrs. Simonian offered a small china bowl to Artoush. 'If the stew is insufficiently spicy, use some of this chutney.' Artoush set his water glass down and just shook his head, no. If it were me, I would have phrased it like this: 'If the stew isn't hot enough for you...' I told myself to shut up.

Emile shifted in his chair and without raising his head, said, 'Mother, maybe it would have been better not to make the stew so spicy. Not everyone is used to it.' Then he looked at me and Artoush, and smiled. I felt he was apologizing.

His mother put two spoonfuls of chutney on the side of her plate and, without looking at her son, said, 'Please don't give me cooking lessons. Okra stew must be spicy.' Then she looked at me. 'I learned how to make this chutney in Calcutta from our cook, Ramu.' She carefully set the bowl of chutney next to the platter of rice. 'Before dismissing him.'

Emile ran his hand through his hair. His fingers were long and thin. Alice would say, 'Sensitive people have long, thin fingers.' She'd hold her hand in front of her face and flutter her fingers. 'Like mine.' I would look at my sister's hands, which were a bit chubby, like the rest of her, and nod yes.

For a while no one spoke. We could hear the frogs and crickets in the yard. The light in the room was so dim that I wanted to get up and turn on another lamp. Mrs. Simonian was eating her food in silence and I felt I should strike up a conversation. The children were laughing in Emily's room. Had they finished dinner? How come none of them had come to tell me, 'I don't like it'? Emile was still looking down, and I could not think of anything to say.

Artoush set his second glass of water back on the table and asked, 'In Masjed-Soleiman, what department did you work in?' Emile looked up and smiled. This time in gratitude, I sensed, for breaking the silence.

I looked at Artoush and thought he and Armen must be in a father–son competition, vying to do things they had never done before. I could not remember my husband ever taking the initiative in a conversation, except to contradict my mother.

Emile raised the napkin and dabbed the corner of his mouth, but before he could answer, his mother said, 'Emile was a top student at university. In India, and of course in Europe, he had outstanding positions. The Oil Company was extremely lucky that my son agreed to its proposal for collaboration. In reality we do not need Emile's salary, but now that I have decided to live in Iran, I thought it would be better for Emile to keep busy. I haven't yet had a chance to hang up his degree certificates from the university. I took the certificates to the most expensive frame-maker in Calcutta and had him frame them, all in betel-nut wood.'

Artoush was still looking at Emile. 'What department did you say you were working in?' As if he hadn't noticed the mother had said a word.

Emile gave a little cough, glanced over at his mother and started to speak. He looked just like his daughter in our kitchen that day, when her grandmother arrived. Tense and afraid.

Artoush only ate the rice, only looked at Emile, and only nodded his head. Mrs. Simonian spooned chutney over her food a second time, with such precision you would have imagined she was measuring out a rare elixir.

I was wondering how, once back at home, I would answer Artoush's reproachful grumbling.

Mrs. Simonian asked, 'What time do your children go to bed?' There had been no peep from the kids for half an hour. I started to worry. 'Usually at eight-thirty, nine o'clock. But on nights like tonight, when they don't have school the next day...'

Mrs. Simonian laid her spoon and fork neatly side by side on her plate and picked up the napkin from her lap. 'Whether they have school in the morning or not is no reason for children to change bedtimes. A child has to get used to a fixed schedule. Emily sleeps at nine o'clock sharp. When Emile was a child I ordered his governess...'

I scooted my chair back and stood up. 'Let me look in on the children.'

Emile got up and gave a slight bow. Artoush took a bite out of a piece of bread.

In a corner of the hallway, a few suitcases were stacked atop each other. Next to them was a statue of a stone elephant. Half of its trunk and part of an ear were broken off. I looked at my watch. It was a quarter after eight.

Emily's room was an exact copy of Armen's, though it, too, seemed a bit larger to me. There was not much in it, except for the metal bed, a small desk, and a crimson carpet. The windows had no curtains, and the room was dimly lit. The twins were sitting on the carpet, and Armen was sitting in the chair at the writing desk. Emily was reclining on the bed. The hem of her white dress had hitched up above her knees, one of her pigtails had come undone, and her hair was falling in her face. She was playing with the ribbon. When she saw me enter, she sat up straight, pulled down on the hem of her dress, and placed both hands on her knees.

Arsineh looked at me, her curly hair spilling out from beneath her orange headband. 'It would be great if tomorrow...'

Armineh, her curly hair spilling out from beneath her orange headband, continued, '...Emily could come to the movies with us.'

Arsineh asked, 'Can you ask for permission for her?'

Armineh cocked her head, 'Please?'

Armen picked up a book off the writing desk and flipped through its pages.

'Are you having fun?' I asked. 'What have you been doing?'

Armineh said, 'We were talking until now.'

Arsineh said, 'Emily was telling us about the schools she's gone to.'

'Now we're going to play Spin the Bottle.'

'Emily has taught us how.'

'Spin the Bottle?' I took a deep breath.

I had met Artoush playing Spin the Bottle at the birthday party of a mutual friend. The guests spun the bottle one by one and had to kiss whomever the bottleneck was pointing to when it came to rest. Once the arrangements were finalized for our marriage, Artoush admitted, 'I tried to spin the bottle somehow so that it would point at you.' After our first anniversary, I was bold enough to say, 'Me too.'

Armineh said, 'The person who spins the bottle...'

Arsineh said, '...gives the person who the bottle points to...'

Armineh said, '...any command he feels like.'

'Neat, huh?' the two of them chimed together.

I let out my breath and laughed. 'As long as the commands are not dangerous.' How innocent children are, I thought.

Artoush and Emile were talking in the living room. Mrs. Simonian was clearing the dinner table – I was surprised she hadn't set her son the task. I helped. As we went back and forth from the dining room to the kitchen, she hitched up her dress and talked on and on. 'I had attendants and servants from birth. Now I am forced to do the work myself. India, with all its problems, had an abundance of maids and servants. In my father's house in Julfa we had all the servants you could want... some families served for several generations in our house.' The pearl necklace kept catching on the dishes and the door handle. 'When we were in Masjed-Soleiman I brought a girl servant from Julfa. She was not quite right in the head. I informed her family, and they came to get her. I believe she wound up in Namagerd, though you probably don't know and don't care where Namagerd is. Can you recommend a good maid here?'

I was about to admit that I do in fact know where Namagerd is, but held my tongue. I thought of Ashkhen, who came round to our place to help out with the housework twice a week, and to Alice and Mother's house once a week. Ashkhen's husband was paralyzed after a back operation and received a pittance of a pension from the Oil Company. Her son had just returned from military service and was out of work, or as Ashkhen put it, 'His job is to hang around the Kuwaiti Bazaar dawn to dusk, stroll up and down along the Shatt al-Arab, smoke two or three packs a day, and chomp on sunflower seeds. He supposes his poor mother, namely me, can pluck money from the trees.' This could work out to their advantage – help for my neighbor and a little extra income for Ashkhen.

Once the table was cleared, I sat down opposite Emile and Artoush, and Mrs. Simonian retook her earlier seat, saying, 'We don't take tea and fruit after our dinner. It inhibits digestion.' Then she asked for the address of the Adib Grocery near our house and jotted down the phone number of the children's piano teacher. 'I've sent Emily to piano lessons since she was seven. She must continue. Of course, I was playing the piano from the age of five.' I almost expected her to say, 'I was performing on the piano.'

Emile was sitting with one leg crossed. He was wearing black patent-leather shoes and black socks. Artoush had one leg crossed as well. His shoes were black and his socks brown. That was my fault. I forgot to lay out his black socks next to his shoes.

I was looking for an opportunity to catch Artoush's eye and signal to him it was time to say goodnight when Armen rushed into the room. His face was red and he could not stop coughing. I leapt to my feet.

'What happened?'

Between coughs he croaked, 'Water!'

Emile jumped up. Artoush also stood up. Mrs. Simonian didn't budge.

I took Armen to the kitchen and poured him some water. 'Did something get stuck in your throat?'

His long eyelashes were matted with tears. He asked for more water, coughed some more, drank again, finally regained his composure and said without looking at me, 'I don't know what made me start coughing all of a sudden,' and walked out of the kitchen.

Artoush had called the twins and was thanking Mrs. Simonian and saying goodbye. Emily, eyes downcast, was twirling the white ribbon around her finger. Was it just me, or was there a half-smile on her face?

As I was shaking hands with Mrs. Simonian and her son, out of the corner of my eye, I saw Armen go over to the twins and whisper in their ear. Armineh tugged at my skirt. 'The movies tomorrow!'

I turned to Emile. 'Would it be alright for Emily to go to the movies with the children tomorrow?'

Emile looked at his mother.

Arsineh tugged at my skirt from the other side. 'Ask her grandma!'

Mrs. Simonian, after ascertaining which cinema and which film, with whom they were going and when they were coming back, and heaven forbid that they eat any sandwiches or chips, finally gave her permission.

The twins, holding each other around the waist, crossed the street ahead of me and Artoush and Armen. Once or twice they turned back to Armen and laughed. I opened the front door and turned on the light in the hallway.

Arsineh said, 'Ahh! It's so nice to have a bright house!'

Armineh said, 'Ahh! And it's nice and cool, too.'

'That was fun,' added Arsineh, 'but their house is very dark.'

'That was fun,' agreed Armineh, 'but their house was very hot.'

Artoush took off his tie and headed for the kitchen. 'Do we have anything to eat?' Armen went to his room and slammed the door.

I sent the twins off to their bedroom, took off my high heels and went barefoot to the kitchen.

Artoush was sitting at the table, staring at the flowers on the ledge. 'Poor guy. Now I know why he doesn't seem normal. With that mother…' A small lizard on the outside of the window screen was staring into the kitchen. I made a hard-boiled egg sandwich. Eggs, whenever and however prepared, were my husband's favorite food.

Just as Artoush was about to bite into the sandwich, Arsineh yelled, 'Tell me where Ishy is, or I'll tell why you were coughing!'

I was about to get up from the table when Artoush caught my hand and said for the umpteenth time, 'Don't interfere. Let them fight. They'll make up afterwards. They'll keep on fighting and making up. Let them be.' Then he smiled. 'Don't worry, they won't kill each other.' Still holding my hand, he stroked the back of it with his finger. I didn't move. How long had it been since he had held my hand? He let go, picked up his sandwich and took a bite. 'Your skin is so dry.'

I looked at my hands. At my close-clipped and unpolished nails. When I shook hands, did Mrs. Simonian notice how chapped my hands were? What about her son? I felt embarrassed at the thought of his kissing my hand. The kids were quiet. Half an hour later, when I looked in on their rooms, all three of them were fast asleep and Armineh was hugging Ishy.

8

On Fridays, when we did not have to rush off to work, we always ate a big breakfast.

The radio was on. I cracked the eggs into the frying pan and told Artoush, who was getting the cheese and butter from the fridge, 'I'll set the table. Go wake Armen so they can make it to the cinema'

From the kitchen doorway Armen said, 'Awake and at your service. Go wake up your lazy daughters. And, by the way, good morning to you.' His hair was all wet and his face all rosy. Artoush looked at me and arched his eyebrows. We both stared at our son.

Armen took a seat at the table. 'What's the big deal? Never seen anyone fresh from the bath before?'

Artoush slid the spatula under the egg, sunny-side up. 'We've had occasion to see a freshly bathed face or two in our day, but not usually a freshly bathed Armen.' He put the egg on Armen's plate and we both laughed. Since the age of ten, getting Armen to take a bath was one of my hardest chores.

Armen was complaining that he didn't like runny eggs when the twins bounced in, wearing their red and blue plaid pinafore dresses over white blouses. They said they didn't want eggs and both asked instead for toast with butter and jam, and chocolate milk.

Over the radio came the pinched voice of the Iranian radio announcer, Forouzandeh Arbabi: 'These are the days of spring blossoms and the rain in Tehran...'

Armen declared loudly, 'These are the days of scorching heat and mugginess in Abadan.'

Arsineh asked, 'What are you talking about?'

Armineh mimicked in a nasal voice, 'He's talking like Forouzandeh Arbabi.'

Arsineh, convulsed with laughter, said through her giggles, 'Are we eating lunch at the Club?'

Armineh added, 'Let's eat lunch at the Club.'

When we were not invited over to someone's house on Fridays, or did not have our own guests, we went to the Golestan Club. The kids liked the Chelow Kebab at the Club, and I thought it was wonderful that we could all be together to eat lunch once a week. Artoush poured sugar in his tea. 'On one condition.'

Armineh quickly swallowed what she was chewing. 'What condition? We've done our homework. We've also practiced the piano. We've also toadied up our room.' She sought her sister's approval, as usual. 'Isn't that right, Arsineh?'

Armen separated the solid and the runny parts of the egg. 'Not toadied. Tidied, you dim...' He caught my glance and did not finish his sentence.

The twins were looking at Artoush. 'What condition? Tell us!' Artoush was stirring his tea.

Armineh said, 'We accept.'

Arsineh affirmed, 'We accept any condition.'

They chimed together, 'What is it? Tell us, tell us!'

Now Armen and I were also looking at Artoush, waiting for his answer. He carefully removed the spoon from his cup, laid it ceremoniously on the saucer, stared out the window, looked at me, then at Armen, then at the twins. Finally he said, 'On condition that my beautiful daughters each give their father a big kiss.'

The twins began to laugh, and both leapt up from their chairs. Armen made a face. 'Hahaha, very funny.' I laughed and started clearing the breakfast table.

Sitting on Artoush's knee, Arsineh said, 'It would be so nice if Emily could come to the Club with us after the movie.'

From his other knee, Armineh said, 'Oh my gosh! We have to go get her.'

Armen pushed back his chair. 'I'll go get her.' Artoush looked over Arsineh's curly hair at me. Armen had already reached the hallway when the twins yelled after him, 'Wait!' and rushed out of the kitchen.

Artoush looked over at the kitchen door. 'Our son has become very meticulous about his manners.' He got up. 'After the movie, I'll pick up the kids from the cinema, and come get you. Call Mother and Alice. Ask them to come too.'

I was taken by surprise. Artoush knew very well that Mother and Alice had no need of an invitation, and would certainly come in any case. And I knew full well that Artoush had no particular desire for either of them to come. So what was the reason for all the lovey-dovey?

From the hallway he yelled, 'After I drop off the kids at the movies, I'll drop in on Shahandeh.'

Aha, I thought. So that's why... 'Wait!' I called out, and ran after him.

He stopped in the middle of the path and waited for me to catch up to him. He was stroking his goatee and chuckling. So I was right! He was horse-trading with me. I stood directly in front of him. 'Didn't you promise me not to go to Shahandeh's?'

He pushed back the hair that had fallen in my face and said patiently, 'I've told you a hundred times. It's not true what you have heard. When was Shahandeh ever mixed up in politics? If one or two folks come around to his store and we chat a bit, so what?' He touched the tip of my nose with his finger. 'Don't worry. I'll only have a little rosewater sherbet and come right back. Shall I bring back some sherbet for you?' And he laughed.

If the weather was hot, Shahandeh would offer rosewater sherbet to everyone who visited his store. And when the weather wasn't hot, it was tea with dried lemon. I had only tried rosewater sherbet once and did not care for it at all.

We walked to the gate together, and Artoush said, 'Maybe he'll even tell an interesting hunting yarn. When I get back I'll tell you all about it.'

'Not that you're any good at telling stories,' I teased. The hunting adventures Shahandeh recounted were interesting, even in Artoush's truncated and lifeless re-telling. I helped him open the garage door. 'There really isn't anything going on at Shahandeh's store? Then why was it closed from

Norouz almost until Easter? The owner of the perfume shop next door said they had come after him from Tehran.'

The sunlight fell on the dark maroon Chevrolet, a twenty-year-old model that was one of Alice's favorite reasons for ridiculing Artoush. He opened the door. 'The perfume-seller was talking nonsense. Shahandeh, like me, did some things in his youth. By now the heroic stuffing has been knocked out of the both of us.' He climbed in. 'We're only going to chat a little. Honest.' After turning the ignition a few times, the car finally started. Artoush was backing out of the garage when the children walked up.

Emily had her hair scraped back off her forehead under a red hairband. Now that her hair was not spilling over her face, her eyes looked larger, her lips and cheeks more prominent. I wondered again whether she was wearing lipstick.

The twins were pouting. 'Emily's grandmother did not give her permission to come to the Club with us.'

'Her grandmother said restaurant food is not good for her.' They each took hold of my hands and swung my arms back and forth. 'You go and ask permission.'

'Please, go.'

'Pretty please?'

Armen, standing a few paces back, was rolling a gravel stone back and forth with the point of his shoe. Emily was looking down. Artoush called from the car, 'Come on. It's late!'

I put a hand on the shoulders of each twin and led them to the car. 'Okay. Maybe I'll go and ask permission for you.'

Arsineh and Armineh scrambled onto the back seat. Armen held the door for Emily to get in, then closed her door and sat in the front seat, next to his father. Artoush headed off and waved. The twins rolled down the window and yelled, 'Permission for Emily! Please.' I nodded and waved goodbye.

I waited until the Chevy reached the end of the street and turned in the direction of Cinema Taj. A warm wind kicked up, gently swaying the Msasa trees lining either side of the street. Our neighbor, Mr. Rahimi, whose garage adjoined ours, was fiddling with his car. His five-year-old son was crying and tugging at his father's trousers. 'Daddy, let's go pol. Let's go pol!'

Mr. Rahimi greeted me and laughed. 'Son, the pool is not open yet.'

The little boy was whining, a packet of Kool-Aid in his hand, and an orange ring round his mouth. In Abadan, the adults used lemon, orange or other flavors of Kool-Aid to create refreshing drinks. But the children loved to take the powder and eat it dry, sticking out their tongues to ask, 'Is it orange? Is it red? Is it purple?'

I asked after Mr. Rahimi's wife, who had gone to Tehran to buy things for her nephew's wedding. Then I said goodbye, opened the gate and shut it behind me. I walked up the path across the lawn. I looked at the red clover in the grass and remembered what Armineh had said. 'Just like violet *Smarties*. Aren't they, Arsineh?' They both loved *Smarties*, colorful round chocolate beans. The branches of the willow tree hung down over the swing seat, and the rose bush was decked with new red blossoms.

9

I went inside and locked the door behind me. In Abadan, nobody locked the door in the middle of the day; I only did so when I wanted to make sure I was alone. My penchant for self-criticism meant that I had challenged myself on this more than once: What does locking the door have to do with being alone? To which I always answered: I don't know.

I leaned up against the door and closed my eyes. After the bright light and heat outdoors, and the noise of the children, the cool, quiet chiaroscuro of the house was lovely. The only sound was the monotonous humming of the air conditioners, and the only smell, a hint of Artoush's cologne hanging in the hallway. I felt like having a coffee.

I looked at the kitchen clock. It was just before ten. Mother and Alice would certainly turn up within half an hour. I'll wait, I thought, so we can have coffee together, and took the pack of cigarettes out of the fridge. Where had I heard that cigarettes would not go stale if kept in the fridge?

I didn't smoke much, but when the house was empty, I liked to sit by the window in the green leather armchair, lean back, puff, and think. In these rare moments of solitude, I tried not to think about daily chores like fixing dinner, getting Armen to study, Artoush's forgetfulness and indifference.

I would reminisce about things I usually didn't have time to think about. Like our house in Tehran – its little yard and big rooms, its long hallway that was dark even in the middle of the day. My father used to come home at noon, wash his hands and face, sit down at the table and eat a big lunch. He ate whatever Mother had prepared that day with great enthusiasm, listening attentively to her recount the morning's events in minute detail: how the watermelon she had purchased proved pale and unripe once cut open. About the rising price of pinto beans. About the fights between me and Alice, which were a daily occurrence. Father would mutter things under his breath that we could not quite make out, or if we could, we would not remember. Then he would get up from the table, thank Mother for lunch, and head down to his room, at the end of the somber hallway. It was a small room with brown velvet curtains, always drawn, and cluttered with stuff that Mother would constantly complain about, saying, 'Why do you keep this junk?!'

After the forty-day commemoration of his death, Mother went into Father's room with Alice and me, and she cried. 'God only knows why he kept all this junk.' The floor-to-ceiling shelves were stuffed with books and newspaper clippings and magazines and half-finished crossword puzzles. There were letters from people none of us knew, not I, nor Mother, nor Alice. There were group pictures of my father with his friends when he was young – friends that none of us had ever seen. Alice choked up and Mother wept. 'For all these years! Why did he hang on to all this junk?' I opened the books and closed them. I examined the broken wrist-watches, recalling, as I turned them over, how Mother always complained of Father's lack of punctuality. In an old shoebox I saw rusty razor blades and in a wood crate, a whole assortment of empty aftershave bottles. As far back as I could remember, Father had a bushy beard and he never used aftershave.

In that little room at the end of the hallway Alice found nothing worth keeping. I took the books, and Mother dried her tears, opened the brown velvet curtains and threw out everything she could put her hands on. With the little room at the end of the hallway emptied, Mother felt her principal duty had been accomplished, and with an uncluttered mind, she sat down to mourn for Father. Since then, the phrase, 'If your late father were alive...' had become her litany.

Little by little we forgot that nothing would have been any different, even if Father were still alive. Father would read his books, solve his crossword puzzles, and eat fatty foods. He would not share his opinion about anything, or, when he did, we would not hear it, or would not remember it. We would get on with our own lives. I would come to Abadan with Artoush and raise my children. Alice would go to England for a few years, ostensibly to study nursing, but secretly hoping to find an English husband. Mother would wash the kitchen floor twice a day, backbite about the sort of women who stored Persian melons and watermelons in the fridge without washing them first, and find some reason to worry every day.

With my head sunk deep in the green chair, I thought of the Simonians. The son's elegant hands, the mother's rhinestone-embroidered shoes, and Emily, who had yet to speak a word to me. I thought about what kind of woman Emily's mother must have been. Mother had said, 'She went crazy and turned up in Namagerd.' I wondered how old I had been the year we went to Namagerd. Eight? Maybe eleven? Or perhaps about the same age as my twins were now.

I heard the gate squeak and craned my neck to see Mother and Alice coming. In the sharp sunlight, with her flappy yellow dress, my sister looked like a big sunflower among the trees and the hedgerows. Mother, wearing a black dress, looked thin and hunched, like a stick of wood. Armen used to say, 'When Aunt Alice and Nana walk side by side, they look like Laurel and Hardy.' My sister was carrying a big cardboard box. I knew what it was without looking. Alice observed her Friday visits to the Mahtab Bakery to buy cream puffs more religiously than her Sunday visits to church.

10

Mother complained about the heat, Alice caught her breath, and then both took their seats at the kitchen table. 'Well?' my sister asked.

There was no need for me to ask, 'Well, what?' On the rare occasions I was invited somewhere without Alice, the next day she would make me recount everything that happened from start to finish, in minute detail, and even then she wasn't satisfied. Her face would wear a doubtful expression that accused me of withholding information.

I stood by the stove, watching to make sure the coffeepot did not boil over. 'Well, we had to go,' I said. 'They're our neighbors, after all.'

Alice laughed out loud. 'You mean it was that bad? Your Professor must have complained up a storm.' Mother laughed as well. I poured the coffee, set it on the table, and sat myself down.

My sister untied the string around the cardboard pastry box and removed the lid. 'I waited for this for half an hour. It's fresh out of the oven. Mr. Mousavi insisted that I get some other pastry instead, but I wouldn't give in. I told him, "You pour three pounds of rosewater into your other pastries." I left out that his cream puffs, on the other hand, are to die for – I didn't want it to go to his head.' She picked up a cream puff between thumb and forefinger, bit in, and closed her eyes. 'Mmm.' That meant it was good. Then she slid the box toward me and Mother, and with a mouth full of cream puff, said, 'Mmm, mmm, mmm!' That meant we should try some. Mother took one out, but I shook my head.

'I just ate breakfast with the kids.'

'The kids are not home? Uh huh! They were going to the cinema. Where is Artoush? Uh huh. He's gone to drop off the kids. Is he coming back? Nope! I bet he's gone to drop in on Shahandeh again.' After her little question-and-answer soliloquy, Mother bit into the cream puff, chewed, and swallowed. 'I've said a hundred times he shouldn't hang around that "brazen hussy."' (Shahandeh had long white hair that he wore in a ponytail, and Mother disapproved.) 'Selling hunting equipment is just a cover.' (Shahandeh had a hunting equipment store near the Kuwaiti Bazaar.) 'What shopkeeper opens on a Friday?' (The vast majority of Iranian stores were closed on Fridays, the Muslim sabbath, but not Shahandeh, who was always open on Fridays, and would only open – 'raise his shutters', as he put it – one or two other days a week.) 'With that giant body and those bushy whiskers, isn't he embarrassed to dress like a twenty-year-old?' (Shahandeh wore loose-fitting bold-colored Hawaiian shirts.) When I gave Mother no answer, she continued. 'I'm telling you, your late father's politicking caused me no end of troubles, and now it's my son-in-law!

Out of the frying pan, into the fire.' As far as I could remember, my father's 'politicking' entailed nothing more than a couple of trips to the Iran–Soviet Friendship Society (and that, only at Artoush's insistence), and loyal listening to the Radio Armenia broadcasts.

Alice tasted her coffee and her face curdled. 'Blech! Bitter as poison.' I slid the sugar shaker in front of her, thinking that the fiasco of the Doctor's marriage might be all but forgotten.

Mother was livid. 'Acho!' Whenever Mother called Alice by this childhood nickname – which my sister detested – it meant she was in high dudgeon. 'There you go again, dipping in the sugar vat?' Apparently the fiasco was long put to rest, if Mother felt emboldened to gripe at Alice about her sweet-tooth.

Alice poured two heaping spoonfuls of sugar in her coffee cup and stirred. She took another cream puff and turned to me, ignoring Mother. 'So tell me about it. What was the son like? Did his mother wear any new jewelry?'

Mother pressed her lips together and turned her face to the ceiling. 'Holy Mary, Mother of God. Here she goes again.'

I wondered how to describe Emile Simonian. What I remembered most was that he seemed to look at you from a great distance and that all of his movements – sitting, walking, eating – were smooth, easy. But that was not what my sister wanted to hear.

'He was tall, well-dressed and...handsome.' As the words came out of my mouth, I regretted saying it.

The third cream puff hung in the air between the cardboard box and Alice's mouth. 'How old?'

I placed my coffee cup back in the saucer and shrugged my shoulders. 'I don't know. Forty, I suppose.' Mother closed the lid on the cream puffs, slid the box over to me and gestured toward the fridge. Alice was looking out the window, paying no attention to us.

Mother said, 'He must be just about that age.' Then she stared at Alice. 'Don't even think about it.'

Alice, her face still toward the window, ran her hand through her hair. 'I have a hairdresser's appointment tomorrow.' Then she looked at me. 'Do you think I should cut my hair short?'

Mother looked at me and shook her head. We both knew by heart the sequence of events that would next transpire. Whenever an unmarried man turned up, Alice first got a new hair-do and then she went on a diet, for a few days or few weeks, depending upon how long the infatuation lasted. And, according to what she told us more than what our eyes could verify, she would lose weight. I got up and took the fruit bowl out of the fridge, telling myself, 'Don't argue, now.'

Alice said, 'Yoo hoo, I'm talking to you. I asked if you think short hair looks good or—'

I began clearing away the coffee cups and hurriedly offered, 'Sure. Why not?'

We heard the brakes of Artoush's Chevy screech, and moments later the twins ran in. '*Hello*, Nanny. *Hello*, Auntie.'

Mother hugged Armineh. 'Again with the *hellos* in English? We're not English. Are we? Say it in Armenian: Barev!'

Alice hugged Arsineh. 'Are you on the children's case again? Is there anyone left in Abadan who does not say *Hello*? You yourself spout English words left and right.'

Mother glared. 'Me? Never!'

Alice glared back. 'You? All the time!' She cocked her head to the right and mimicked Mother. 'The kitchen *fan* is broken.' She cocked her head to the left. 'Alice has gone to the *hospital*.' Again to the right. 'The *store* had no *twist* bread, so I bought *rolls*.' Again to the left. 'Kids, be careful you don't fall off your *bicycles*.' She stared right at Mother, 'Armen's *tenni shoes* are worn out. And by the way, it's *tennis shoes*, not *tenni shoes*.'

The children laughed, and Mother gave Alice a dirty look. Alice went on, 'Yesterday one of the doctors told a funny story.'

Armineh sat facing Alice. 'Auntie, you tell it to us and then we'll...'

Arsineh sat by Armineh's side. '...then we'll tell you about the movie.'

Alice asked Mother, 'What happened to the cream puffs? Did you sneak them back to the fridge again?'

'Auntie, tell us,' said Armineh.

'Tell us, Auntie,' said Arsineh.

I grabbed Armen's arm, whose hand was headed for the refrigerator door. I wagged my finger at him, warning, no cream puffs for you.

'One of the English engineers went on a site supervision call to I don't remember where exactly,' began Alice. 'The foreman was supposed to act as his interpreter and translate what the engineer said for the workers. So the engineer says in English, "Tell them to bend the pipes," and the foreman turns around and shouts to the workers, "Attention, guys! He says to *bend the pipes*."'

We all laughed, except Mother, who glowered at us and said, 'It wasn't funny at all.'

Armineh said, 'But the film was really funny.'

Arsineh said, 'But Cinema Taj was like a refridgerator'

'That's how cold it was.'

'Mommy, what about permission for Emily to come for lunch?'

'Did you ask?'

'Call her.'

'No, go to their house.'

'No, Auntie. We don't want chocolate. It will spoil our lunch.'

'Mommy, please. Go get permission for Emily. Please.'

I put my hand on my head. 'Goodness gracious, already. I'm going.' And I got up. As I left the kitchen, Armineh and Arsineh were sitting on their auntie's and grandma's knees respectively, taking turns retelling the plot of the film.

As I crossed the street, I thought to myself, 'I hope my sister will not try out her usual scheme on Emile.' Normally I would tell myself, 'Maybe this is the one…' But this time I entertained no illusions whatsoever. I was sure this one was in no way, shape or form good for Alice.

My nose was assaulted by the smell of sludge in the gutter.

The door opened before I could lift my finger from the doorbell, as if they had been waiting for someone. Without returning my greeting, Mrs. Simonian said, 'No. There's just no way. Restaurant food does not agree with Emily. She has to have a rest now.' Through the cracked-open door I could see Emily's tearful face.

On the way back home, my critical streak lashed out at me: 'Serves you right! You just have to dance to whatever tune the children fiddle, don't you?' I answered back, 'I'll never subject myself to that again!'

The children were disappointed that Emily wouldn't be joining us. 'I don't feel like going to the Club,' Armen said.

'Great,' I responded. 'Stay home and study.' And with that encouragement, he piled into the car ahead of everyone else.

I sat with Mother and Alice in the back of the Chevy. Armineh sat in Alice's lap, and Arsineh, after making Armen swear to 'No teasing, I mean it!' sat up front, between Artoush and Armen.

The twins frowned from north Bawarda all the way to Braim without saying a word. Armen was taking driving pointers from Artoush. Alice and Mother were arguing about the date of the Lenten fast. In the end, Alice said, 'Eastertime is so far away now, and anyhow, I for one am not going to fast. I fasted this year, and it was enough for seven generations!'

'You have to fast,' said Mother.

'I'm not going to,' said Alice.

'What the hell do you mean, "I'm not going to?" You have to.'

'I'm not going to.'

Mother hissed just like an angry cat and pinched Alice's forearm hard. 'Ouuuch!' cried Alice. The twins cracked up laughing and their frowns melted away. Mother and Alice's fights, real or pretend, were the best way to make the twins laugh.

11

At the door to the Club, Alice whispered in my ear, 'Invite them over, please.'

I drew a deep breath and returned the greetings of Mr. Saadat, the manager of the Golestan Club, and asked after his wife, who had just given birth to their fourth child two weeks earlier. Artoush always shook hands with Mr. Saadat, and it always pleased me. I rarely saw other members of the Club shake hands with the manager.

The twins yelled out, 'Hey! Mimi!' and ran off in the direction of a classmate of theirs, a very delicate girl whose name was Marguerita, though her mother insisted on calling her Mimi. Up until a few months ago, Mimi, or Marguerita, lived in north Bawarda. When the kids were little, they were frightened of Marguerita's father, a tall, very rotund man who sported a thick beard. They called him 'Golirra.' I had heard from Artoush that the rank, or as the Abadanis would put it, the *Grade* of the 'Gorilla' had been raised, and he got himself a house in Braim. When they lived in Bawarda, Marguerita had many times come home from school with the twins and stayed at our house quite late, until finally her mother would arrive to pick her up with a wishy-washy apology. 'Sorry. It's so late. I got caught up.' It was well known to all the Armenians in Abadan what caught up Marguerita's mother: gambling and lounging about the Milk Bar, a new café that had recently opened.

Alice took my hand and headed off. 'Come along.'

No need to ask where we were going. Whenever we went out, the first thing Alice did was find a mirror and make sure her hair was not mussed up and her lipstick not wiped away. And no need to ask why I should tag along, either. Alice could not possibly contemplate going to the ladies' room alone.

Marguerita's mother was in the restroom teasing her hair. Her name was Juliette, but she insisted people call her Zhou Zhou. On the sink next to her purse stood a small aerosol can of Taft hairspray. The last time we had seen one another, in a ball at the Boat Club, she was a brunette. Now she was a redhead. Same color as her lipstick.

She saw us in the mirror, and turned around to give us a lukewarm greeting. 'Well, well!' she said. 'Fancy meeting you here.' The humanitarian aim of this sentence was to ask what we low-*Grade* residents of Bawarda were doing in the Golestan Club, which she considered the exclusive preserve of the high-*Grade* residents of Braim.

Alice drew a deep breath and puffed up her chest. I realized she was about to – in her words – 'run Marguerita's mother through the wringer and hang her out to dry.' Alice glanced at herself in the mirror, and once assured that her hair was in place and her lipstick fresh, she turned to Marguerita's mother. Before I could do anything about it, she asked,

'Excuse me, Juliette. What *Grade* did you say your husband holds?'

Marguerita's mother arched her eyebrows into virtual half crescents. 'It's Zhou Zhou. Fifteen. Why?'

Alice smiled. 'How interesting. So he still has three *Grades* to go before he reaches my brother-in-law.' Then she threaded her arm in mine and said, 'Phew! The smell of hairspray's about knocked me unconscious. Come on, Clarice.'

Outside the restroom, I protested. 'Why do you tell her such fibs? Her husband and Artoush are at the same *Grade*.'

Alice let go of my arm and waved at someone. 'It was the right thing to do. Keep that monkey-lady from going around and showing off in people's faces about the *Grade* of her gorilla man. If the Professor would knock off this "comrade" nonsense of his and get a house in Braim like any normal person would, we wouldn't have to put up with the pretentious airs of every nouveau riche in town. By the way, did you hear what I said before we walked in? You will invite them, won't you?' All of a sudden she gave a broad smile and a loud 'Well, hellllo!' and went up to a couple whom I could not recall. I had heard what she said before we walked in. And no need to ask who she wanted me to invite.

Artoush was talking to the head waiter by the door to the dining hall. I walked up to him and on the way peeked into the assembly hall, the double doors of which were wide open. There were thirty or forty women sitting in seven or eight rows of chairs, facing a table covered by a green baize cloth. On the tablecloth stood a vase full of asters, behind which a woman stood giving a speech. From her chignon and the bow in her hair I recognized her immediately. It was Mrs. Nurollahi. I always marveled at how she could arrange her hair in such a tall chignon. Armen called Mrs. Nurollahi's bowtie hair ribbons, which always matched the pattern of her dress, 'the trademark of Father's secretary.' When I reprimanded him – 'Be nice!' – Artoush would laugh. 'She is a capable woman. I suppose she does talk a bit much and maybe once in a while gets worked-up over nothing.'

Armen was pulling Arsineh's hair. 'Stop it,' I said, and grabbed Armineh's hand – she was lurching toward Armen to defend her sister.

Artoush said, 'There are no free tables. We have to wait half an hour.' Then he turned to Armen. 'I hear that you are itching to lose a few games of ping-pong to me.'

Armen laughed. 'No way! I'm itching to win.'

The twins jumped up and down. 'The winner gets to buy ice cream for everyone after lunch!' Artoush took the twins by the hand, and they went over to the ping-pong tables with Armen.

I called out after them, 'I'll wait here, then,' but they did not hear.

Out of the corner of my eye I saw Mother and Alice talking to a couple who were distantly related to us. I did not have the energy either for the woman or for her husband. They were members of a religious movement, Mary's Disciples, and were always proselytizing, insisting that we come to their meetings. In order not to catch their eye, I started reading the noticeboard for the events scheduled in the assembly hall:

WOMEN AND FREEDOM –
A TALK BY MRS. PARVIN NUROLLAHI
BEGINS AT 11:30 A.M.

I looked at my watch. It was nearly 12:30, so the talk must be winding down. I stepped in to the room, reflecting that I had not known until now that the first name of Artoush's secretary was Parvin.

I sat in the first empty seat. Two women, one elderly, the other young, looked at me from the adjoining seats, nodding their heads and smiling. The elderly lady was eating peanuts from a bag held between her knees, and the younger one was chewing gum. Mrs. Nurollahi was saying, 'Let me repeat once again that the first demand and primary goal of the women of Iran is the right to vote.'

The last time we had Nina and Garnik over to our place, Garnik and Artoush got into a long argument. In the end, Garnik asked, 'Why do we have to get ourselves mixed up in it?'

Artoush asked, 'We are Iranians, are we not?'

Garnik answered, 'We are Armenians, are we not?'

Nina said, 'What is all this voting stuff about?'

Mrs. Nurollahi's voice was high-pitched, and she drawled the end of her sentences. 'In conclusion, I remind you that we have been struggling for this cause for a long time now. The women of Iran have raised a great cry. The problem is that their cry has not been united, and has never been coordinated and directed toward a single goal...'

The elder woman smiled and leaned toward me to offer some peanuts. I smiled back and declined with a wave of my hand. The young woman next to me was listening to the talk, nodding her head in rhythm to her gum-chewing. Mrs. Nurollahi said, 'And now, to close with a flourish, allow me to read a poem for you.' I remembered that I needed to put the freshly ironed sheets away in the bedroom drawers. Mrs. Nurollahi read:

Awake, sister!
In a world where Djamila Boupachas write decrees of
    national Freedom
In their own blood across the page of history
Fetching eyes and ruby lips
Are no longer the measure of
Womanhood

The elder woman whispered in the ear of the young woman, loud enough for me to hear, 'They're not talking about our Miss Djamila, are they?'

The young woman said, 'No, Mother.' She shifted her stance and grumbled, 'You don't understand anything!'

The elder woman's hand hung motionless in the peanut bag. 'What do you mean I don't understand? I understand perfectly!' The sound of clapping mingled with the crinkling of the bag.

The women got up from their seats. A small group headed off toward the exit. Others mingled, talking and congratulating Mrs. Nurollahi, whose chignon was visible above all the other heads. I bid farewell to the elder lady and her daughter and came out of the room.

Artoush and the children were standing by the door of the dining hall, while Mother and Alice were still talking with the couple from Mary's Disciples. I motioned to Alice that we were going in to the restaurant. Artoush and I and the children followed after the head waiter, who showed us to our table. Artoush was right. Mrs. Nurollahi was a capable woman. I knew she was married, with three children. Like me. Despite that, she was working, and was involved in social activism, too. What did I do beside housework? I returned the greeting of the head waiter and thought, 'Mrs. Nurollahi is a capable woman.'

The dining hall of the Golestan Club was crowded, like every Friday, and, as usual, swimming with acquaintances of ours. Luckily, we were seated at a table far away from Marguerita and her parents. Soon Mother and Alice found us. Mother was saying, 'Nonsense, they are a very fine couple.'

'I didn't say they were bad people. I said they talk a lot.'

'They make up for it with a house so clean it sparkles.'

Alice looked at the kids and crossed her eyes. 'What's that got to do with the price of eggs?!' The twins burst out laughing.

We ordered Chelow Kebab and Mother told Artoush three times to tell the waiter to make sure her kebab was very well done. 'And have him take away these awful eggs, too.'

Armineh and Arsineh said, 'No! We want to play with the flour.'

I gave the dish of flour and cracked eggs to the waiter. 'Thanks. We won't be having eggs.' Some people liked their

Chelow Kebab in the old-fashioned style, with a raw egg yolk, so on Fridays the Club decorated the dining hall tables with deep dishes full of flour in which several egg shell halves were nestled, serving as little egg yolk bowls. The twins loved playing with the flour and once or twice had spilled the egg yolks onto the table, so that the waiter was obliged to change the white cotton tablecloth and the green felt mat underneath. Mother detested egg yolks with Chelow Kebab.

Alice took a piece of bread, scanned the entire circuit of the room, and then started in. 'Do you see Dr. Salehi-Fard's wife?' Dr. Salehi-Fard was the Chief of Surgery at the hospital. He was recently married, and now I remembered that it was him, the man Alice had waved to earlier and exchanged kisses with his wife. 'She looks and acts like a hick, but see what a husband she caught? Do you see Dolatarian's wife? I don't know why people say she's so chic. Is that thing on her head supposed to be a hat? It looks like a baby bath. Does she imagine a woman can turn herself into Jackie Kennedy just by slapping on a hat?' The woman described by Alice was the mother of one of Armen's classmates, a boy who once received a good beating from Armen for calling Armineh and Arsineh 'twin fillies hitched together like draft horses to a buggy.'

Alice asked Armen, 'Aren't you going to have any salad? Pass it over here.' She tipped Armen's salad onto her plate and looked over at the door. 'Whoa! What are Manya and Vazgen doing here? Onions in a bowl of fruit!'

Manya was the twins' art teacher and Vazgen Hairapetian the school principal. They were a young childless couple whose only concern in life was the Armenian school and its pupils. They were coming over to our table. I told the children to stand up in the presence of their teacher and principal. Artoush also stood up, and after exchanging greetings, invited them to sit with us. Vazgen said, 'Just for a few minutes.' He sat down and explained, 'We are guests of Mr. Khalatian. Otherwise we're complete outsiders at the Golestan Club.'

Alice tried not to look at me, and said, 'What a thing to say!'

Manya got into a conversation with Mother and Alice and kidded with the twins, as usual. 'Are you two sisters, or Xerox copies?'

Vazgen turned to me. 'The translation of the book I was telling you about is finished. Do you have time to read it? I'd be grateful.'

Vazgen and Manya produced a monthly children's magazine in Armenian called *Lusaber*. On a few occasions I had translated some poetry or stories for it, and Vazgen would sometimes give me material from the magazine to comment on before publication. When they had gone to their table, Arsineh asked, 'What book, Mommy?' Armineh echoed, 'What book?'

The day I was summoned to the school about Armen beating up the Dolatarian boy, Mrs. Dolatarian (elegant and petite, jade-green business suit, hair in a French twist) conceded that Armen was in the right, while I took the side of her boy. We made both boys apologize to one another. Afterwards, Vazgen talked about the book *Little Lord*

Fauntleroy and mentioned he was translating it into Armenian.

'Little Lord what was it now?' asked Alice as she burst out laughing.

Mother said, 'Manya has no equal. Despite all her work, you should see her house. Always clean and tidy. Fresh and spick and span. That's what you call a real woman!'

Armen took the grilled tomato from his plate and put it on Arsineh's plate. Arsineh sneered, and Armineh muttered, 'Why do you always use our plate like a garbage can?'

Artoush lifted the tomato off Arsineh's plate and moved it to his own. 'Does Vazgen really find the time to do translations after all the work he does? Why don't you do some translations?' I looked at him for a moment. He was smiling at me.

Mother said, 'When would she find the time? It's been six months since she washed the bedroom curtains.' And she stared at me. 'If I'm lying, go right ahead and say so.'

I cut up the twins' kebabs. Was it Artoush's smile, or his tone of voice, that reminded me of the days when we were newly engaged?

12

The children were at school, and Artoush was at work. I had straightened up the bedrooms, the dusting was done, and dinner was on the stove. The phone rang.

'If I don't call you, you'll never think to ask how I'm doing, will you?' It was Nina.

When I launched into an explanation of how I had been thinking of her for several days and wanted to telephone her and just didn't have the time, she laughed and cut me off. 'Don't explain. I know you are busy. What with the way you constantly needle yourself about the minute details of everything, and then there's your mother's pickiness, and Artoush's grumpiness.'

One of Nina's virtues was that she never got offended. She always said, 'When I put myself in so-and-so's position, I see they are right.' The way Nina saw it, everyone always had a good reason for what they did, no one was ever to blame, and people never did things in a mean spirit or with an ulterior motive. And yet...and yet...here she was talking about 'Artoush's grumpiness'? Why did everyone around me think my husband was grumpy?

To change the subject, I asked about Sophie and Garnik, and about her son, Tigran, who had been accepted to the University of Tehran. Nina asked after the kids and Artoush and Mother and Alice, and then talked about how happy she was with her new place, and that the neighbors were not bad people.

'In the house next door is this bachelor Dutchman. He's practically two meters tall, and he's a little loony, worse than me.' In the midst of raucous laughter, she explained that the Dutchman sunbathes on the lawn at three in the afternoon, smack in the middle of the yard, with the sun blazing away overhead. And that the lady across from them is Jewish, and asks Nina every Saturday to go and turn on the outside lights for her. She had not yet met her other neighbors.

One of Nina's faults was her talkativeness, especially on the phone. I was worried about the food on the stove. I butted in, 'Nina, I've got food on the stove...'

'My gosh!' she hurriedly exclaimed. 'I'm sorry! I completely forgot why I called. Come over for dinner this Thursday. Tell your mother and Alice, too. Actually, I'll call her myself – I don't want your sister to get her knickers in a twist.' And she laughed again. 'Garnik's niece is here with us for a few weeks from Tehran. The poor thing's just gotten divorced. I want you to meet her. Some of the things she does remind me of you. Thursday, don't forget! Come early so the kids can play together. Sophie really misses the twins. You'd think they didn't see each other every day at school.' Finally she said goodbye.

I hung up the phone and went to the kitchen to stir the food. As I turned off the stove, the phone rang again. I went back into the hall.

'I had not pegged you for one of those women who are constantly on the phone.'

One of my faults was never being able to think of good comebacks. When people talked rubbish I would just keep quiet. I kept quiet and Mrs. Simonian kept on talking. 'The other night you told me you would send some woman to our house. There's no sign of her. I don't appreciate empty promises.'

There was a limit to my never being able to think of good comebacks and to keeping cool and quiet. I drew a deep breath, twisted the phone cord tightly around my wrist and said with a voice rather louder than normal, 'In the first place, Ashkhen's name is not "some woman." She is a respectable lady who happens to work to make a living. In the second place, she has no telephone and I have to wait until Saturday when it's our house's turn in the schedule, and third—'

She cut me off. 'Today is Saturday.'

I was caught off balance. 'Yesterday she called to say she can't make it, because—'

She cut me off again. 'You said she didn't have a telephone.'

I was about to blow up. 'Her son telephoned.'

She was quiet for a few seconds. Then her tone changed. 'So, please don't forget and…I've set aside a jar of chutney for you.'

I was dumbstruck. I couldn't make sense of her hot and cold behavior. I said I would speak with Ashkhen, thanked her for the chutney, and put the phone down. I had better warn Ashkhen what she would be getting herself into.

13

The children's piano teacher was an English woman, fair-skinned and blond. She had married an Iranian man, and despite living for many years in Iran, her Persian was much worse than us Armenians. Before the children's lesson began, she told me, 'My telephone number…you, to Mizzus, Mizzus, what is her name? Your neighbor.'

'Simonian,' I said.

She clapped her hand on her freckled forehead. 'Ahh! Simonian. She called today. She very strange woman. She say come tune our piano. I say I am no piano tuner. She spoke with bad manners.' She arched her thin blond eyebrows and shrugged her delicate shoulders. She waved her upturned fingers in the air a couple times, with their red polished nails, beckoning the children to follow her to the piano room.

I took a seat in the parlor, feeling embarrassed, as if I was the one who had done something awful. While waiting for the children to finish their lesson, I glanced over the plaid easy chairs, the chintz drapes, the little statues, the large paintings, the silver and china dishes, and waged an internal struggle: 'What does it have to do with you? You are not responsible for the wrong-doings of anyone else. Artoush is right. You should not socialize much with this family.' Taking in the room's decor, it occurred to me that dusting all these tiny statuettes, heavy busts, paintings, and dishes must take quite a long time.

On the bus on the way home I tried to explain to the twins why they should not ask after Emily so much. 'Emily has more homework, and her classes are harder than yours. And I suppose her grandmother does not like Emily to go out of the house too much. Everyone has their own ways, and we have to respect that.'

Arsineh blew away a curl that had fallen over her forehead into her eyes. 'But Emily is our friend. We like her a lot.'

Armineh put the piano book down on the seat next to her and took her sister's hand. 'Every day she says "I wish I could come to your house."'

Poor Emily, I thought. If it were me, I would also long to get away from that jail and its jailer.

'Can we go to the *Store*?' asked Armineh.

'Can we buy *Smarties*?' asked Arsineh.

We got off at the stop near the *Store*.

The supermarket was cool and fragrant, as always. The twins ran straight for the candy counter. 'Basket or cart?' the clerk asked me. 'Basket, please.' I hooked the shopping basket over my arm and headed directly to the health and hygiene section. A woman was leaning over her grocery cart looking at the shelf of soaps and lotions. Her cart was full of different kinds of Cadbury chocolates. We smiled at one another and, as though obliged to explain, she said, 'I'm taking souvenirs for some Tehranis who rarely get their hands on imported chocolates.' She laughed and I laughed back. 'They also asked for soap and lotion. I'm not sure which soap to pick.'

I picked up a bar of Vinolia soap and put it in my basket. 'I always take Vinolia for souvenirs.' She picked four bars of the soap and dropped them in her cart, along with three jars of Yardley hand cream. She said goodbye and, with some difficulty, got her cart to roll forward. I took a jar of Yardley and placed it in my basket.

I made the circuit of the store and got two boxes of Nice cookie wafers, the kind Artoush liked, and Haliborange vitamin syrup for the children.

Arsineh and Armineh turned up with their hands full of chocolates. Armineh said, 'You told us to remind you to...' Arsineh finished, '...buy bread and milk from the *Dairy*.' I told them to return half of their chocolates to the candy counter, and then we went over to what the Abadanis called the *Dairy*, a little room attached to the supermarket, and bought rolls and milk.

When we arrived home, exhausted by the heat, Artoush's car was in the garage.

Armineh said, 'Oh, goody! Father is home.'

Arsineh said, 'Father is home. Goody!'

We could hear voices in the living room. Armineh set her piano book down on the telephone table. 'Do we have guests?' Before I could say that the piano book does not belong on the telephone table, Arsineh picked it up and said, 'We have guests.'

I wondered who was here. Alice was working the afternoon shift this week, and Mother would always sit in the kitchen, and Armen must be in his own room, because the music on his portable Teppaz turntable was loud enough to hear three houses away. Armineh looked at me. 'Maybe it's one of Father's acquaintances.'

Arsineh said, 'The green Cadillac was not in the garage.' She plunged her hand into the grocery bag and fished out a box of Smarties.

Armineh stroked her chin, as if to play with a beard, in imitation of Artoush. 'Actually, I forgot to tell you. A few of the fellows are coming over.'

Arsineh burst out laughing. 'Manners!' I reminded her, and she obligingly stifled her laughter.

'A few of the fellows' referred to three middle-aged men who sometimes came to our place. They were not Armenian. They would sit, not on the living room sofa, but at the dining table, and when I took tea in to them, they would thank me profusely. Artoush would close the door behind me as I left the room, and for an hour or two I would only hear muffled voices.

Armineh turned to her sister and mimicked one of the three, the tall fellow who spoke in a staccato fashion. 'Par-don me...Would it be pos-si-ble to leave the Ca-dil-lac in the ga-rage?' The first time the tall fellow came over, he asked to leave his green Cadillac in the garage, because the sun would damage its paint. It became a habit every time he came over; even in twilight, when there was no sun, he left the Cadillac in the garage and closed both of the double doors.

Angry at Artoush for forgetting to tell me that he was to have guests, I yelled at the twins, 'Wash your faces and hands and do your homework.' When the twins ran off to their room, I went to the kitchen.

I had seen the green Cadillac in front of Shahandeh's store a few times, under the blazing sun. When I mentioned this to Artoush, he shrugged. 'Well, there's no garage near Shahandeh's store.'

I began putting away the stuff I had bought. I did not know the names of these three people, and I did not want to know. 'Won't it cause problems to have them come over here?' I had once asked Artoush after they left. 'Don't worry,' he said. 'We're just shooting the breeze.'

I put the bread in the breadbox, grumbling to myself, 'Just shooting the breeze, my foot!' and went to the living room.

There, instead of 'Father's acquaintances,' as the twins put it, I saw Emile Simonian, who got up as I walked in, said hello and extended his hand. I shook it and quickly with-drew my hand. The hand cream was still on the kitchen table. We exchanged pleasantries and I asked, 'Care for coffee?'

While the coffee was brewing, I washed my hands at the kitchen faucet, opened the Yardley hand cream and rubbed some on my hands.

I headed for the living room with a tray of coffee and wondered how it came about that Artoush had invited Emile over. Artoush said, 'Did you know that Emile is a mean chess player?'

Well, there was my answer. I thought of our honeymoon in Isfahan and Shiraz. For hours Artoush, with infinite patience, had tried to teach me to play chess, but I never learned.

Emile lifted his coffee cup and looked at the window. 'What pretty drapes.'

I had embroidered the lace flower trim along the hem of the drapes myself, and liked them quite a lot. But no one (other than Mother, who had said, 'Your tastes take after mine') ever complimented the drapes. As Artoush set up the chess pieces I left the room. I told the twins to bring their dictation notebooks to the kitchen and told Armen to turn down the record player.

I was thinking about what to fix for dinner when Armineh and Arsineh ran in, pouting.

'My dictation notebook is missing.'

'My pencil case is missing.' They stomped on the floor in unison.

'That Armen!'

'That Armen!' I said, and got up.

Armen's door was locked, as usual. Instead of knocking, I jerked on the doorknob, twisting it left and right several times. The second I said, 'Again, you took...' Armen shouted from inside the room, 'The cabinet in the living room.' Still facing the closed door, I said, 'You have a real sickness, you know,' and headed for the living room.

Emile looked up. The top button of his shirt was undone, revealing a fine gold chain. I opened the door of the china cabinet. Emile asked Artoush, 'What was going on today? Everyone left early.'

Artoush stroked his beard, his eyes on the chessboard. 'There was a speech. Why didn't you come?'

'A speech?'

'Pegov was speaking.'

'Pegov?'

'Nikolai Pegov, the Soviet Ambassador.'

'I see.'

I collected the dictation book and the pencil case from the china cabinet and returned to the kitchen.

I was boiling macaroni noodles for dinner when the doorbell rang. It was Emily, conveying a message from her grandmother that they were waiting on her father for dinner. Emile jumped up. 'I wasn't paying attention to the time.' He reacted just like his daughter, the first time her grandmother had come after her.

Artoush looked like a kid whose toys had just been yanked away from him. The twins pleaded, 'Let them stay for dinner.' I forgot all about those limits on socializing and my vow 'never to subject myself to that again,' and told Emile, 'Why don't you stay for dinner? I'll call your mother.' Artoush affirmed the invitation, and the twins each grabbed an arm, tugging me toward the telephone. Armen's door was open, and he was leaning on the door jamb.

Elmira Simonian not only agreed to let her son and grand-daughter stay, she even agreed to come herself. After this quick and unexpected acceptance, the twins jumped for joy, and Emile and Artoush returned to their chess game. Seeing Emily's smile, I thought 'the innocent child.' My back was to Armen, so I didn't see if he was happy or not.

14

They sat cross-legged on their beds, clutching Ishy and Rapunzel, respectively.

Armineh said, 'You didn't tell us why, but we finally figured out all by ourselves why Emily's grandmother never got bigger.'

Arsineh, with great gravity, explained, 'Because she didn't get vaccinated.'

Whenever it was time for the twins to get a shot, I had to cajole them with pleas, explanations, and warnings, including: 'You won't get bigger if you don't get vaccinated.'

Artoush laughed when I told him half an hour later what they had said. I sat down beside him. 'Mrs. Simonian has a lot of Dr. Jekyll and Mr. Hyde in her. You start thinking she is a selfish, beastly creature, then she does something totally unexpected, something that makes you want to like her. Those were wonderful stories she told! And you have to admit that her piano playing was flawless.'

After dinner, first Emily and the twins had played the piano. Then Mrs. Simonian had played the difficult parts of their lessons for them, before taking song requests, and finishing up with some old Armenian melodies. I believe that even Armen didn't notice that Mrs. Simonian's feet did not reach the pedals.

Artoush yawned. 'They are not bad people. Nothing wrong with Emile's chess playing, either!'

'Where did the political discussion lead?' I inquired.

He clasped his hands behind his head. 'Nowhere. Emile lives in his own world and marches to his own tune.'

I picked a pistachio shell off the carpet. 'What world is that?'

He let his hands drop, drawing them across his goatee. 'Oh, I don't know. Literature, poetry, that sort of thing.' I juggled the pistachio shell from one hand to the other. Mrs. Simonian had said, 'No matter how hard I tried, he didn't learn to play piano. Instead, he began reading books and composing poems before he even started going to school.'

I tossed the pistachio shell in the ashtray. 'Well, what's wrong with reading books?'

Artoush stretched his legs out on the coffee table in front of the sofa and looked at the blank TV screen. 'Nothing wrong with it at all. As long as it has a point, or offers a solution, or teaches people something, and isn't simply an amusing pastime. Emile doesn't seem to be living in this world.'

I twirled a strand of hair around my finger. 'You mean to say that anyone who reads or loves poetry is not living in this world?'

He yawned. 'Poems and stories don't pay the rent. Oh, by the way! Mrs. Nurollahi said she wanted to ask you something. She said she would phone.'

What could Mrs. Nurollahi want with me?

Mrs. Simonian had said, 'A very important journal published a number of Emile's poems. One of his stories won an award.'

What could Mrs. Nurollahi want with me?

Artoush asked, 'Did you figure out what ever happened to Ishy and Rapunzel?'

After the Simonians had left, Ishy and Rapunzel were missing. We all suspected Armen, as usual. But Armen, who usually gave a mischievous smile and eventually admitted where he had hidden his sisters' toys, was serious this time and even had a tear in his eye as he protested, 'I swear to God, to the Christ, to Mary, to all that is holy, I didn't hide them.' Finally, Artoush found Ishy and Rapunzel outside, in the yard, beneath the window of the twins' bedroom.

I tucked the strand of hair I was twirling behind my ear. 'I don't think it was Armen's doing.' Artoush closed his eyes and leaned back in the sofa. I stared at the dark TV screen. So, could it have been the girl's doing?

Artoush opened his eyes, stood up and stretched. 'Will you get the lights, or shall I?'

'I will,' I answered.

While I was clearing the dinner table, Emile had asked, 'Clarice, can I lend a hand?' Was it his offer of help, or his calling me by my first name, that made me happy? I turned out the living room lights and before retiring to the bedroom, put the jar of chutney that Mrs. Simonian had brought in the back of one of the kitchen cupboards. It was the cupboard where I kept things I rarely used.

15

Alice sat down at the kitchen table. She had her hair cut short, layered, and teased to the utmost. Her head looked round as a ball. 'I came straight here from the hairdresser.'

I jumped in preemptively, 'Oh, your hair looks great. Did you go to Angele's?'

She smiled. 'Are you kidding? Angele doesn't know how to do short hair. I went to the Shemshad Salon; they have a new hairdresser from Tehran.' When she spied last night's washed dinner plates in the dish rack, she was livid. 'Did you have guests?' She posed the question much the same way one might ask, 'Did you kill somebody?'

I started putting away the plates. My rational side reminded me for the thousandth time, 'You don't need to explain. Just say, yeah, we had guests. Nothing more.' I put the last spoon away, closed the drawer and wheeled around to face Alice.

'Yeah, we had guests.' And I told her who it was.

She frowned. 'Why didn't you let me know?'

Before I could stand my ground on not needing to explain, my emotional side capitulated. 'It all happened quite suddenly. And you were at work at the hospital last night.'

Instead of grumbling or picking a fight, as was her habit, this time Alice picked an apple from the fruit bowl and said nothing. Angry at myself for having gone ahead and explained, and also surprised at Alice for not having bickered, I sat down across from her. She ate the apple down to the core and said, 'You could have told them to come to Nina's on Thursday night.'

In order to keep my cool, I tried to think about something else. I stared at the flowers outside the window. I had never been able to get it through my sister's head that if a person gets invited somewhere, it's not right to show up with an uninvited guest of his own accord. And I could not convince her this time, either.

She raised her eyebrows. 'Don't be silly. You don't have to stand on formalities with Nina. But, fine. It doesn't matter much. I've made my decision. Do you have a cigarette?' I got up without a word and brought her the pack of cigarettes. So, my sister had decided to lose weight. I lit a match for her.

She puffed clumsily at the cigarette and let out the smoke. 'As long as Mother is not here to raise a fuss, let me say that whatever faults and drawbacks Simonian may have are of no importance to me. The truth is that I'm tired of being lonely, and I'm tired of Mother's grumbling. So what if he's been married before? You were right. One can't have cake and eat it too. He comes from a decent enough family, and he is educated… Hey, careful! You've burned your fingers. Where is your mind?'

The match had burnt to the base. I tossed it into the ashtray. Mother had warned me on the phone, 'If Alice turns up, no matter what she says, don't argue. This time she's really gone off the deep end.' I guessed that meant that they had argued again. Now I was sure. I remembered a joke. This man says, 'I've decided to marry the king's daughter.' They tell him, 'The king's not going to give you his daughter.' He says, 'I've made my decision, so the matter is half resolved.'

My sister had decided to marry Emile Simonian, so as far as she was concerned, the matter was *fully* resolved.

Alice grabbed another apple. 'When his mother dies, her jewelry will go to me.' And she laughed uproariously. 'The only problem is the girl. But you said she's not a naughty kid. I've got no patience for raising kids, but you will help me out.'

And after having settled the matter just like that – cut and sewn and worn from whole cloth, as Mother would say – she got up.

'Okay, I'm off. I need navy blue shoes to go with my new two-piece white suit.' My head was spinning and I do not think I even returned her goodbye. Alice left, smiling.

Before I could make it to the hallway to call Mother, the phone rang. Mother had beat me to it. 'I know. I know. I've been filling her ears from last night until now. It's like talking to a brick wall. The sooner she sees this lout, the better. Maybe she'll drop the crusade.' When I hung up I was mad at Mother, too. What right did she have to call someone she had never set eyes on a 'lout'?

I sat down again at the kitchen table. My hand found my hair. I was twisting my hair around my fingers and letting it go. Twisting, letting go. It was not a difficult thing to picture, the first meeting of Alice and Emile Simonian: my sister is made up to the nines and in the first half hour gives a complete report of her virtues, her education, and her social position. She offers an opinion about everything from cooking and housekeeping to politics and global economics. Then she speaks of her many suitors (some of them of course imagined), explaining that she refused their every proposal. Finally, she speaks about her student days in England. My straight hair was twisted like a spring. I coiled it behind my ear and latched onto another strand.

My greatest hope and aspiration was for Alice to marry. Several times I had suggested possible candidates, but my sister would grimace as though I had offered her a poisoned cup. 'You have got to be kidding! You mean I'm so hopeless that you have to find me a husband?'

Every time I twisted my hair around my finger Nina would say, 'Turning into Louis the Sixteenth again? Let go of your poor hair!' I let go of my hair and stood up. I paced up and down the room in search of a solution. Finding none, I vowed that if my sister would give up this crusade, the very next day I would buy everyone at the almshouse lunch and dinner.

16

When the children came home from school, Emily was with them.

Immediately I asked, 'Did you tell your grandmother before coming over?' Emily nodded her head and lowered her eyes to the floor. All this shyness was beginning to try my patience.

'We just went over and got her grandmother's permission,' Armineh explained.

'Emily has some problems with math,' said Arsineh. 'She came to get Armen's help.'

Before my surprised gaze could settle on my son, Armen ran off to his room, saying, 'I'll be right back.' Quite a day for the unexpected! Math was Armen's arch nemesis, right after, or perhaps on an equal footing with, the bane of his life, Composition.

I forgot about their after-school snack until the children asked, 'What do we have to eat?'

I started making excuses. 'I was busy. I didn't have time to prepare anything.' The twins stood there wide-eyed, looking at me with heads cocked at an angle.

'What were you doing?'

'Why didn't you have time?'

Irritated, I said, 'There is bread and cheese. Help yourself, and don't ask so many questions.' They took a step backward and looked at each other. I put my hand on my forehead, leaned against the wall and closed my eyes.

Armineh stepped forward and took my hand. 'Don't you feel well?'

Arsineh took my other hand. 'You don't feel well?'

I badly wanted to tell them, 'No, I don't feel well.'

The doorbell rang, leaving me no chance to figure out what was making me feel ill.

I withdrew my hands from the twins' grasp and headed for the door, telling myself, 'God help me through this.' I braced myself for yet another strange occurrence, feeling, as I opened the door, like Alice in Wonderland. In any other circumstance, the similarity of the names of my sister Alice and the little heroine of that book would have seemed amusing. But it was not some other circumstance – I was not feeling well, and it was not amusing.

It was the Company electrician, come to repair our yard lights. He was a young man I had not seen before, very thin, with a large birthmark on his cheek.

I accompanied him from one end of the yard to the other so he could test every lamp. At each light he paused to talk, explaining that he was newly employed by the Oil Company, and now that he had a good job, he had decided to marry. From childhood our electrician had fancied his maternal cousin for a wife, so his mother had long ago persuaded her sister to promise him her daughter's hand. And finally, he arrived at the conclusion that one of the lamps had a short. That much I had figured out myself. Then he said his voltmeter was broken and, God willing, we might have one he could use.

I was sure we had a voltmeter, but could not find it after searching all through the toolbox. Armen had probably taken it again. I knocked on his door and went in. 'Do you have the voltmeter?'

He and Emily were sitting on the desk, their feet swinging over the edge. They both leapt down to the floor. Armen, flustered, said, 'No, I don't have it.'

On my way back to the yard, it occurred to me, 'Strange way to study!'

The electrician asked, 'Can you borrow one from a neighbor?'

Mrs. Rahimi was in Tehran. Mr. Rahimi would certainly not be home at that time of day. I did not know my other neighbors well enough to feel comfortable asking to borrow something from them. 'Well, yes. Wait just a minute.'

I crossed the street and rang the Simonians' doorbell. Emile would not be back from the Company yet. I was praying that his mother had a voltmeter and would not be out of sorts. Emile himself opened the door. He went to fetch a voltmeter and walked back with me to our yard. 'Maybe the electrician will need a hand.' I don't know why I did not protest at this (at least to make a pretense of being polite and saving him the trouble), and I did not ask myself what he was doing home at this time of day. I was feeling a bit better now. Let Alice build castles in the air. She might not be so dumb after all.

17

Emile found the problem with the wiring before the electrician did, and the entire time he was fiddling with the wires, the electrician stood idly by, talking about his marriage and how he might be able to get a house in the Bahmanshir or Pirouzabad neighborhoods, and that, God willing, they would go on pilgrimage to Mashhad after the wedding. In the end, he gathered his stuff, and as he was leaving, he said with a laugh, 'With a neighbor like the Engineer, here, why call us?'

He was almost at the gate when I called out, 'Wait!'

I ran inside, opened one of the kitchen cabinets and took out a box. I went back to the yard and handed the box to the electrician. He stared at it. 'Chocolate from the *Store*?' His eyes lit up.

'Take it for your fiancée,' I said. He was delighted. He thanked me and left.

Emile was watching me. His hands were blackened and dirty, so I invited him inside to wash up. While he washed his hands, I fixed two glasses of Vimto fruit cordial I had bought from the Kuwaiti Bazaar. I was the only one in our household who liked Vimto.

Stepping into the kitchen, he looked all around. Then he smelled his hands. 'What fragrant soap, what a pretty kitchen, what a lovely drink.'

I don't know why the smell of Vinolia soap reminded me of my father and our house with the dim hallway in Tehran.

He sat down at the table and looked out the window. 'You built that ledge yourself, didn't you? Our kitchen window doesn't have a ledge.'

None of the homes in Bawarda had window ledges. We had just arrived in Abadan, and I was pregnant with Armen when Mr. Morteza built the kitchen window ledge for me.

Emile took a sip of his drink. I expected him to say it was tasty, but he did not. He was still looking out the window. 'The sweet peas are fading a bit.'

Mr. Morteza had run his dirt-caked hands over the ledge, which was still covered with brick and mortar dust, and said, 'This ledge is perfect for sweet peas. Their fragrance will bowl you over.' I did not know what kind of flower sweet peas were, in fact had never even heard of them before. A couple of weeks after Armen was born, Mr. Morteza came over one day for an unscheduled stop with a flower box fastened to his bicycle rack. He set it on the ledge, adjusted its position, and said, 'Sweet peas! Just a little something to welcome the newborn.' It was the first time I had seen the little blue and pink and white blossoms. How did Emile know the names of such flowers?

'I have to change its soil,' I said.

He drank the Vimto. 'I planted sweet peas in Masjed-Soleiman. I've ordered soil and fertilizer for our yard here.

When it's delivered, I'll change the soil in this flower box for you.'

'The Company gardener does that stuff for us,' I said.

He put the glass down on the table. The chain around his neck had caught on the top button of his shirt. He untangled it. 'I like digging in the dirt, the soil, and the roots. Watching something grow that you planted with your own two hands gives you a good feeling, no?'

A ridiculous smile settled on my lips.

He laughed. 'Of course, I'm no green thumb, like you.'

Seeing my confused expression, he added, 'I heard from the twins that it was you who grew the flowers you brought my mother that night.' I felt myself blushing. Was it because he had addressed me with the familiar form of the pronoun 'you,' or because I was not used to receiving compliments?

'Did you know that electrician?' Now he was using the formal form of 'you' again.

'No,' I said. 'That was the first time I saw him. He's just started work for the Oil Company.'

He looked at the cross around my neck. 'So how did you know he's getting married?'

I straightened the cross, which had gotten twisted. 'He told me so.'

He looked at the sweet peas. 'I know why. Everyone enjoys talking with you. Talking with you is comfortable.' He looked at me. 'A person feels like he's known you for years.'

The twins came bouncing and sliding up. 'Our homework is finished.' 'Emily's not finished yet with her work?'

It only now occurred to me that I hadn't heard a peep from

Armen's room for over an hour. As I started to get up, Emily walked in, her math book and a notebook under her arm. Armineh and Arsineh went over and attached themselves to either of her arms.

'Shall we play house?'

'Or jacks?'

Emily looked at her father. Emile took the last sip of Vimto and set the glass on the tray. 'Grandmother is all alone. She's got her headache again. Maybe it's better if...'

Armineh cut in, mid-sentence. 'Well, let grandmother rest. Emily can stay with us.'

Arsineh said, 'Well, you can stay, too. That way, grand-mother will get a good long rest.'

Emile chuckled and looked at me. 'Wouldn't imposing upon you two nights in a row be quite cheeky?'

I was sure that he was merely trying to be polite. 'Stay,' I said. 'Artoush, wherever he is, will soon turn up.' Before the sentence had completely left my mouth, I heard the Chevy come sputtering up our street.

Armineh and Arsineh jumped up and down. 'Stay! Stay! Please.' Then they pinned their eyes on me.

'I'll telephone Mrs. Simonian,' I agreed. We had all quickly learned that permission – not only for Emily, but also for her father – rested in the hands of the grandmother.

I returned Artoush's greeting while he let the twins climb up his back like it was a tree, and dialed Elmira Simonian's number, wondering how she would react. Her voice sounded tired and listless. 'It's not up to me. They can decide for them-selves.' And she hung up.

I started making dinner – cutlets and French fries. The unexpected occurrences of that afternoon and my sister's strange conviction seemed like a long ago memory. What had made me so mad? It wasn't the first time that Alice had arrived at this kind of decision. There was the Armenian doctor at the hospital, after all. And the brother of a friend who came from Tehran. The reason I had felt queasy this time was that...

My self-critical streak butted in: '...was that what?'

I poured the oil in the frying pan. It was that I was tired. It was because...I don't know. Emile and Artoush were playing chess in the living room, and the children were running around outside in the yard.

I was thinking about Elmira Simonian as I flipped the cutlets over. Mother had said, 'Her father's house was like a palace. More than fifty rooms, a huge garden, servants, and retainers. The nurse who committed suicide was English. They said the lady, despite her dwarfish stature, had a hundred admirers, both before and after marrying. Dashing, debonair European men would come to Isfahan just to see her and attend her fashionable parties.'

I peeled the potatoes and figured that they must have spun a whole-cloth about her out of a single strand of yarn, the stories sounded so exaggerated. After all, short as she is, how...

I was trying to imagine Mrs. Simonian in her youth when Armen and Emily, breathless and sweaty, burst into the kitchen. Armen got the pitcher of water out of the fridge and poured some, first for Emily, then for himself. Emily's hair

111

was sticking to her forehead and her eyes were sparkling. It occurred to me that if the grandmother, in her youth, looked like her granddaughter does now...I put the pitcher, which Armen had left on the counter, back in the fridge...maybe what people said about her is true.

I plopped the potatoes into the hot oil. Mother had said, 'What a wedding her poor father threw for his daughter! An orchestra from Tehran, a chef from France. He bought the oldest wines from the cellar of Levon the wine-merchant. He invited a crowd of grandees, from courtiers to foreign ambassadors.' I turned the potatoes over and thought, after the luxurious life Mother had described her leading, this house in north Bawarda must seem quite contemptible. I remembered the dim empty rooms of the house; the quite expensive and once beautiful tablecloth and cloth napkins; the tarnished, almost black, silverware; and the chipped china. Only the twin candelabras retained their long-ago luster and brilliance, along with that wooden cabinet.

I was standing over the potatoes so they would not burn, lost in my imagination. Where was Elmira Simonian when she first spread out that cotton tablecloth in her dining room? In her house in Calcutta? Or in her apartment in Paris, which she said was opposite Notre Dame? I remembered the long tablecloth almost touching the floor on all four sides of the table, so it must have been designed for a much larger table, a twelve-person setting maybe, with high-backed plush velvet chairs. The hostess – all made-up, her hair jet black, dressed in a gown with a lace collar, maybe, wearing long earrings to match her heavy diamond necklace – would raise a crystal-cut wine glass to her red lips. Her dark eyes must have sparkled like her granddaughter's did a few seconds ago, over the rim of the glass.

Emile's voice – saying, 'It smells so good' – cut off my reverie about his mother's parties in her youth, and I looked down at the potatoes, which were starting to burn.

'Oh, no!' I shouted, and without thinking, picked up the hot frying pan with both hands and put it on the counter. I didn't feel the burn until I let go of the pan. I burned my hands on a regular basis while cooking or ironing, so I was used to the pain of it and did not usually cry out, but this time I could not suppress a yelp. I was drenched in sweat.

Emile shouted, 'What have you done to yourself?' He grabbed my shoulders and led me to the table, pulling out the nearest chair for me. 'Let me see.'

I sat down. Why was he using the formal 'you' again? I looked down at my palms, turning redder by the second. He poured water in a glass and brought the glass to my lips. 'Don't you worry. I'll take care of it in a moment.' He set the glass on the table and rushed out of the kitchen. This time he had used the informal 'you' again.

Worse than the pain and the worry about whether I would be able to work with my hands for the next few days, and what I would do about meals tomorrow, and who would wash the dishes, and a dozen other what-will-happens and who-will-do-its, was the muttering of Artoush, who had come running into the kitchen in response to my cry. He was standing over me, grumbling as he always did when such things happened.

'I've told you a thousand times to be careful. If the potatoes burn, let them burn! Why don't you think what you are doing to yourself? Why are you making French fries and cutlets in this heat, anyway? We could have ordered food from somewhere. And don't worry, restaurant food never killed anyone. You've inherited this irrational finickiness from your mother. I wish your sister was half as finicky as you...'

I tried not to hear it. I had understood years ago that Artoush shows his love for people by chastising them when something happens to them. It was the same thing whenever one of the children fell down or got sick or had a pain somewhere. If he seized the opportunity to criticize Mother and Alice at every turn, that was only because Mother and Alice did the same thing to Artoush. I had long ago learned how to play the role of mediator. He was now walking round and round the table, and around me, talking away. It was making me dizzy, and the burning in my hands was getting worse when Emile returned with a large brown jar. Without a word, he dug his hand into the jar several times and rubbed a cream of some sort, black and somewhat sticky, on both of my palms. Artoush stood silently, watching over us. Eyes fixed on my palms, I suddenly felt very hot, and my hands began to burn once again, as if still stuck to the sides of the frying pan. Then my palms started to throb, until they gradually grew cooler and cooler, and finally the burning and the throbbing stopped. I was drenched in sweat.

When I raised my head, Emile was watching me with a smile that seemed to say, 'Didn't I tell you I would take care of it?'

18

The three of us were sitting at the kitchen table. As he peeled potatoes, Emile was explaining the properties of the Indian burn cream. He had dumped the burnt potatoes in the garbage pail, and picked out several fat spuds from the basket near the refrigerator. He was now peeling off the skins, and Artoush was trying to lend a hand. I wondered how many times in his life Artoush had peeled potatoes, and how many times Emile had? Listening to Emile, I was still holding my palms open flat. 'One of our cooks, who was from the south of India, brought two jars of this cream for my mother many years ago.'

The twins came running in.

'Ramu?' I asked, immediately regretting the question. It was an unhappy reminder.

He put the knife down on the table. 'It was Ramu's father.' He was quiet for a minute, then picked up the knife again. 'I've had it tested several times in different places, and no one was able to figure out the ingredients. They could only say that it contained roots and leaves of various plants, a fact which I had already figured out on my own.'

Artoush closed the refrigerator door and sat at the table. 'What did the children want?' I asked.

'Water,' he said.

By the time Artoush had patchily removed the skin from a couple of potatoes, Emile had peeled the rest and cut them into even strips. He poured them into the strainer and got up. 'Only one member of Ramu's family knew how to prepare that cream, and he taught it to only one other person before he died.' He put the strainer in the sink and turned on the faucet. I noticed that when his mother isn't around, he does not speak so formally.

The phone rang. In the hallway someone picked up the receiver, and a few moments later, Armen was calling out, 'Mommmm! Telephone. Mrs. Nurollahi.'

I yelled back, 'For me or for your father?'

'For you.'

I got up. 'Will you be able to hold the phone?' Artoush asked. Emile turned his head back from the sink. The water was pouring over the sliced potatoes in the strainer. Was it my imagination, or did he look at me with worry?

I opened my hands and closed them. They hurt much less now. I nodded, indicating that I could manage, and went to the hallway. Through the door to the living room I saw Emily and Armen sitting in the easy chairs. Emily was recounting something, animatedly gesturing with her head and hands. If I did not know better, I would have supposed her a young woman rather than a girl. Armen was in the chair facing hers, his chin resting on his hand, watching raptly.

I picked up the receiver and wondered what Mrs. Nurollahi wanted with me. I looked at my hands, with a new appreciation for their importance.

Mrs. Nurollahi, as usual, greeted me warmly, asking after everyone at length, including each of the children one by one, before getting to the point. She had a good memory. She remembered not only the names of the children, but what grade they were in. She even remembered the cold the twins had caught a few months back. Finally, she said, 'I saw you last Friday at the talk at the Golestan Club. I'm sorry that I didn't get an opportunity to say hello.'

There was no hint of reproach in her voice. I was embarrassed. I should have gone up to her after her talk to congratulate her, and had not done so. Mrs. Nurollahi did not give me an opportunity to explain and apologize, and did not seem to expect it.

'I wanted to ask if you would be so kind as to attend the next meeting of our society? The Armenian ladies have not been inclined to join in with us. I know that you have your own society, a very active one, but as you know, the Majles elections are coming up, and as you are also no doubt aware, because of the suffrage issue, the coming year will be an important one for Iranian women...'

I did not know that the Majles elections were coming up, and had only heard here and there about the issue of women's voting rights. I reproached myself: you, and most other Armenian women, act like you are not living in this country! I felt embarrassed and ashamed.

'I have a couple of questions I wanted to ask,' said Mrs. Nurollahi. 'Would it be possible for me to come see you some time, at your convenience?'

To make amends for my ignorance, I instantly agreed. 'Of course. I would be delighted.' Before hanging up, she asked, 'By the way, do you have any gathering planned for the 24th of April this year?'

I hung up the receiver and headed back to the kitchen. Mrs. Nurollahi, who was not Armenian, knew about the genocide that had begun on 24 April 1915, and although I was born in this country... Again I felt embarrassed. She had said, 'We must learn a lot of things from our Armenian friends.' Surely she said this merely to be polite?

I sat down again and looked at my hands. There was no trace of any burn. Artoush bent down over me, caressed the back of my hand and whispered in my ear, 'Does it hurt?' He was smiling, and I knew he was trying to be nice. I smiled back and shook my head no.

I looked at Emile. He was facing us, strainer in hand, looking at me. The water was off. We looked at one another for a few seconds. Then he asked, 'Where's the oil?'

I jumped up. 'You shouldn't bother!' I reached out to take the strainer from him, but he drew it back.

Artoush shifted from one foot to the other. 'Is it absolutely necessary to have French fries?'

'You go check on the kids,' I said. Looking greatly relieved, he left the kitchen.

I looked at Emile. He gave the potatoes a little toss to turn them over in the strainer. 'I guess I am one of the few men who likes to cook.' The top two buttons of his shirt were undone and his gold chain was showing. He looked toward the door of the kitchen and lowered his voice. 'On the other hand, I hate politics. But it seems Artoush…' He looked at me expectantly.

I said, 'No. Well, yes. I mean, to the extent of reading the news and well, sometimes…' I turned around and took the tin of oil from the cabinet behind me.

He took the tin from my hands. 'I've never liked politics. I can't make head or tail of any of these movements or isms and their platforms. I'd rather read books. If the world is ever destined to get better, and I for one have my doubts about that, it won't be through politicking, right? What do you think?' Instead of a reply, I gave him a stupid smile.

Together we fried the potatoes and made salad. He talked about Indian food, about various spices and their properties. We talked about our favorite writers and the books we had read. He asked me to call him 'Emile' rather than 'Mr. Simonian.' It also occurred to me that, when his mother was not around, he was quite easy and pleasant to talk to.

While I set the table, Artoush and Emile bent over the chessboard. 'Will it be alright if I take some food for your mother?' I asked Emile. 'With her headache, she probably didn't feel like fixing dinner.'

He looked at me for a moment and then said, 'Yes. Maybe. I guess so.' Just the mention of his mother made his tone of voice change.

19

I put a plate of cutlets and French fries on a tray, alongside a small bowl of salad, and covered it all with a large napkin to keep a zillion insects from getting in the food as I crossed the street. Although the yard lights were on, I plodded down the entire length of our path, tray in hand, with high and exaggerated steps, setting my feet down firmly on the ground. This was my own special method to alert the dumb frogs not to jump under my feet and startle me. The children and Artoush laughed whenever I put it into practice.

Mr. Rahimi was watering the yard and singing loudly, as always. Armen said that Mr. Rahimi's voice was so bad that Mrs. Rahimi forbade him from singing inside the house. 'That's why Mr. Rahimi waters the front and back yard and half the street three times a day.' Although not a day would go by without the twins quarreling with their big brother and winding up in a fight, even Armen's not-so-funny jokes got Arsineh and Armineh laughing. Mr. Rahimi's voice is not all that bad, I thought to myself as I crossed the street. Suddenly one foot slipped. Armen was right. Mr. Rahimi had watered the entire width of the street.

I opened the metal gate to the yard of G-4. The yard lights were not on, but the flowerless front yard and the yellowing lawn, parched dry in places, were visible in the moonlight. Stalks of ivy stuck to the walls of the house like spider webs. Last year this wall was completely green. Instead of ringing the doorbell, I tapped a few times on the door. The house was dark. I thought she might be asleep and was about to turn back when the door opened. In a long-sleeved nightdress buttoned up to the neck, she stood there looking at the tray in my hands, which due to her stature was literally right in front of her face. Then she tilted her head upward.

'Sorry,' I said. 'I brought you a few cutlets, but if you are resting...'

The moonlight was shining on her face. Her eyes seemed red and puffy. She smiled wanly. 'Very kind of you. Come in.' She stepped aside for me to enter. Her voice was different from the tired, impatient, and angry voice on the phone. She was tired, but not angry or impatient. 'Do you mind if I lie down? I don't feel very well.'

She turned on the hall light and headed down the hall toward the bedrooms. The metal trunks were gone, but the elephant with the broken trunk was still there. The door to Emily's room was open. On the floor I saw some crumpled scraps of sheet music, a pair of scissors and some torn strips of white cloth.

Mrs. Simonian's bedroom was dark, with only a small bedside lamp turned on. The window had no curtains, and one corner of the Persian rug was flipped over. There were a few photos on the bed and a couple of half-open albums on the floor. She took the tray from my hands, set it on the nightstand, and removed the napkin. For a moment she looked at the plate of food and the bowl of salad. Then she turned back. 'Thank you for thinking of me.' The lamplight fell on her face. Now I was sure she had been crying.

In an effort to break the silence, I said, 'Try a little. They say that partaking of food is beneficial for a headache.' Why was I talking like a book?

She pushed back the pictures that were spread over the bed, ran her hand over her hair, sat down and motioned for me to sit. She picked up one of the photographs. 'I don't have a headache.' She looked at the picture for a few seconds and then held it out to me.

It was one of those old-fashioned pictures taken in a photographer's studio. For a second I thought it was Emily in a dark buttoned-up dress, sitting straight as an arrow on a high-backed chair. She had a large bow on her head, and her hair hung in ringlets down to her shoulders. There was a cat sitting on her knees, and her legs below the knees were outside the camera frame.

She took the photo out of my hand. 'It's not Emily, it's me. A little bit older than Emily is now.' She turned the photograph over and then gave it back to me. 'Elmira Haroutunian – Autumn, 15 years of age' was written on the back. The handwriting was uniform, thick and bold.

She leaned back on the headboard and stared at the ceiling. 'My father would bring a photographer to our house several times a year, or take me to the photographer's studio. He insisted the photos be taken from the knees up, with me seated, so that my height would not be obvious. He thought that, because I was short, I was going to die young. He used to say that he wanted to have pictures of me after I died.' Staring at the ceiling, she sneered. 'I made my father understand that I did not intend to die before him. Same for the doctors who said I would die if I ever gave birth.' She held out a few other photographs to me and then leaned back against the headboard again, closing her eyes. I noticed that she was not speaking as formally as usual, and wondered why.

I looked through the photos. All of them were more or less the same as the first: on a bench in the garden, next to a big bush (probably an eglantine); in front of a fireplace framed with decorative plasterwork; on a chair with a fan in hand and a dog, only the head of which was visible, resting on her knees. On the back of each photo, in that same bold, uniform hand, was written: Elmira Haroutunian, at thirteen, at sixteen, at twelve.

I was looking over the photos again when she opened her eyes, sat up straight and ran her hand over her forehead. 'Forgive me for going on and on. I sometimes reminisce about the past. Thank you for coming. Now…if you permit me…' As I said goodbye, she asked me, 'The burn on your hands is better?' I nodded and, with a wan smile, she nodded back.

In bed that night I told Artoush, 'It's as if she's been taking revenge on people all her life.' When he did not answer, I turned my head to look at him. He was asleep. I turned out the light and listened to the monotonous sound of the air conditioner. How I would have loved to see the rest of the photographs.

20

Nina lived in one of the large houses in Braim, within a block of the community pool. As we got out of the car, Armineh said, 'Sophie is so lucky.' Arsineh said, 'It's not two minutes from the pool!'

As Artoush parked the car, Armen shouted, 'Careful, now. Don't get any scratches on dear ole Chevy.' The girls laughed. Not a day went by without someone poking fun at Artoush's old Chevrolet.

Before we made it inside the yard, Sophie came running out of her house. 'We bought rabbits!' she yelled. In we went.

Nina was showing us around the house and Mother was nagging under her breath in my ear. 'Look at this mess. You'd think they just moved in yesterday.'

We got to the kitchen, which was big and inviting. Nina poured sherbet into some glasses and said, 'You see? I still have a lot of things we haven't unpacked yet. If a body didn't know better, they'd suppose we moved in only just yesterday. Call me the messiest woman on earth!' She laughed heartily.

Mother and Alice exchanged a knowing look.

Garnik stepped into the kitchen with Artoush just at that moment to say, 'They call you the merriest woman on earth.' He took the tray of sherbet from Nina's hands. 'Let me get these for you, my love.'

Alice muttered under her breath, 'Some girls have all the luck!'

Artoush tried to stifle a yawn and, hands in his pockets, followed after Garnik. The evening barely under way, and he was already bored.

The living room was large too, and cheerful. The girls had scattered the toys we brought for Sophie across the carpet and were busy at play.

Garnik wove his way between the kids with the tray of sherbet, pretending to step on the toys. The twins and Sophie screamed and laughed. Nina said, 'What lovely gifts! Thank you, children.' Then she turned to Armen, who was standing by the window. 'Why are you standing? My, how you have grown, young man! When did you grow so handsome? You must have lots of girls at school fainting over you, no?'

The girls looked at Armen and covered their mouths with their hands to hide their tittering. Armen glowered at all three of them and sat down in the chair by the window. Mother pulled her skirt down over her knees and pressed her lips together. Alice checked herself in the mirror of her compact case. Her Coty face powder made me sneeze.

Nina turned to me. 'Now let me open my present. What a huge box! You're putting me to shame, Clarice.' She set the box on the coffee table in front of the easy chairs and tore open the wrapping paper.

I saw the big Grundig tape recorder on the floor, in a corner of the room. A few large reels of tape were piled next to it, and it was Vigen's voice we now heard, singing, 'You, my rival, my foe...' We had a similar tape recorder in our house.

Alice whispered in my ear, 'You see? Mrs. Keeping-up-with-the-Joneses ran right out and bought herself a matching tape recorder.'

Nina was on her knees by the table, the bunched-up wrapping paper in her hand, looking at me. 'Did you see the tape recorder? I haven't had a chance to buy a stand for it yet. Garnik promised to record Sophie's singing and the poems she recites. I told him he should follow Artoush's example of recording the twins. We have nothing from Tigran's childhood except for a couple of pictures which you have to squint at with a magnifying glass to figure out who's who. At least we'll have some mementos from Sophie's childhood.'

I told her, 'I just hope that Garnik doesn't saddle you with the responsibility of dusting the tape recorder and all those tapes, like Artoush did to me.'

Nina laughed aloud. 'No way! Garnik learned from day one that his wife is not in that line of work. I only know how to give orders. I told him, it has to be just like the one Clarice and Artoush have.'

I looked at Alice, who turned her eyes away from me and snapped the compact case shut with a clack. She told Garnik, who was standing in front of her offering the tray of cold sherbets, 'None for me – I'm on a diet. Do you have any English songs?'

Garnik held the tray out for Mother and asked Alice, 'Do you like Nat King Cole? My niece brought a whole reel of his songs from Tehran. And no diet for you tonight! You're not going to copy those phony women in Tehran, are you? A woman should have some meat on her bones.' He repeated Mother's shibboleth: 'If I'm lying, Mrs. Voskanian, go right ahead and say so.' He shook with laughter.

Someone said, 'There you go again, gossiping about Tehrani women.' All eyes looked over to the doorway.

She was of medium height. Neither thin nor fat, with shoulder-length blond hair and honey-colored eyes. She was wearing backless high-heeled shoes and a white sleeveless blouse with small red polka dots. Garnik set the tray down on the table and opened his arms wide. 'And here we have Violette, my niece from Tehran!'

The Tehrani niece stepped forward, shook hands with everyone and kissed the twins, who were staring at her, open-mouthed.

Armineh said, 'How beautiful you are!'

Arsineh said, 'Just like Rapunzel.'

Violette tossed back her head and laughed. 'I don't know any Rapunzel, but I wish that everyone had your taste!'

Nina scrunched the wrapping paper again and said, 'Everyone knows you are beautiful, lovely, and sweet. Only your idiot of a husband did not realize it. Look what Clarice brought me!' She picked up the china statuette from its box and held it up. 'Wow, how pretty!'

Violette bent over the table to touch the statuette, facing Mother and Alice and with her back to Artoush and Armen.

There was a short slit in the back of her skirt. Artoush turned away to face the window. Armen shifted in his chair. Alice just stared at Violette and Mother took quick sips from her drink.

Garnik, Artoush, and Violette took the children into the backyard to see the rabbits Garnik had bought that day. Mother asked Nina about her son, Tigran. 'Is he staying in the dorm or renting a room?'

Nina threaded her way through the toys scattered on the carpet and sat down opposite us. 'He stayed in the dorm for a few weeks. Then he went to stay with Garnik's aunt – Violette's mother. To tell you the truth, I don't want him to mix much with other students. They're all cooking up something or other these days, and who are we to play around with politics? If we Armenians know what's good for us, we'll just keep our heads down and see to it that the hat we're wearing doesn't blow away.'

Mother bent over and picked something off the carpet that was so small no one could have said what it was, and tossed it in the ashtray. 'Yep. Who are we to meddle in matters of state? That's what I told my late husband, God rest his soul, but...'

Alice faked a yawn and said, 'My goodness, there she goes again.'

Mother elbowed her in her chubby forearm. 'Knock it off with your "there she goes again." Am I lying?' Alice looked at me and laughed.

Sophie was at the window showing us one of the rabbits. Nina waved to her. 'Poor Violette was only divorced a couple of months ago. Her husband was a real nut-job. The poor girl didn't even have permission to walk to the end of the block without him. He acted all jealous and would throw these fits. And if anyone at a party, or in the street, looked at Violette, holy mackerel! "I know there's something going on," he would say. "Why are they looking at you? Are you some kind of a show dog for them to eyeball?" She just couldn't put up with it any more. And the promises he'd made before they got married: I'll buy you a house, I'll take you to Paris, to London. He didn't make good on a single one of them, and to top it off, he was going to drive her crazy. She did the right thing to divorce him. Even after the divorce he cooked up a new quarrel every day. He would phone her, follow her, pop up wherever she happened to be. Just a few weeks ago, he blocked the poor girl's path on Naderi Street in Tehran – right in front of Khosravi's Piroshki Place – and caused a scene. We thought if she comes to Abadan for a while, maybe the crazy creep will let go. You've no idea how sweet a girl she is. God grant her a good husband.' Mother stared straight at Nina, and Alice fixated on the half-filled glasses. I will bake piroshkis for the kids one of these days, I promised myself.

Nina gathered up the box with the china statuette and the wrapping paper. She looked toward the door, leaned forward, and beckoned us closer. She lowered her voice: 'Keep it between us – Violette doesn't know yet, but...' She looked at me. 'Do you remember the Dutchman I told you about on the phone? If he and Violette get along, it wouldn't be a bad match. I've invited him over tonight.' She stood up and laughed. 'He seems a little screwy to me. But, then, most foreigners seem a bit bonkers to us Iranians. If he marries Violette and they leave Iran, wouldn't that be a triumph! Violette is not made for life in Iran.' She tucked the empty box and the wrapping paper under her arm. 'Let me go throw these away.'

On her way to the kitchen, she told Mother, 'Oh, you'll never guess what I've made for dinner. Lubia polow! See what a homemaker I've become? It's about time to marry me off, no?' She laughed heartily. I looked over at Alice. She was pouting. Talk of marriage always does it, I thought. God give Mother patience tonight.

As soon as Nina was out of the room, Mother started her muttering. 'I've told you a thousand times you should stay away from this couple. Not an ounce of dignity or morality. Whatever passes through their heads comes straight out their mouths, right in front of the children! They talk about marriage and divorce like it's a dress you buy and return if you don't like it. We should never have come. It's all Clarice's fault that...'

I jumped up. 'I'll go help Nina set the table.'

In the kitchen, Nina asked me, 'All by your lonesome?' She looked to the doorway and when she was sure that Mother and Alice were not behind me, she giggled and said in a low voice, 'Actually, I brought Violette with me to Abadan because...' She looked again toward the door and almost whispered, 'Because Tigran had a terrible crush on Violette.'

My jaw dropped and I looked wide-eyed at Nina. 'What?'

I pictured skinny, quiet, and shy Tigran. He wore glasses and was always studying. Always top of his class. He did not go to the movies or to clubs, and he did not have any friends. His hobby was tinkering with electronics. Mother had often said, 'Isn't that amazing? Such a well-behaved boy from such frivolous parents!'

Nina was explaining. 'When Violette got divorced and returned to live with her mother, Garnik's aunt, Tigran was also living there. After a few days I saw that the boy had gone all loopy. He either listened to love songs or would sit in a corner and stare at Violette, like a dog before its master. And don't imagine that Violette was flirting or anything like that. She's not like that at all! I'm a woman, too, and no idiot. I know what's what. No. It was not Violette's fault at all. It's no sin for a girl to be pretty. Her looks set her apart from other women, so people gossip about her. That's why I said Europe would be good for her. Over there the streets are full of blond-haired, fair-skinned women. I did some investigating, and the Dutchman's assignment is almost over. Let's see what we can do tonight.' She took the salad out of the fridge. 'Maybe we'll be able to accomplish a good deed.' And she laughed from the bottom of her heart.

The twins ran into the kitchen. Armineh said with pouting face, 'Uncle Garnik bought Sophie...'

Arsineh's lip curled, '...bought Sophie a hula-hoop.'

Then the two of them started in. 'Uncle Garnik said that a hula-hoop is not bad for the back.'

'It's not bad at all.'

'All the kids have hula-hoops.'

'Please get one for us.'

'Please, please get one!'

Garnik shouted from the living room. 'I'll get you one, not to worry. Come on out here, now. The rabbits have joined the party.'

'Yippee!' and 'Fantastic!' shouted the twins, as they ran out.

Nina picked up the fruit bowl. 'I don't know who started circulating the rumor that hula-hoops cause backaches. No one spins a hula-hoop twenty-four hours a day. Relax. They'll play for two or three days and then toss it in a corner of the yard. Can you bring the dessert plates?' And she headed for the living room.

Violette was sitting on the carpet, cradling one of the bunnies. Her tight black skirt had hitched up, and her white un-stockinged knees were on display. Sophie and the twins were sitting around her, each with a bunny in their arms. Armen was petting Violette's bunny.

Mother was staring straight at the empty drink glasses. Alice had practically turned her back on Mother and was staring at the bare wall of the room. Her crossed leg was kicking rapidly up and down. Mother and Alice are fighting, I said to myself. Garnik was asking Artoush's advice about where to install the new air conditioner. Before coming over, I had warned Artoush, 'Don't get into any political arguments.'

I was helping Nina set the dinner table when the bell rang.

It was the tall Dutchman, with very short, straight hair, the color of straw. His freckled face was a tad reddened, most probably from sunbathing. He shook hands firmly with each of us, one by one, even the children. He spoke in Persian,

'Greetings! I am Joop Hansen. I am very pleased to meet you, sir.'

Violette, sitting there on the floor, raised her rabbit-less hand slightly and said, 'See what a lovely rabbit I have?'

In order to shake hands with Violette, Joop Hansen practically knelt on the ground. 'Exceedingly pretty is the rabbit.'

Violette only smiled. The Dutchman's somewhat formal, somewhat broken Persian did not surprise her nor make her laugh. I remembered that Nina had said, 'Garnik's niece reminds me of you.' I thought Nina had lost her mind. I did not see the slightest resemblance between myself and this woman, neither in her looks, nor in her behavior. Though I would not have minded being like her at all, in either department.

Joop Hansen had a pleasant manner and smiling face. He asked Artoush not to call him Mr. Hansen, and to speak Persian rather than English, saying, 'For speaking Persian I am most eager.' At the dinner table, when he offered the platter of pilaf to my sister, Mother and Alice both smiled for the first time that night.

Alice thanked him and explained she was eating salad. Joop raised his blond eyebrows. 'Why? Do you not like Lobiya pilof?'

'I like it,' said Alice, 'but…'

Joop set the platter down on the table, picked up the salad bowl and offered it to Alice. 'Ahh! You must be on a diet.' He pushed his chair back and looked Alice over carefully. 'You don't need any diet. To my considered opinion, you are very, very excellent as you are.'

When we returned home, Artoush picked my dress off the bed, where I had tossed it. He turned it over this way and that, and said, 'If I had not seen it on you tonight, I'd have thought it belonged to the twins.'

I snatched the dress from him and hung it up in the wardrobe. 'Don't joke. Go ahead and say I'm too thin.'

I heard him say behind me, 'To my considered opinion, you are very, very excellent as you are.' Then he laughed aloud. 'At that instant you could have lit a score of 100-watt bulbs with the light in your sister's eyes.'

I turned down the covers on my side of the bed. 'Violette has a nice figure, no?'

Artoush turned down the covers on his side. 'Does she have a nice figure? I didn't notice.' He began humming Nat King Cole's 'Mona Lisa.'

'Thank you for not arguing politics with Garnik.'

He made a face at me and, mimicking Joop, said, 'Your wish is my command.'

I tried not to laugh out loud and wondered why people thought of Artoush as grumpy. I asked him, 'Are you coming to the 24th of April ceremonies on Thursday?'

He closed his eyes and yawned. The only thing he said was, 'Hmm...' which surely meant no. I turned out the night lamp.

21

The auditorium at the school was full. Wreaths of white gladioli with wide black ribbons were pinned to the walls at regular intervals. Mother was grumbling at Alice. 'I told you we'd be late. But no, off you go to the hairdresser on a day of mourning! Would the sky have fallen if you'd waited a day?'

I pointed Nina out to Mother – she was waving to us from the second row, where she had saved us seats. We threaded in between the chairs and through the people, saying excuse me a dozen times until we finally made our way to Nina.

Alice – half-seated, half-standing – looked over her shoulder to scan the entire hall. She began to report who was there and what they were wearing. Nina handed me the evening's program and asked, 'What kept you?'

Mother answered, 'Lady Alice went to the hairdresser.' Again she harrumphed: 'The hairdresser on the Day of Mourning!'

Nina whispered in my ear. 'You never know, maybe the Day of Mourning will turn out to be her lucky day!' She giggled and looked around her. 'But looks like only old hags and geezers have turned out. Did you leave the kids with Artoush?' (She did not ask why Artoush had not come. There was no need to explain.) 'Garnik insisted that Sophie must come too.' Dropping her voice an octave or two, she mimicked him. '"Children must learn from this age what our people have suffered." But the little squirt threw such a tantrum that her Papa eventually gave in. I left Violette at home, too, on the pretext that Sophie not be all alone. What would Violette do here, anyway? She'd be bored. To be honest, if Garnik were not the Master of Ceremonies, I would not have come myself. So, tell me, what's new?'

Before I could say nothing was new, she began exchanging pleasantries with a woman sitting in the row in front of us, whose husband was the first speaker of the evening. I read the program:

* Talk by Robert Madatian on the 24th April Mass Murders
* Report of the Church & School Association on the construction of a memorial

Intermission

* Reminiscences of Mrs Khatoun Yeremian, eyewitness to those terrible events.

The lights in the auditorium dimmed and Garnik came up to the microphone. He gave the welcome and then Madatian began his speech. I remembered the 24th of April commemoration many years ago, when Artoush and Madatian got in a heated argument. Things would have gotten out of hand if not for Garnik, who diffused the situation with joking banter and pleasantries. After that incident, I had told Artoush time and time again, 'Why insist on political differences on this of all days? It makes no difference whether one is a leftist or a conservative. All these people got massacred! Even if you're not Armenian, you have to feel something, you have to grieve, and you should take part in the commemoration.' Artoush would always reply, 'I do feel grief, but I will not take part.'

I was listening and not listening to Madatian's talk. We heard the same things over again every year – some statistics and some slogans, that's about it. Nina looked over at me several times and then looked pointedly in the direction of Mrs. Madatian. She put her finger to her lips to say that she must keep quiet, since it would surely offend the lady if anyone talked during her husband's speech. Mrs. Madatian turned around several times to stare down the people behind her, who apparently did not know the speaker was her husband, and that they must keep quiet. Everyone was whispering to their neighbor and fanning themselves with the program. I fanned myself too, and tried to remember whether I had given the twins their Haliborange that morning. I had, I now remembered, because they had complained:

'But what about Armen?'

'But how long will we have to take this syrup?'

'But if we take it to keep from catching cold, why doesn't Armen?'

Mr. Madatian waved his notes excitedly and after a few more long sentences, concluded his talk. I clapped along with everyone else. A few people sitting near Mrs. Madatian congratulated her. She smiled and thanked them, as if she herself had given the talk, and when her eyes lit upon me, she turned away.

Mother was exchanging greetings with a woman a few rows behind us. Alice leaned over to me across Mother, who was sitting between us. 'Guess who's here? Mrs. Nurollahi! Sitting in the back of the auditorium.' I was about to turn around, when Garnik came on stage and began to read the report about the construction of the memorial. On one of the occasions I was summoned to the school over Armen's trouble-making, Vazgen Hairapetian had shown me the sketch of the memorial monument. It was a large rectangle made out of grey stone. Carved on one side was a woman carrying her lifeless child in her arms, and engraved on the other side were the dates of the genocide. Garnik announced that the monument was nearly completed and would be erected in the school yard the following year, in front of the door to the church. He then thanked all those present for their financial and moral support and announced a fifteen-minute intermission.

Mother said she was going to stay in the auditorium to chat with her friend, who had just come back from Julfa, and was sitting a few rows behind us. Nina said she was going backstage to see what Garnik was doing, and took Alice along with her. I headed over to one of the exits that opened on to the schoolyard. Just in front of the doors, I stood aside to let a man carrying some sandwiches and Pepsis pass by. In one corner of the school yard, a good-sized crowd was mingling around the buffet table. I exchanged greetings with several acquaintances, and then saw Manya coming toward me.

As usual, she was jumpy and excited. The white collar of her blouse was turned up on one side. I said hello and straightened her collar. 'The wreaths and the ribbons are beautiful. I'm sure they were your idea.'

She pushed aside a sweep of hair from her perspiring forehead. 'Did you see the black armbands on the ushers?'

Of course I had seen them. The night before, Armen took the telephone into his bedroom, locked the door and talked for half an hour. He then came out to the kitchen, where Mother and I were washing vegetables, and announced that he had decided to be one of the ushers for tomorrow's program. And that Miss Manya had said the ushers need to wear black armbands. 'Again you have to wait until the last minute?' I chided. 'Where am I going to find black cloth in the middle of the night?' His grandmother came to the rescue. If there was anything her various trunks and boxes didn't lack, it was black cloth. I told Manya, 'Everything turned out splendidly. Thank you for all the trouble you've gone to! The next program must be the end-of-year celebration?'

She said hello to someone passing by and turned back to me. 'Yep. We'll hold the end-of-year celebration here in the yard. I'm building a stage for it.' She gestured toward the end of the yard, which was full of bricks and beams and planks. Then she put her hand on my shoulder, which was not an easy reach, considering how much shorter Manya was than me. 'We'll start practicing in a day or two.' Her hand slid down my shoulder to my arm. 'I have a neat idea for the twins. Vazgen found a pretty poem by...I forget who it's by, but the poem is called "The Four Seasons." I thought it would be cute if the twins take turns reading the parts of the seasons. Armineh as spring and fall, and Arsineh as summer and winter. That way they'll have time to go backstage and change costumes for each season. And as for the costumes...'

I spotted Armen standing by one of the auditorium doors, talking with Emily and two high-school-age boys. With his navy blue pants and white shirt he looked more like a young man than like my little boy. I wondered if Emily had come with her father and hoped Alice would not see Emile here. I said to Manya, 'As for the costumes, it will naturally be me who should sew them?'

She let go of my arm and covered her mouth to hide her tittering. 'Yep. That's why I was looking for you. It won't be difficult. Four simple long dresses with wide sleeves. But the colors should all be different. Pink for spring, for example, green for summer, orange for fall, and white for winter.'

On the other side of the yard I spotted Emile talking to the priest and his wife. Fretting again, I hoped that Alice would not show up in the vicinity. Then I remembered that, fortunately, the two of them had not been introduced and would not recognize one another. 'I could even sew something on each dress particular to the season. Like flowers for spring, wheat stalks for fall.' Emily's headband fell on the ground.

Armen bent over before the two other boys could and picked it up. I lost sight of Emile in the crowd.

'What a great idea!' agreed Manya. 'By the way, Vazgen has finished the translation of *Little Lord Fauntleroy* and...' She stopped mid-sentence, staring directly behind me. What was she looking at with that vacant grin? When I turned my head around to see, Emile shifted his gaze from Manya and greeted me. Both of them now stood looking at me. I introduced them and they shook hands. Manya straightened the collar that I had already straightened for her.

'You were saying, about the translation...' I prodded Manya.

'What?' She seemed to have just woken from a trance. 'Oh, yes, the book. The translation is finished. I'll give it to the kids to bring to you. Please read it soon and return it. We intend to print it before the end-of-year celebration.'

Emile said, 'I guess you are the one who planned the program tonight? Congratulations. It was very interesting.'

Manya blushed and called out 'Coming!' to one of the ushers who was calling to her. Then she shook hands with Emile, saying, 'I am pleased to make your acquaintance,' and left. Was it my silly imagination or did they hold hands for noticeably longer than was necessary?

I looked around. Fortunately Alice and Mother were nowhere to be seen. Emile was wearing a white suit with very thin blue stripes. His tie was black.

He was watching the people around us talking, smoking, and having drinks and sandwiches. He said his mother had not come, so he came to save Emily from being all alone.

Well, and out of some curiosity, too. 'I wanted to get acquainted with the Armenians of Abadan.' He turned around to face me. 'If all the women here are like you and Miss Manya, Abadan is not such a bad place.' He laughed at his own joke. 'But between the two of us, the program was a bit tedious.' He said he was thinking about going back home and returning later to fetch Emily. I was happy that he was leaving, and in order to keep him from coming back and meeting Alice, I insisted that we would give Emily a ride home. He thanked me, said goodbye and left.

I looked through the crowd trying to find Mrs. Nurollahi. I did not, and so returned to the auditorium. Maybe Alice was mistaken. Why should Mrs. Nurollahi come? She did not speak Armenian, and the ceremonies for the 24th of April were not particularly interesting.

The crowd gradually re-assembled in the auditorium. Mother was in a good mood after chatting with her friend from Julfa. Nina was making arrangements to invite Mrs. Madatian for dinner, and as soon as I sat down, Alice said, 'Shushanik and Janette must have made a killing! All the lovely ladies have new clothes on, head to toe. All, it seems, in black.' Shushanik and Janette were two of the most famous dressmakers in Abadan.

Garnik came to the microphone and waited for the room to quiet down. Then, in a tone at odds with his usual cheerful, laughing voice, he introduced Khatoun Yeremian, from the city of Van, now resident in Tehran. She had been an eyewitness of those bitter times and was now, for a few days, a most welcome visitor in Abadan. He gestured toward the back of the stage. We all looked in that direction. One of the usher boys came and placed an armchair in front of the microphone. An elderly woman, walking with short, shuffling steps and leaning on the arm of another usher, came onto the stage. She was frail and thin, wearing a black ankle-length skirt, with a large black shawl covering her white hair. With the boys' help, she sat down. Garnik lowered the microphone for her. The woman laid her bony hand on the heads of each usher and mumbled something sotto voce, which I took to be a prayer of benediction.

We all watched her in silence. For a few seconds she looked back at us, then began to speak in a weary voice. She spoke in a different dialect from ours, in the western Armenian of the city of Van, saying things like 'a wee bit' instead of 'a little bit;' and 'gusto,' in place of 'joy.' She said that before talking about those days of hardship, she wished to speak 'a wee bit' about the days of 'gusto.' She wished, she said, to journey with us to the past.

She spoke of her childhood home in the city of Van. In their yard there were two pomegranate trees, a few olive trees, and over in one corner, a brick oven in which her mother used to bake Lavash bread. There was also a small flowerbed where they planted marigolds. She spoke of her father, who came home every day from his cloth shop in the bazaar of Van with bags of fruit under his arms. Sometimes he brought home left-over scraps from the huge cloth-bolt rollers for Khatoun and her sister. From those scraps, their mother would make rag dolls for her two girls. Their older brother would draw faces for the dolls with a piece of charcoal. In fact, he was always drawing or painting, using whatever was at hand for his canvas. On Sundays the whole family went to the city church, which was on a wide boulevard with rows of willow trees and poplars. The girls, holding their rag dolls under one arm, walked hand in hand with their mother, weaving through the willows and poplars and counting the red fezzes of the men, some of whom would stop to exchange greetings with their father. 'Old customers of the shop,' Father would say. 'God-fearing and conscientious.' On Fridays, the sound of the muezzin could be heard from the neighborhood mosque. As the Muslim neighbors returned home from their Friday congregational prayers, Father would tell them, 'May God accept your prayers.' Whenever Mother made yoghurt soup, she poured some of it in clay bowls to send to her Muslim neighbors. She would decorate the surface of the soup with marigold petals. In return, the neighbors would send over baklava for her.

Mrs. Madatian took out a handkerchief from her black patent-leather purse. No one in the room was fanning any more.

Khatoun fell silent for a few moments. With bowed head, she twisted the two ends of her shawl around her hands. 'And then came the black days. There came a day when Father returned home earlier than usual, empty-handed and distraught. He told Mother that the Armenians had closed up their shops. The soldiers had set fire to the few shops that remained open, and plundered sacks of rice and wheat from another. Father said, "We must leave." Mother clawed at her cheeks, "We are ruined."'

Once again Khatoun fell silent. She drew a deep breath, slapped her knees several times with the palms of her hands, and rocked left and right, her frail body swaying. Then she shook her head and said, 'And we were ruined.'

As I went to open my purse, Alice held out a small packet of tissues. I took a tissue and passed the packet to Nina. Mother was shaking her head back and forth and muttering, 'God deliver us from evil.'

The only sound in the auditorium was breathing, inhaling and exhaling, and Khatoun's weary voice. 'The door of the house was wide open. Mother was crying, filling up the knapsacks and trunks, fastening them shut. Father was shouting, "We have no room, woman. Leave this junk behind. There is not much time. Hurry." Mother was wailing. "Wait a wee bit. Just a wee bit." My sister and I stood under the pomegranate trees, stupefied, clutching our rag dolls. Brother was cursing. He kicked the marigolds and spoke of revenge. We climbed on the cart, sat on top of the knapsacks and trunks, and headed off. The streets were thronged with other carts, buggies, horses, mules, and whatever else could carry a person or his belongings. It was a maelstrom of dust and wailing and cursing. The rag dolls got lost, and my sister and I cried. First for our dolls, then for Father, then for Mother, for our brother and for one another.'

The packet of tissues passed hand to hand and was soon empty.

That evening I stretched out my feet on the coffee table and leaned my head back against the sofa cushion. I twisted my hair around my finger and looked at the painting above the television. It was a watercolor of the Ejmiatsin Cathedral in Armenia. I don't remember who had told me that the church in Abadan was modeled on Ejmiatsin. I wondered why Manya was flustered when Emile came over to us. Good thing that Alice had not seen Emile! Why did Emile tell me the program was tedious when he told Manya it was interesting? I spoke aloud to the painting: 'Poor Khatoun.'

From behind his newspaper Artoush inquired, 'What's that?'

'Poor Khatoun, her mother, her father, all those people,' I said. 'You should have come.'

A page turned.

I was looking at Ejmiatsin. 'All those people, living happily side by side for all those years. What happened? For what reason? Whose fault was it?' I was twisting a lock of hair around my finger. 'We can't do a thing about it except pay our futile empty respects and hold memorial gatherings. You should have come.'

Another page turned.

I said, 'You'll never guess who came. Mrs. Nurollahi. Alice saw her. But maybe she was mistaken.'

He folded the newspaper, played with his beard and laughed. 'So she came after all? She asked me for the day and time of the commemoration. When she saw that I didn't know, she went to ask some other Armenians. Shall I get the lights or will you?'

'How come you didn't know the day and time? Why isn't it important to you? Why didn't you come?'

Artoush stood there. He stroked his beard and looked at the painting of Ejmiatsin. Then he asked, 'Do you know where Shotait is?'

When I did not reply he put his hands in his pockets and went over to the window. He looked out at the yard for a while. Then he turned around. With the point of his toe he drew a circle around one of the flowers in the design of the Persian carpet. 'It's not far. Right next door, about four kilometers from Abadan.' He looked out at the yard again. 'If you want, I'll take you, so you can see for yourself. Ask Madatian and his wife to come, and Garnik too.' He turned around to look at me. 'Women and men and children and oxen and goats and sheep all live together in a hut.' He took his hands out of his pockets and undid the band of his wristwatch. 'We'll have to go in the daytime, because they have no electricity in Shotait. Remember to bring water, too, because they don't have plumbing.' He wound up his watch. 'We have to be careful not to shake anyone's hand or caress the children, because we could get either tuberculosis or trachoma.' He started walking toward the door. 'Tell Mrs. Madatian not to bring English chocolates for the kids there, because I don't suppose the children of Shotait have ever seen chocolate in their lives. And tell Garnik not to wear his Italian shoes because the mud and dung will come up to his ankles.'

I was staring at Ejmiatsin. Artoush reached the door, then walked back, stood right in front of me, and stared me in the face. 'Tragedies happen every day. Not just fifty years ago, but right now. Not far away, but right here! A stone's throw from the heart of green, safe, chic, and modern Abadan.' He strapped his watch back on. 'And at the same time, you are right. Poor Khatoun. Poor mankind.'

And he left the room.

22

I was making Chombur for the children's after-school snack: breadcrumbs with cheese and ground walnuts on top. I heard the drawn-out hiss of the air brakes of the school bus in the street.

I wiped my hands on my apron, waiting for the sound of running footsteps. Hearing nothing, I went to the hallway and opened the front door. They had reached the middle of the path and Arsineh, head downcast, was crying. Armineh was carrying both their satchels in one hand. Her other hand was resting on her sister's shoulder, and she was whispering in her ear. There was no sign of Armen.

Alarmed, I ran out to them. 'What happened? Did you fall down? Did you have a fight with someone? Are you sick?'

Her crying intensified and in between sobs, she stammered out, 'What did I do? I didn't say a thing. It was the kids at school who said it. They're the ones who laughed.' The intense crying made her cough.

Armineh quickly confirmed, 'Arsineh's right, Arsineh is right.'

I washed Arsineh's face and hands, sat her on a chair in the kitchen, made her swallow a few gulps of water and said, 'Now tell me what happened.'

They looked at one another. Arsineh looked straight down, laced her fingers and twisted her hands. Then Armineh thrust out her chin, took several steps back, set her hand on her hip and took a stand right there in the center of the kitchen.

'Until now, we kept quiet for Armen's sake, and didn't spill the beans. Today on the bus, instead of thanking us, he slapped Arsineh in the face, in front of all the kids! Now it's time to tell you the whole story.' Armen was in love with Emily, she explained. Emily wants to make Armen jealous by joking and laughing with other boys in school. Today, somebody wrote in big big letters above the seats on the bus: 'Armen loves Emily, Emily loves no one.' The kids on the bus all laughed, Armen accused Armineh and Arsineh of writing it, and smacked Arsineh in the face. Armineh took a deep breath and continued the story. 'That night at Emily's house, the reason Armen coughed was that…'

Arsineh said, 'Don't tell on him!'

Armineh said, 'I am telling! Why shouldn't I? That night Armen coughed because, playing Spin the Bottle, Emily made him drink a whole glass of vinegar. And she even poured a whole bunch of the chutney her grandmother made into it.'

I sank into the chair.

The idea of drinking a whole glass of vinegar with that chutney made my throat burn something awful. The twins stared at me, their jet black hair spilling out from under their color-matched headbands and their chubby cheeks all ruddy as they waited anxiously for my reaction.

What was happening? What had I been thinking? How had I not noticed? I wiped the sweat off my forehead and asked, 'Where is Armen now?'

They shrugged their shoulders and looked at me with pouting faces.

I looked at the sweet peas, blowing in the breeze. It was near sundown and the ledge was in shadow. A bee was buzzing around one of the flowers.

Arsineh's eyes were still red and Armineh was searching in her satchel for something. She took out a notebook and a book, and held them out to me. 'Miss Manya gave this for you.' It was the manuscript of the translation of *Little Lord Fauntleroy* with the original English text.

I told them to sit and have their snack, and went off to the living room. Back in the green leather chair, my gaze settled on the bare windows whose drapes I had washed that day. I thought of Emily. Was it really possible? Artoush had said, 'What a sweet girl.' I had thought, 'How shy.' I thought of the glass of vinegar and chutney again, and I don't know why but it reminded me of the day Armen was born.

Artoush's cousin had come to visit us from Tabriz with her husband. At lunch, Mother and Alice were there too. I was going back and forth between the kitchen and the dining room, and hearing snippets of conversation.

'This is an unprecedented cold spell!'

'It may even snow.'

'Snow? In Abadan? Don't be silly. We're not in Tabriz, you know.'

'Clarice, don't walk so much. It's not good for you.'

'Are you kidding? Today she followed the gardener all around the yard and drove in the stakes for all the tomato plants.'

'She drove in what?'

'They drive stakes in the ground next to tomato plants to train them while they grow. They twine the branches around the stakes.'

'People don't grow tomatoes at home, in Tabriz.'

'What do they ever grow at home, in Tabriz?!'

It was the first time I had planted tomatoes. Every morning, the first thing I did was go to the backyard and check on my still green and very tiny tomatoes.

That evening we went to Khorramshahr to drop off Artoush's cousin and her husband at the train station. On the way back, near the outskirts of Abadan, my contractions started, so we headed straight to the hospital. It was the middle of the night when Armen was born. I lay awake until morning, shivering in the Oil Company hospital bed. I assumed that all my cold and shivering was a result of giving birth. But when Alice and Mother came to the hospital that morning, they were wearing their thick woolens.

'It was freezing last night!'

'The temperature went down below zero centigrade.'

'It never got this cold in the past fifty years.'

'All the plants and flowers in town are shriveled up, blackened in the frost.'

'The tomato plants...' I exclaimed.

Mother picked up Armen in her arms. 'A whole city full of plants and flowers and tomatoes aren't worth a single hair of the head of my grandson.'

Alice kissed Armen on the head with a hearty laugh. 'What hair?'

When I got back home from the hospital I went straight to the backyard. The hard frost had shriveled all the tomato plants. I sunk to the ground and broke into tears.

'Aren't you ashamed to cry for a few lousy tomato plants?' chided Mother.

Artoush slid his hands under my arms and scooped me up.

Alice said, 'Post-partum depression.'

Mother replied, 'What nonsense. Take the child inside; don't let him catch cold.'

In the room we'd set up for Armen, I looked at the curtains I had embroidered with my own hands, and the colorful photos of mice and cats and rabbits we had hung on the walls. I turned down the baby blanket that Mother had knitted for the crib and laid Armen down to sleep. I wiped my tears and said, 'My poor little baby.'

Now, leaning back in the leather chair, I wiped my tears and gazed through the window at the cloudless sky. Someone had given a glass of vinegar to 'my poor little baby.' It made me sad. I wished that he was not so grown up. When he was little, he only did what I wanted him to do – ate only what I wanted him to eat, went only where I wanted him to go. And now... Now someone had made him swallow a glass of vinegar, and I hadn't even noticed. My thoughts turned to Emily. Where had she learned to do such things?

I still had the notebook in my hand. I opened it to Vazgen's steady and legible handwriting. He always wrote with black ink. I'll read it later, I thought. I closed the notebook, set it on the bookshelf and returned to the kitchen. Arsineh and Armineh were whispering together. When they saw me they jumped up.

'Armen just came in and went to his room.'

'Was it wrong for us…'

'…to tell you?'

'You won't punish him, will you?'

'You won't punish him, will you?'

I assured them that they had done nothing wrong and that I would not punish Armen. I told them to go do their homework.

I knocked on his door. 'It's not locked,' he said.

He was stretched out on the bed, arms behind his head, staring at the ceiling. I sat down beside him. Years ago I had replaced those embroidered curtains in his room. I had given away the baby crib and packed away the baby blanket in a suitcase in the storage room. What had I done with the pictures? I couldn't remember. It had been a few years now since those pictures of the mouse, the cat, and the rabbit had given way to posters of Alain Delon, Kirk Douglas, and Burt Lancaster. Posters of Claudia Cardinale and Brigitte Bardot.

I looked at him and felt I was seeing a stranger. Until that morning, my fifteen-year-old boy had still been my poor little baby, and now…I looked at his eyelashes, still the same as when he was a child. Long and up-turned. He still had a mark near his left eye from the chicken pox, which he got when he was a year old. I was noticing it all for what seemed like the first time in fifteen years. I was trying to figure out what to say to him when he, still staring at the ceiling, came to my aid.

'I know what I did was wrong. It was not Arsineh's fault.'

Any other time, slapping Arsineh in the face would be reason enough to give him a good scolding and a nice long lecture, but now I only wanted him to talk about the deeper subject at hand, for me to talk to him, and for us to talk together, about Emily and – it was difficult for me to voice this aloud – about being in love.

I did not know where to begin or how. I looked at the map of Iran on the wall above his bed. My eyes circled around a lake and I leaned in closer to read its name: Bakhtegan. I remembered my appointment with Mrs. Nurollahi and wondered why it was that I knew the names of all the cities on the map of Armenia without ever having seen them, and yet did not know the names of the lakes of Iran?

I tried to recall how I felt during my engagement to Artoush. It was the only time in my life I would consider myself to have been in love. I could not remember much of it. The time between our first meeting and the engagement was not long, and the marriage followed not long after that. A week after the birthday party of our mutual friend, I ran into Artoush near our house. I was surprised first, and then felt happy.

Artoush seemed to be surprised as well. 'What an interest-ing coincidence!'

'Yes, what a coincidence!'

One day, later on, we were walking down Saadi Avenue eating piroshkis we had bought at Bakery Mignon. He asked me, 'You mean you did not realize I came around on purpose?'

Surprised again, I asked, 'How did you know where I lived?'

With great gravity, he explained, 'Yes, indeed, it was extremely difficult to find your address, but...' I don't know what he saw in my eyes that interrupted his monologue and made him laugh. 'Well, I asked around.' Then he put his arm around my shoulder. 'It's this innocence about you that I like so much.'

My eyes fixed on Lake Bakhtegan, I wondered whether it was innocence or idiocy.

Armen, still staring at the ceiling, asked, 'Did you and Father fall in love with each other before getting married?'

I was caught off balance. Unexpected questions, unforeseen behavior, anything I could not prepare myself for ahead of time made me lose my poise, and Armen was a master at it. Now he was staring at me instead of at the ceiling, waiting for an answer.

I got up and went to the window. I thought of the day many years ago when the high school algebra teacher unexpectedly called on me out of turn, and I did not know how to solve the equation on the blackboard. I could feel the eyes of my classmates boring through the back of my head and I saw the teacher out of the corner of my eye waiting impatiently, rapping his fingers rhythmically on the table. My heart was pounding and sweat was pouring off me. I kept repeating to myself, 'Oh God, help me. Make it end quickly.'

My heart was not racing now, nor was I dripping with sweat, but I wanted it to end quickly. With my eyes on the jujube tree and my back to my son, I told him, 'I was just like you, I did not really like math.'

Armen did not come out of his room all night and when I called him to dinner, he shouted from his room, 'I'm not hungry.'

The twins ate dinner in silence, brushed their teeth in silence, got their pyjamas on and went to bed. They did not ask for a story, nor did they try their usual tricks to stay up late. Neither Rapunzel nor Ishy went missing that night.

23

Artoush was sitting in front of the television. In one hand he held a book of chess strategy and with the other he was stroking his beard. The chessboard was open on the table.

I sat down beside him and watched a few minutes of television. There was a documentary on about the date palm orchards near Ahvaz. 'Mother is right,' I said. 'From now on we had better keep a bit of distance from the Simonians.'

His hand hung motionless on his beard. 'Why?'

I recounted the story. He listened to the part about the glass of vinegar and chutney. When I got to the part about the handwriting in the school bus he laughed. At Arsineh getting slapped by Armen, he returned to his book and the chessboard. 'Don't take it too seriously. That's how kids are. By the way, Emile said he was taking the afternoon off tomorrow to come over and change the flowerpots with you? Or plant flowers? Something like that. I don't remember exactly.'

For a few moments I forgot about Armen and Emily and the glass of vinegar and keeping a bit of distance from the Simonians. I twirled my hair around my finger. 'How interesting. So he did not forget.'

Artoush moved the pieces around. 'He didn't forget what?' In the documentary an Arab man was about to climb a palm tree.

'A few days ago he said he would come over so we could change the soil of the sweet peas. I thought he was just saying it to be polite.'

Artoush raised his head and looked at me for a few moments. 'Sweet peas?'

'The sweet peas on the kitchen ledge.'

'The kitchen?'

I drew a deep breath, sunk back in the sofa, and fixed my gaze on the television. The Arab was shinnying swiftly up the palm tree. 'We have a house, this house has a kitchen, the kitchen has a window, and on the ledge of this window we have for years had a flower box, and once a year I plant sweet peas in this flower box, and twice a year I change the...' The Arab had reached the top of the date palm.

Artoush twirled a chess piece in his hand. 'Ahh.' Then he sneered. 'He's taking the afternoon off to change the soil in a flower box? Really, now!'

'He didn't take the afternoon off for our flower box. He wants to plant some flowers in his own yard.' I remembered the glass of vinegar and chutney again. 'But I believe it would be better to keep a distance from the Simonians.'

He closed the chess book. His finger was saving his place. 'Making mountains out of molehills again? They're kids. They fight, they make up. They fight again. What does our keeping a distance or not have to do with these things?'

You are only worried about losing a chess partner, I said to myself. To Artoush I said, 'You're right. There's nothing I don't make a big deal out of. Every time I talk to you I'm making a big deal out of something.'

For a second or two he looked at the ceiling, then at the television, then he stood up. He tossed the chess book on the table and left the room. A black pawn tumbled over and rolled under the chair.

The TV announcer, Mrs. Doorandeesh, smiled. 'And I wish you a pleasant evening.'

I was choked with emotion, almost in tears.

24

Alice was so excited she could barely talk straight. 'He telephoned. Can you believe it? He phoned the hospital. He invited me to dinner at the Club.' She was laughing, hiccupping, and walking round and round me and Mother and the kitchen table.

Mother got up, opened the fridge, poured a glass of water, gave it to Alice and said, 'God help us. She's gone stark raving mad.'

My sister finally calmed down. She did not touch the sweets and did not drink any coffee, but related all the details, whether pertinent or not, of Joop Hansen's phone call. Then she got up, slung her purse under her arm and headed for the door. Her foot caught on the chair, she bumped into the table, almost tripped headfirst into the wall, but finally made her way. Breathlessly she announced, 'I made an appointment with the hairdresser. I have to be at the Club at 8:00 p.m.' And with another hiccup, she was off.

We stared down at the table, Mother at the sugar shaker, me at the salt shaker. Finally Mother asked, 'What do you think?'

Her anxious, worried face made me laugh. Any little thing made my mother anxious and everything made her worry. She was constantly worrying about Alice not being married yet, but whenever any man showed up in her life, it scared Mother. I myself was surprised by the Dutchman's behavior at Nina's dinner party and the attention he had paid to Alice. I was even more surprised that he had now, just a few days later, invited her to dinner. But I was also glad. First of all, because my sister would now certainly put aside the weird plan she had hatched for Emile Simonian, and secondly because, I told myself, 'Who knows, maybe...'

Mother seemed to read my mind. 'It's impossible. Nina said the guy liked this Tehrani woman...What was her name? Garnik's niece. So why did he telephone Acho?' Now that Alice had gone, Mother was scot-free to call her by her child-hood name with no fear of stirring up a bout of bickering and complaining.

I got up and slid the window screen aside to water the sweet peas. I tried to portray this relatively odd development for Mother in a positive light, but my reasons seemed unconvincing even to myself.

Mother was sitting straight up in the chair, arms folded on her chest. All she said was, 'It's impossible. The lout probably has some scheme in mind.'

The previous night's scene flashed in my mind. 'Emile said he is coming to change the soil in the flower box.' For an instant I was glad, then I remembered the black pawn, which must still be lying on the living room floor, underneath the chair. I expected the choking emotions to return, but they did not. Better to wait for the soil to be changed and then water the flowers, I thought.

I put the water pitcher on the counter and turned around to face Mother. 'Maybe he really liked Alice. What could be better?' I looked at the clock. 'Wouldn't it be better for you to be home? Make sure she doesn't overdo the make-up, as usual. I have to make a snack for the children. It won't be long before they get back from school.' I wanted to talk to Emile about Emily and Armen, and I thought it would be easier if Mother were not there.

Mother was so engrossed in the idea of Alice and the Dutchman that she made no protest about it being a long time yet before the children got home or before Alice's date. She repeated several times, 'Holy Mary, guide us through this,' and left.

I stood there in the middle of the kitchen for a moment. The two halves of my mind were at war. Finally, one said to the other, 'It's no sin to look neat.'

I went to the bedroom, combed my hair, and put on some lipstick. Then I washed my hands, rubbed on some hand cream, and looked at the clock. I wished I knew what time he was coming.

I thought about all the things I had to do. Iron the twins' uniforms, straighten up Armen's dresser drawers, collect the laundry from the clothesline in the backyard. Instead of any of that, I went to the leather chair in the living room and opened the manuscript of *Little Lord Fauntleroy*.

The nineteenth century. An American woman marries an English man who is heir to the title of 'Lord'. As usual, Vazgen's translation was straightforward and smooth.

Does Mrs. Simonian know that her son is coming to our house? Why shouldn't she know?

The elder lord is upset that his son has married an American woman, and he deprives him of the title.

The twins would surely like this story. I never put on lipstick at home.

This sentence is too long; let's break it in two. Where's my pen? The kids must have taken it again. Nothing is ever in the right place in this house!

Together, the lord's son and the American girl have a boy of their own.

'You make mountains out of molehills.' He wastes hours and hours talking about things that have no relation to us whatsoever and lets the things that affect us directly just slide by. What could be more important than the children?

The lord's son dies. What a selfish person the grandfather is! The poor American girl!

Artoush is selfish. Really selfish. The doorbell rang and I jumped up. Before reaching the hallway I wiped off my lipstick with a tissue.

He was wearing brown trousers with a white short-sleeved shirt. He set the sack of dirt under the kitchen window in the yard. I went over to pick up the flower box, but he said, 'Leave it. Don't touch the soil, either. Just give me a trowel.' I remembered the incident with Shahandeh.

We had bought two suitcases at the Kuwaiti Bazaar. With one suitcase in each hand, I was walking behind Artoush to the car, which we had parked near Shahandeh's store. Shahandeh came out of his store to say hello and chat. He looked at the suitcases, then at me, then, with a laugh, he said to Artoush, 'Doc, you've got yourself a pretty porter!' That night Artoush said, 'Shahandeh is a jokester. What he said didn't upset you, did it?' It was not Shahandeh, I thought, who turned me into his porter.

Emile changed the soil in a jiffy and stood up. 'Well, our work is done.'

'You did the work. I just watched.'

He wiped the sweat from his forehead with the back of his hand and looked at me. 'Let's not stand on ceremony; use the informal "you."' And he smiled. 'So, watering the flowers is "your" job. Do "you" still have that nice-smelling soap?'

I watered the flowers. The two halves of my mind renewed their struggle. The first half would give no quarter to the other. 'Why in such a rush? You always coil the hose around the faucet; why did you just toss it on the ground? Why are you looking at the clock again? And you remembered that Artoush said he would be late today, but you don't remember the reason why he will be late?' Then the other half cut in. 'I want to talk to him about Emily and Armen before the kids get home. That's all.'

I made coffee and insisted we sit in the living room. I had washed and ironed the drapes and hung them back up again that same morning. I thought we would talk after coffee.

The manuscript of Vazgen's translation and the English copy of *Little Lord Fauntleroy* were on the coffee table. He picked up the book and leafed through it. Then he looked at the Armenian manuscript. 'Did you translate it yourself?'

I set the cups down on the coffee table and before I could explain, he said, 'I remember now. The book that Miss Manya spoke about?' I said yes, wondering whether he had remembered the book, or Manya.

He went over to the bookcase and bent over to read the titles. 'You have just about all the works of Sardo, except one or two.'

I don't know how I got started, but I did. I talked about which of Sardo's novels I liked and which I did not like, and why, and about Mr. Davtian's opinion of Sardo – and that Mr. Davtian is the owner of the Arax bookstore, and Arax is in Tehran at the Qavam al-Saltaneh intersection, and it's a bookstore I really like, and it's the first place I visit whenever I go to Tehran, and I stay there for hours, and I've arranged with Mr. Davtian to send me books from Tehran, and he sends them, and of course I haven't read all of Sardo's works... I talked and talked and talked.

When the children appeared in the doorway with their satchels dangling from their hands, I wondered how I had not heard the school bus drive up.

Emile just watched me the entire time, his elbow on the arm of the easy chair, and his hand under his chin.

25

I was washing eggplants when Alice and Mother came in.

Instead of saying hello, Mother grumbled, sat down in the chair and fixed her eyes on the ceiling.

Before she had even sat down herself, Alice launched into her report of the events of the previous night. 'First off, he gets an "A" for social graces. When I walked into the restaurant he immediately got up from the table and bowed.'

I was going to ask why he had not come to pick her up, but I caught the words in my throat and asked instead, 'Do you want coffee?'

Excited, she shook her head no, sat down, and breathlessly continued. 'He talked about everything. About his mother, who lives with her sister near a small city in the south of Holland. It's a small house near the forest, just like those cottages you see in postcards...'

I started making coffee for myself and Mother, who was now frowning at Alice.

Alice pushed her chair back, got up and headed for the refrigerator. 'He showed me a picture of his house, along with a few pictures of his mother and his aunt.' She opened the refrigerator door while fetching a glass with her other hand. 'His poor aunt is crippled and gets around from here to there with a wheelchair...' She filled her water glass. 'Joop said because of the heat in Abadan, we must drink a lot of water.' She took two gulps. 'Joop's aunt is an angel, so kind and lovable.' She took another drink. 'His mother's just like the aunt. A gem, kind and lovable.' She finished the rest of the water. 'The poor thing has been taking care of her sister for years and only recently has started to complain a little of backache.' She set the empty glass on the counter. 'Joop said his mother and her sister don't socialize and don't go out. All they want is for Joop to marry and bring his wife to that pretty little house and live happily together ever after.'

I removed the coffee pot from the burner, turned off the stove and poured the coffee for myself and Mother.

Alice was walking round and round, looking everywhere but at me and Mother. 'The house is isolated, not a soul for miles around, and if you look out of the window early in the morning, you can see deer. Isn't it dreamy? At night you can hear the jackals howling.'

Mother said, 'Holy Mary, Mother of God!'

I washed the empty glass, set it in the dish rack and sat down at the table. Alice sat down as well. 'What a nice man! How sensitive, how likeable, how kind. He asked me about everything. Where I studied nursing, how long I've been working.' She laughed. 'He first thought I was an ordinary nurse. Later, when he understood I'm an operating-room nurse, I think he was quite *impressed*.' She looked at Mother. 'You know what *impressed* means, right? You could see it meant something to him.' Then she looked at me. 'He asked me when I was hired, how much money I'll receive in Company pension if I retire. Well – he asked me about every-thing. If he had no particular intentions, he wouldn't ask that, would he? What do you think?'

Instead of answering, I offered her an almond cookie.

Mother retorted, 'Your sister thinks you're an ass, just like I do.'

Alice, seemingly oblivious of what Mother had said and what I had not said, pushed the cookie away and stood up. 'Thursday, which I have *off*, he's invited me to go with him to Kut-e Abdollah. He has to check in on a project or some-thing there, smack in the middle of the desert. I've offered to make sandwiches so we can have a picnic right there in the middle of the desert and go for a hike. Joop is in love with the desert and the sand and the sun.' She said 'the desert and the sand and the sun' as if she was reciting a line from some love poem. Arms spread wide apart, head tilted slightly upward, her gaze on the window.

All at once, Mother erupted, 'Why can't you understand?!'

Alice was livid. 'It's you who don't understand! He told me himself that he fell in love with me from the moment he laid eyes on me.'

Mother began shouting and screaming. I looked at the cookie in my hand, with a bite already missing from it. Did I even like almond cookies? I tossed it into the ashtray and stood up.

I began peeling the eggplants. Why was my sister so dumb? Why was my mother repeating things she had said a thousand times before, some relevant to the situation, some obviously not? Why did I feel so poorly? When I cut my finger, I cried out, more from shock than from the pain.

Mother jumped up. 'What happened?'

I washed off the blood in the sink. 'It's nothing.'

Mother and Alice resumed their bickering. I asked myself, 'Why did that happen?' and reasoned: The glass of vinegar and the spicy chutney, the unpleasantness with Artoush last night, Alice's foolishness, the shrewdness of the Dutchman, Mother's yelling and screaming, and...what had Emile Simonian thought of me? How long had I talked to him non-stop? Half an hour? An hour? I was flushed with embarrassment.

Mother was looking for someone to blame. 'It's all Nina's fault. I told you a hundred times we shouldn't socialize with them.'

Alice said, 'Don't yell and scream for no reason. What has Nina got to do with it?'

As Emile was leaving, he had said, 'Thank you. For the coffee and the interesting ideas.' He must have been mocking me. He must have been mocking me, and it served me right.

Mother slammed the salt shaker on the table. 'You mean you can't understand that the creep is looking for an indentured servant to work as a free nursemaid?'

Alice slammed down the fruit knife on the table even harder. 'None of you understand!'

I laid out the eggplant in the strainer. My self-critical streak berated me: 'Let it be a lesson to you never to show off again!' I sprinkled salt on the eggplant. My generous streak came to my defense: 'She wasn't showing off, she was just talking

171

about the things she likes.' Some salt got into the cut and stung my finger. I sucked on the cut and looked at the sweet peas. That unrelenting critical streak challenged me again: 'Since when do we ever talk about the things we like?' My generous side searched for a counter-response.

Mother's voice brought me back to attention. 'Hey, where have you gone to, Clarice? Say something.'

Still sucking my finger, I wheeled around to face Mother. Just then the twins walked in. 'Our homework is finished.'

I plucked my finger from my mouth, pointed at the door and shouted, 'Out!'

The pair of them stared first at me, then looked to Mother, who was fanning herself, then to Alice, who was nonchalantly peeling an apple, and then stared back at me. They had figured out some time ago that when I had no energy, I would not oppose them. They both cocked their heads.

'May we…'

'…ask Emily…'

I cut them off. 'Out!'

Mother turned back to Alice. 'After all, you can't see a person just one time and…'

'Twice,' Alice interjected.

'However many times,' said Mother. 'If your father, God rest his soul, were alive…'

I closed my eyes and put my hand to my forehead. Should I tell Alice once again, 'You are right'? The twins had not reached the end of the hallway when the doorbell rang.

'Hello, Auntie Nina.'

'Hello, Auntie Violette.'

'What a pretty dress, Sophie!'

'How wonderful you all dropped by!'

How wonderful you dropped by? Mother had such a look on her face that I was convinced she was going to pick a fight with them. Alice set the apple down on her dessert plate. 'It's Nina? How wonderful!'

Nina's voice was calling from the hallway, 'Where is the mistress of the house?'

I got to the hallway. I kept insisting that we sit in the living room, but Nina said no. 'I have missed Hansel and Gretel's cottage.' She came into the kitchen. 'Well, well! Mrs. Voskanian and Alice are here, too. Barev, Barev!'

Alice went up to Nina and Violette with open arms, and hugged and kissed each of them. Mother did not return Nina's greeting. Violette looked around and said, 'What a cute kitchen.'

Alice told Nina, 'I was just telling Clarice how badly I miss you.' Mother glowered at me and Nina and Violette and at the walls of the kitchen. I was about to ask if there were enough chairs for all of us when the doorbell rang again, and I heard Armineh and Arsineh's voice in the hallway.

'Hello, Uncle Emile.'

'Hello, Mrs. Simonian.'

'We were just coming to get you, Emily.'

'Everyone's in the kitchen.'

I had no time to think or move. The mother and her son were standing in the doorway of my kitchen.

For a moment there was silence. The only sound was Violette humming a tune under her breath. She had opened the window screen and with her back to us was smelling the sweet peas.

My sister was the first to speak. She went straight up to Mrs. Simonian and offered her hand. 'Good afternoon. My name is Alice Voskanian, Clarice's sister.'

The twins, who were standing behind the Simonians with Sophie and Emily, giggled and before my gaze could lock on theirs, they ran off. In a normal situation, the unusual tone of Alice's self-introduction and her beefy body, in contrast to the little limbs of Mrs. Simonian, would have made me laugh.

Now Alice was shaking hands with Emile. 'I'm pleased to make your acquaintance. I have been looking forward to the opportunity of meeting you, sir, and your distinguished mother. Clarice has spoken highly of you.'

When had I spoken highly of them? Why was Alice speaking like a book? Why was the whole city gathered in my kitchen that afternoon?

A voice said, 'What fragrant flowers!'

We all turned to the window. Violette in her red blouse, white flared skirt and hoop earrings was leaning back against the window frame. Backlit by the sunlight pouring in through the window, her hair looked even more flaxen than usual.

Once I had introduced everyone, I suggested we retire to the living room. Mrs. Simonian said that they were on their way to the Kuwaiti Bazaar and they had dropped in along the way because Emile wanted to give me something. Then she nodded to Nina and turned to Mother, who was asking something.

Alice threw Emile and his mother a contemptuous glance, which neither of them noticed, grabbed Nina by the waist and headed for the living room. 'I'm glad to see you. I was going to call you tonight.'

Mother was talking to Mrs. Simonian. 'Your late father was a friend of my late father. My parents were invited to your wedding. Not me, of course, as I was just a child, but...'

I repeated my suggestion that we go to the living room. Mrs. Simonian muttered something inaudible and turned back to her son. I also turned back to her son. Our gaze followed Emile's gaze all the way to the window. Violette was twirling a white sweet pea in her hand and smiling.

Mother said, 'It was a pity you had to sell that beautiful, large house. I was telling Clarice the other day...'

Mrs. Simonian said, 'Emile!'

Mother said, 'I was telling Clarice...'

Mrs. Simonian repeated Emile's name a bit louder, then turned around and stalked out of the kitchen.

Practically running, Emile trailed after his mother, and I practically ran after him into the yard. In the middle of the path, he turned around and held out a package to me. 'Yesterday I opened a box of books and...'

Mrs. Simonian yelled, 'Emily!'

I reached out, took the package, and looked at it. When I looked up again, no one was in the yard and the gate was half open. I returned to the kitchen.

Mother was wiping the counter with a cloth. It was Mother's habit to work quickly, but when she was angry her movements became jerky and rapid, like in a silent film.

Violette was staring at Mother. When she saw me, she marveled, 'How quickly she works. By the way, your neighbor is such a cute little woman. But she seemed to be mad about something, no?'

Mother spun around to Violette. 'Of course she was mad. She was mad because I asked why she sold such a pretty house. She was mad because she realized I know her whole life story, top to bottom, and she can't put on her airs in front of me. She was mad because I said that I was a child at the time of her marriage. I wasn't lying, though.' She turned her back on us and once again laid into the counter with all her might.

Violette, her mouth half-open, watched Mother's hands for a few seconds, making rapid swirls on the counter. Then she brushed aside a strand of hair that had fallen in her face. 'I see, so that's why she got mad.'

I took the cloth from Mother's hands and sent her with Violette to the living room. When I was alone, I pressed both hands to my head for a moment, drew a deep breath, then set out the coffee cups on the tray and the coffee pot on the stove. I did not feel well at all. I was tired and mad, indignant even. At Alice? At Mother? At Nina, who had turned up unannounced, or at myself, for running after Emile and his mother? The coffee began bubbling up the sides of the coffee pot. As the ripple in the coffee pot drew smaller and smaller, my breathing sped up. Right at the moment when I should have turned the burner off, two voices said in unison, 'Mommm-mmmy! May we...'

I turned around and shouted, 'No, you may not!'

At the sound of the coffee boiling over, I spun around, looked at the half-empty coffee pot and the dirty stove top, and closed my eyes.

I heard Armineh's voice in the hallway. 'She got angry because the coffee boiled over.'

Arsineh said, 'No, she was angry first, then the coffee boiled over.' I rinsed the coffee pot under the faucet and measured out the coffee, the sugar, and the water again.

When I came into the living room with a tray, Alice was telling Nina, 'What trouble? It's no trouble at all. I'll call Garnik right now.' When she spotted me, she said, 'We've arranged to eat dinner together. Will you phone Garnik?' I do not know what look she saw in my eyes, but she added, 'I'll call him myself.' And she went into the hall.

I set the coffee cups out on the table, sat down next to Nina and tried to listen to what she was saying. Mother was sitting on the edge of one of the dining chairs. Her lips tightly pursed, she was staring at the carpet.

Alice came back into the room. 'Garnik said he's caught a cold and is afraid to give it to us. He said Nina and Violette needn't worry. Have fun, he said. Really, what a wonderful man!' Then she looked at me. 'Scoot over. I have something to tell Nina.'

I was about to get up when the sound of yelling and shouting suddenly filled the hallway. Then the loud slamming of a door, and the breaking of glass. Then Sophie screaming: 'Ouch! My hand, my hand!'

We all ran to the hallway. The transom window above Armen's door was broken, and shattered glass lay scattered all over the floor. Sophie, pressing her wrist to her body, was screaming, while the twins were yelling, 'Sophie cut her hand!'

I could not breathe. God forbid it cut the poor child's artery!

Nina gripped my arm. 'Dear Jesus, Lord, and Savior! Oh no, what's happening to me?! What will I do?'

Sophie was bent over double, screaming, and would not let go of her wrist. The twins were hanging onto each other, crying. Mother was behind us, slapping her cheeks, saying, 'Satan, be cursed!'

Alice bounded up to Sophie with unexpected alacrity for such a heavy-set body, yanked on Sophie's arm and yelled, 'Let go. Let me see what happened.'

Everyone was suddenly quiet and Alice lifted Sophie's wrist. She held it up at an angle where everyone could see the little scrape.

Alice bent over and stared Sophie in the face. 'Two days ago they brought a little mouse to the hospital who had suffered a similar misfortune. Do you know what happened?' Sophie looked at Alice with her tear-stained eyes and Alice said, 'It died,' and gave a laugh.

Nina let go of my forearm, went over to hug Sophie and said, 'Thanks be to God!'

Mother left off slapping herself and said, 'Thanks be to God!'

In my heart, I echoed, 'Thanks be to God!'

The twins hugged Sophie, who said with pouting lips, 'Ouch!'

Alice came over to Nina. 'Clarice will put some antiseptic on it now. Come, I have to tell you the rest.'

Sophie, seeing her mother leave, started to cry again.

I went into the bathroom, got the bottle of Dettol and a cotton ball from the medicine cabinet, and returned to the hallway. Sophie was still crying. Nina was hugging her again. The twins were shouting at Armen's closed door, 'It was your fault.'

Armen yelled from inside his room, 'I had nothing to do with it.' And Mother was yelling at the kids, 'Quiet!'

I noticed Violette at the hallway mirror, holding a decorative hairpin in her teeth and straightening up her hair. Where had she been all this time?

Alice shouted at me, 'Hurry up, will you? You sure are taking your sweet time.' And she snatched the Dettol and the cotton wool from my hand.

The front door opened and Artoush walked in with Emile.

'We thought we'd sneak in a game of chess before dinner...' ventured Artoush. Emile, as if he were reading my mind, offered, 'Mother's headache has recurred and...we did not go to the bazaar.' Then they both saw the glass on the floor.

Sophie, seeing there were fresh onlookers, began to cry once again, and Alice quickly dabbed the scrape with antiseptic. Nina and the twins and Mother together recounted the incident for Emile and Artoush.

My eyes settled on Violette. She smiled and the hairpin fell from her mouth onto the floor. Her hand went to cover her mouth as she said, 'Whoops.' She bent over and picked up the hairpin. Through the open collar of her blouse, I saw her black lace camisole. How white her skin was!

I was cleaning the coffee stains off the stove and thinking what to make for dinner for all these people, and wondering why I should have to make dinner for them, and by what right had Alice invited all these guests to my house, and what the devil was wrong with Armen, and why were the twins making so much noise, and why does Nina laugh so loud, when Artoush came up behind me and said, 'What's for dinner?'

I tossed the washcloth into the sink. 'Nothing. Go get something from the Annex.'

He was surprised at first. Then it seemed to make him happy. 'The curry at the Annex is not bad.' Then he seemed to recall that he did not like spicy food. 'I'll get *fish and chips* as well. How many are we? I'll take a count.' And he left the kitchen.

The kids loved the fish and chips at the Annex restaurant. I had made it for them myself a couple of times, but each time they pouted. 'It's not as tasty as at the Annex.'

After acting up for a minute or two, the Chevrolet finally started up and headed off, and Mother came into the kitchen. 'So the Doc got his wish and went out to get food, huh? He's probably gone out to get Döner Kebab. Hmmph! Or samosas, which a whole host of flies have marched over. Disgusting!'

Violette came into the kitchen. She was pulling on the strap of her camisole to adjust it. 'They said they are going to get food from the Anicks? I went with Nina and Garnik to the Anicks last night and had curry. It was delicious.'

Mother, as if taking the precise measurement of Violette's height, looked her over from the top of her hair – which seemed deliberately out of place – to the tips of her high heels. 'Not Anicks, but Annex. Their food is all right, for people who have never tasted home cooking.' Louder and with more emphasis than the two previous times, she repeated her 'Hmmph!' and 'Disgusting!' and left the kitchen.

Violette laughed. 'My English is wretched.' Then she asked, 'Are you making salad? Shall I help?'

If it were some other time, I would certainly have said, 'Don't trouble yourself; I'll make it.' But this was no other time. I set a fat onion on the table and said, 'Peel this.'

26

My day began badly.

When Artoush asked, 'Have you seen my glasses?' I shot right back with, 'Is there a big sign on my forehead that says "Bureau of Lost and Found"?'

I had no bread to make sandwiches for the kids' recess snack. I gave the twins money to buy crackers, and their eyes lit up. 'No chips or other junk food. Only crackers, and only after lunch.' I tried to remember what the school cafeteria was serving for lunch that day, and whether it was a dish the children liked or not. I could not remember the lunch menu schedule, but I did remember what Nina would say. If I said something like, 'They are serving lamb shanks today and the kids don't like it,' Nina would frown and reply, 'If they don't like it, tough. A child should learn to eat whatever is put in front of him.' I smoothed out a wrinkle near the hem of Arsineh's uniform, wondering if Nina might not be right.

Armen tucked the money in his pocket and left the house without saying goodbye. He had argued several times with the twins, had not spoken to me or his father, and had barely eaten anything since the day before. I could not work up the energy to lecture him about not leaving the school grounds again during recess to buy a snack. 'Only Mama's boys bring their snacks from home,' the high-school-age boys would say. So, to prove their manhood, they would appoint one boy each day to sneak off the school premises and buy Lavash for everyone at the nearby bakery. God only knows how many times I had to go to the Principal's office because Armen was the one who had slipped out. Each time he promised not to do it again, but he was a habitual offender.

I went out to the yard hand in hand with the twins. Half-way down the path, I gestured toward Armen, his back to us as he opened the gate. 'Now what's the matter with him?'

The twins looked at each other, then at me, and finally shrugged their shoulders. I asked, 'Is it because Emily did not come over last night?' This time they avoided looking at one another and tried not to laugh.

The school bus picked up the kids and headed off, the sound of the engine fading farther and farther away. I closed the gate, walked up the path, and came inside. I was about to close the front door and breathe a sigh of relief about being alone until the afternoon, when I heard the faint whirring of the Chevrolet's ignition.

The Chevy's failure to start was part of our daily ritual. Artoush would open the hood, engrossed in the old, and in places rusty, guts of the machine. Then he would play with some of the hoses, which connected something to something else (and I was fairly sure that Artoush did not know either). 'It won't start?' I would ask Artoush, and he would say,

'Hmmm.' I would stare at the engine with him for a few seconds, thinking of it as a terminal patient, kept alive with transfusions and drugs. 'Shall I call a taxi, or call Mr. Saeed?' were my next lines. If Artoush was late, he would say 'Taxi,' the way a surgeon might tell a nurse, 'Scalpel.' And if he was in no hurry, and the car could not be coaxed into coasting by fits and starts to the repair shop, he would say, 'Call up Mr. Saeed,' the way a surgeon might tell a nurse, 'Give him a pint of blood.'

Mr. Saeed was the owner of a repair shop near Cinema Khorshid. Every time he saw Artoush and his Chevrolet, he would laugh, clap his blackened hands to his head with its even blacker frizzy hair and say, 'Dear ole Chevy broke down again?' Mr. Saeed would come stand over the Chevy, and nearly every time he did, he would tell me, out of Artoush's earshot, 'Mrs. Doc – pardon me for meddling – but if you just nag a bit at your husband like other ladies do, the Doc will certainly buy the latest top-of-the-line model.' And when I explained that the Doc had grown rather fond of this car, Mr. Saeed would shake his head and mutter, 'Well, if you want to know the truth, I can't make head or tail out of you and the Doc. Customers from the Oil Company, as soon as things take off and they get a salary raise and a *Grade* increase, go right out and trade in their house and car for better ones. But the two of you...' I would take him tea or sherbet and tell him, 'Salary and rank don't decide what house you live in or the car you drive.'

He would knock back the sherbet or tea and say, 'They don't?'

I did not go out and stand beside the hood to participate in the usual ritual, but instead stayed in the hallway, leaned up against the wall, and closed my eyes. 'Oh God, make it start.' I wanted to be alone. I wanted to be alone right away. My head was pounding and I had no patience for anything.

When the engine finally turned over, I opened my eyes. But I waited until Artoush had backed out of the garage and turned into the street, and until the sound of the engine faded into the distance, before saying, 'Thank you, God.'

I went to the kitchen, sat down at the table and yelled at myself. 'What the hell is your problem?' I drew a Kleenex out of the box and dabbed my eyes, remembering my father.

Whenever I felt really bad, I would think of Father, and whenever I felt really glad, again I would think of him. Like when a plant clipping I had put in water actually sprouted roots. Or when I tried out a new recipe and it turned out delicious. Or when Armen got good grades. I began to tear the Kleenex into pieces and wondered why I think of Father whenever I'm feeling especially bad or glad.

I raised my head up and looked at the two paintings I kept taped to the refrigerator. The twins had done one of them, a Mother's Day gift from the year before. Two hearts and big colorful flowers, with 'I love you' written inside each of them. The other one Armen had done, when he was four or five years old. Using yellow watercolors, he had painted the outline of what was supposed to be a woman. In the woman's hands, which did not look like hands, was a green ring that looked like a head with two eyes. When I asked him what he had drawn, he said, 'Mommy, holding Armen.' Chin in hand, I gazed at the painting and thought, 'I will never be able to hold you like that again.'

My eyes roamed to the counter and I saw the package that Emile had put in my hand the day before, when both he and I were running after his mother in the yard. How had I forgotten the package until now? I took it to the living room. What with the chaos of the previous afternoon and evening, it was not so strange I had forgotten. I leaned back in the leather chair and opened it.

It was one of the books by Sardo that I said I had not read. He had inscribed on the flyleaf: 'For Clarice, to whom I could listen for days and days.'

I closed the book. The room was not that cool, but I felt cold. I re-opened the book and read the sentence again. I traced the handwriting with my finger. What an elegant hand, I thought. Even, proportional, diagonally slanted. My handwriting in Armenian script was stiff. I wrote in block letters and my 'O's looked like little rectangles. Emile's handwriting was cursive, with neat angles, and...supple.

Little by little my queasy, listless feeling began to lift. Like boiling water evaporating bubble by bubble. I felt a burden had lifted. I felt better. 'So he was really interested in what I said? So I hadn't bored him?' I remembered his hand under his chin, and his wristwatch, with its white leather band. In the yard two frogs were calling to each other back and forth. I looked out the window. 'Maybe these two enjoy chatting with one another, too.' The bougainvillea seemed to be nodding to me through the window.

I turned the book over and read the blurb on the back. This man has been in love with this woman since they were young, and his sole desire is to be united with her. Now engulfed in political affairs, he is uncertain whether to choose love, or as he puts it, his responsibilities to society. I returned to the flyleaf and read Emile's inscription one more time. I leafed through the pages, then opened to the first chapter and began to read. The hero of the story was undecided; the heroine attempted a variety of stratagems to win him over, until the phone rang. I looked at my watch and could not believe it. When was the last time I had read a book for such a long uninterrupted stretch?

27

On the phone, Nina's motor was, as Garnik would put it, running at full speed, her voice ringing out like a bell. 'I, for one, am still in the dark. Are things really and truly getting serious, or is Alice building sandcastles in the air again? The minute Violette heard, she said it was obvious off the bat that Joop liked Alice. So how did we miss it? Clueless me, trying to fix him up with Violette! But I guess it did not turn out too shabby. Alice is first in line.' She chuckled loudly. Then her voice lowered to a whisper. I heard her say 'Emile Simonian' a few times and when I asked, 'What did you say?' she answered, 'Nothing. Will you come with me this afternoon to drop by the bazaar? Sophie is nagging me to buy her a beret.' She gave me no chance to answer yes or no, ending with, 'So, see you this afternoon. Violette says hello. Bye for now.'

For Alice to divulge a relationship that had barely even sprouted yet, much less borne fruit, was not terribly surprising. But what was that Nina had said about Emile? Why was she whispering, and why had she said 'I'll tell you later'?

I went to the backyard, checked on the vegetables I'd planted, and picked a few tomatoes. I turned my head to look up at the jujube tree. Wedged between the branches were two nests. A nice plump sparrow flew up in the branches and settled on one of the nests. It had something in its beak – bringing food for its babies, I thought. It was very hot and everything was quiet. I went back inside, singing a song to myself.

For their after-school snack, I made what the kids liked to call 'Cheese in the Oven' sandwiches. I cut up some rolls, laid a slice of cheese on each, and put them in the oven. While waiting for the bread to toast and the cheese to melt, I wondered how many after-school snacks I had prepared up to that day. How many lunches? How many dinners? The metal gate squeaking and the sound of feet running up the path interrupted my calculations.

Sophie said, 'My mom said to come to your house. She should get here herself in a minute or two.'

I told them to wash their face and hands, have their snacks and get ready for their piano lesson.

Armineh said, 'It would be super if Sophie came to piano class with us.'

Arsineh said, 'It would be super duper if Sophie came to piano class with us.'

Both of them turned to Sophie. 'When you hear Miss Judy speak Persian...' began Armineh.

'You'll die laughing...' finished Arsineh.

I shouted, 'Armen, snack!'

He shouted back from his room, 'I'm not hungry.'

The girls muffled their laughter. When I looked at them, Armineh said, 'I swear, we don't know anything, but...'

Arsineh continued, 'But we heard he made up with Emily.'

Sophie said, 'That's probably why he's not hungry.' The three of them burst out laughing.

The phone was ringing in the hallway; I went to get it. Mrs. Simonian said that she had heard from Emily, who had a piano lesson scheduled, that the twins also had their piano lesson that afternoon. Since Emile would be coming home late due to some business that had come up, Emily should come with the twins. Mrs. Simonian herself had a backache and could not take Emily. Not so much as a 'please,' or an 'if it wouldn't be too much trouble.' Not even a proper hello and goodbye.

Before I could put down the receiver, Armen popped out of his room.

'Shall I go get Emily?'

I raised a quizzical eyebrow, and he fell to stammering.

'Uh, well...Emily said on the bus that she has a piano lesson and, uh, well...I decided to take piano again.'

I laughed when I saw the comical look on Armen's face, forgetting all about the sting of Mrs. Simonian's rudeness. Just at that moment, Nina opened the front door. 'Oh my gosh, I'm baking in this heat.' With no thought of hello, Armen slipped between the two of us and shot out the front door. Almost at the end of the yard, he turned back and shouted 'We'll wait for you at the bus stop.'

Nina looked at me. 'What's come over that one?' I stared up at the ceiling.

'He's in love!'

I waited for her rollicking laughter, but she just shook her head. 'It seems like they've poured something in the water supply these days!'

I called out toward the kitchen, 'Kids, let's go.'

Emily was wearing a white blouse and black trousers, a piano book pressed to her chest. She was leaning up against the bus stop sign, her head down, pushing a little stone back and forth with the tip of her toe. Her long straight hair was spilling over her face. Armen paced back and forth in front of Emily, waving his hands and talking. He fell silent as soon as we walked up. Emily swiftly raised her head and said hello. The hair fell to either side of her face.

'What a sweet girl,' Nina said.

I asked myself, 'Is she just a girl?'

Emily looked at me for a moment. Why did it feel like she had read my mind? She tucked a wisp of hair behind her ear and smiled, not unlike the smile the twins offered when they wanted something.

The bus arrived, and when I got on, the driver greeted me. I was surprised to see him. 'Hello, Mr. Abdi. Weren't you working the Refinery route?'

He laughed. 'What can I do, ma'am. I got promoted. What about you? Are you well? We are grateful for all the troubles you went to for us.'

'What trouble?' I protested. 'How is your boy?'

The kids filed past the driver one by one, each saying 'Pass.' Mr. Abdi laughed and said, 'Day before yesterday there was a Tehrani riding the bus. He heard the passengers from the Oil Company sayin' somethin' and not payin' for the ticket. 'Stead of saying "pass," he said "gas."'

I laughed and Mr. Abdi pressed the button to close the door. He turned his face to me. 'Thanks God, our son is much

191

better. We brought him home. Your sister was very kind. Many thanks.' Nina nudged me from behind. 'Hey, get a move on, already.'

The bus had only a few passengers. The twins and Sophie went to the back, Armen and Emily sat directly behind the driver, and Nina led, almost pushed, me to a seat far away from the children. I was explaining, 'His son was sick, and I asked Alice to look in on him at the hospital...' when Nina cut me off.

'Yeah, yeah, yeah. The sun would never rise if it weren't for your making buddies out of all the Oil Company drivers, gardeners and plumbers, would it?' She looked behind her and leaned in close to my ear. 'Tell me about your new neighbor. Isn't his name Simonian? He's a widower, right?'

I stared at her for a few seconds. Why had I not understood earlier? Now that I had understood, why did I suddenly feel empty? Why was it so hot? Why was it taking so long to get there?

By the time we reached Miss Judy's house in south Bawarda, I had told Nina everything I knew about the inhabitants of G-4. As we approached the stop, I stood up, pulled the cord and told Nina that while the children were at their lesson, we could go buy that hat for Sophie and come back. Nina looked at me, confused.

'What hat?'

I motioned to the kids to get off, and said to Nina, who was still sitting, 'Get up. Here we are. Didn't you say you wanted to buy a beret for Sophie?'

She got up from her seat. 'For the moment I've got more important things to do than buying hats. Let's see, you are not invited anywhere on Thursday night, are you?' The instant I said no, she said, 'Then you'll have guests.'

I said goodbye to the driver, and was the last one to get out. I reprimanded myself. 'A beret in this heat? As Mother would say, "You really are an ass!"'

28

After the kids' piano lessons, we all took the bus home. When we got off at our stop, I looked over at Emily, who was walking with the kids toward our house. Before I could venture a word, she said, 'Grandmother said for me to stay at your home for a couple hours.'

I remarked to myself, 'Grandmother assigns everyone his appointed task.'

I went in the kitchen, only to find that Mother and Alice had turned up before we got back. Time and time again I had explained to Mother that I gave them the spare house key so they could open the door in case of an emergency when we were out of town. It had no effect. Mother and Alice were in the habit of popping over unannounced, and if it happened we were not at home, they would just dig out the key and let themselves right in.

Alice was sitting at the table, filing her nails. Mother was standing on a chair dusting the clay jugs atop the cabinets. As I walked in, instead of returning my hello, she blurted out, 'What am I going to do with you and the junk you display all over the house? Just like your father, God have mercy on him.'

'Who asked you to go climbing up there? Ashkhen dusted all the cabinets last week,' I said.

Mother stepped down off the chair. 'Ashkhen's dusting is good for nothing.' As Nina walked in, Mother greeted her enthusiastically. So, her pique with Nina had come to an end. I heard Artoush drive up in the Chevrolet.

Nina and Alice greeted each other with kisses, and Nina told her about Thursday night's dinner party. Sophie and the twins jumped up and down, clapping.

'Oh boy! A party!'

They hopped over to Emily. Armineh said, 'You must come too!'

Arsineh added, 'Do come!'

Armen looked at Emily. Emily looked downward. 'If Grandmother allows...'

Nina said, 'Don't worry, your grandmother and your father are invited too.'

Alice put on her lipstick without a mirror. 'Joop just loves Persian food.'

Mother said, 'Clarice will make Fesenjan for him.' So her pique with the Dutchman had come to an end, too.

Arsineh told Armineh, 'Now do your impression of Miss Judy. Come on, do it!'

Armineh stood on her tiptoes and pointed her index finger at Armen. 'This time you serious learn piano, or you play hokey again?'

Arsineh answered in the role of Armen, 'I am serious about it.'

Armineh arched her eyebrows and pursed her lips. 'Then you, Emily, here in *living room*, until I call!'

Sophie held her hand to her stomach and said, amidst her laughter, 'That's exactly how she talks!'

Nina lovingly pinched Armineh's cheek. 'You little rascal.'

Mother grinned, saying, 'That's my lovely, witty girl!'

Alice, her lipstick canister and nail file in hand, doubled over laughing.

Emily cast a sideways glance at Armen, who said, 'Hardy har har.'

When Artoush came in, the twins jumped into his arms. 'Daddy, we're having guests Thursday night! Sophie, and Emily, and everyone, and all…'

All the way home from the piano class I had wanted to say something, wanted to tell Nina no, but she never gave me the chance. Now, as I tried to open my mouth again, she put her hand on my shoulder. 'I'll help you out. You won't have to lift a finger.' She slipped her arm behind my back and practically pushed me out the kitchen door. 'You just go invite the neighbors. I'll take care of the rest.'

Artoush kissed the twins. 'Not a bad idea. Emile and I will play some chess.' I left the kitchen, thinking, 'If only I had thrown that black pawn into the garbage pail.'

I do not know if I closed the front door behind me or not. I headed down the path, opened the gate, but instead of crossing the street, I followed the drainage channel toward the neighborhood square.

I was mad. At Nina for twisting my arm to hold a dinner party because she wanted, as she put it, to fix Violette up with Emile. At Alice, who only thought of herself, and at Mother, who only thought of Alice. At the kids for being happy, and at Artoush, who only thought of chess. Why wasn't anyone thinking of me? Why didn't anyone ask me what I wanted?

My compassionate streak complied. 'So, what do you want?' I answered, 'I want to be alone for a few hours a day. I want to talk to somebody about the things I like.' My critical streak leapt in. 'Which is it? To be alone, or to talk with somebody?'

I passed by a eucalyptus tree, reached out and picked a leaf, crumpled it up in my hand and smelled it. I walked on a few paces and tossed the mashed-up leaf in the gutter. 'I want to know what decision the hero of Sardo's story takes in the end.' The words came out, and I took a sudden step backward, having almost stepped on a dead frog, flattened on the sidewalk. It looked as though a fat tire had run smack over it. I muttered under my breath, 'Curse this city and all its frogs, lizards, and water snakes, dead or alive.'

I reached the square, angry, grumbling, on edge. The sun had set, but it was still hot. A stench rose off the drainage channel. I sat on one of the benches lining the square, a row of Msasa trees and oleander bushes, with their pink and white blossoms, behind me. In the square, under the water tower, a skinny cat was chasing something. A frog, maybe, or a lizard.

A hot gust blew over me and dropped what looked like a pea pod into my lap. For a second, though, I mistook it for a worm or a locust, and instinctively flicked it to the ground, shivering with disgust. I thought how, ever since arriving in Abadan, life seemed like a constant struggle against a multiplicity of winged bugs and creepy crawlies. Ever since I was a little girl, insects were revolting to me, and still were. That, and all the smells that washed over me in Abadan, gave me a constant feeling of nausea: the smell of gas from the refinery, the rancid smell from the drainage channel, the smell of fish and salted shrimp mixed with the Arab perfumes in the Kuwaiti Bazaar – it all combined to make me feel sick whenever I went shopping. Of course, along with all that, perhaps the main culprit was the heat and humidity. Why had I come to this city? Why didn't I just stay in Tehran?

I thought of our house in Tehran. What a pretty little yard it had. I remembered the little lane and its tall plane trees. Summers when we or one of the neighbors watered the trees, you could smell the wet soil. Winter mornings, before even getting out of bed, I could tell if it had snowed. The light that came streaming in through the bedroom window after a snowfall was different from the light on other days. I remembered snowy days, going to school with gloves, a hat, and a woolen scarf that Mother had knitted for me. What a wonderful sound the crunch-crunch of the snow made under our boots! How many years had it been since I'd seen the snow, or worn my overcoat and gloves, or warmed my hands in front of the heater, or watched the frosty breath come out of my mouth?

I shooed away a mosquito that was trying to fly up my nose. Why had I come to Abadan in the first place? Why hadn't I stayed in Tehran? Because Artoush got hired by the Oil Company, because Alice got a job in the Oil Company hospital, and because Mother came with Alice to Abadan. Had Mother come to be with Alice, or to be near me? Has anyone ever done anything just for my sake? What had I, at the age of thirty-eight, ever done solely for my own sake?

It was getting dark. The square was empty, with no one about. Through the boxwood hedges ringing the houses, I could see the lights coming on one by one. I turned my head toward our street. I had to go back. The thought of all the things I had to do depressed me: making dinner, planning Thursday's party, a brewing argument with Armen about the pants he had been nagging me to buy for ages and which he would certainly want to wear on Thursday night, and above all, inviting Mrs. Simonian. Demanding, selfish harpy, I thought. She imagines everyone's her personal maid and servant. Instead of all these tasks I did not like but had to do, I just wanted to lean back in the easy chair and find out what the hero of Sardo's story would choose in the end: love or responsibility?

A dark shadow turned the corner and I leapt up. In the fading twilight I could not see well. It must be one of the children. They must have gotten worried. I started heading toward it, then almost ran, then stopped in my tracks. Mrs. Simonian also stopped in her tracks. She was wearing a white crew-neck blouse with black pants, just like her granddaughter's outfit from that afternoon. Wearing flats, she seemed even shorter than usual.

She stood motionless for a moment, then continued on her way, and without looking at me, said, 'So, you like to take walks, too.' It was not a question. I did not know what to do, whether to walk with her, or not. She stopped and turned around. 'You were on your way back home.' Again, not a question. 'Shall we walk together a little ways?' This time it was a question. It even had the hint of a request about it.

I walked beside her, feeling ashamed for having called her in my head a 'demanding, selfish harpy.' Something in her voice made me feel sorry for her. We walked back to the square in silence and, heading toward the bench where I had been sitting just a few minutes before, my neighbor asked, 'Shall we sit here a while? I'm tired.'

The bench was tall for her, but she sat with ease, neither hopping nor jumping, but rather gently pulling herself up onto the seat. She's had a whole lifetime to practice, I thought. A whole lifetime of practice, just to sit down.

It was dark and muggy, and the air was still. I heard the monotonous ribbeting of the frogs in the drainage channel and the sound of splashing every time one of them jumped. I smelled my hand. It still smelled of eucalyptus.

A bicycle circled around the square, with a large box fastened to the back. It was Hajji, or as the kids called him, 'Bread Man,' an old man who sold Lavash in the mornings and evenings at the Oil Company locales. He must have been on his way back home to Ahmadabad and the tiny, dusty, dirty lane where his house was. He'd have more than an hour left to pedal. A few years earlier, his son had drowned in the Shatt al-Arab river, and I paid a consolation visit to Hajji's wife, who, as he said, was just dying of grief. When Mother and Alice found out that I had gone to see Hajji's wife, they said, 'You're crazy.'

Artoush said, 'It was a good thing you did.'

Before the forty days of mourning for the boy were over, Hajji's wife set herself on fire and died.

Hajji remarried two months later. 'Won't you take a wedding gift for Hajji?' laughed Mother and Alice. Artoush just shook his head, and I stopped buying Lavash from Hajji.

'What a lifeless city,' Mrs. Simonian said.

I thought I would broach the matter of Thursday's dinner party and kill two birds with one stone. 'The family who used to live in G-4 – you saw them yesterday at our house – have arranged...'

She did not let me finish. She turned her head to face me and spoke very deliberately. 'I saw them. Let me guess. They want to invite my son and because they want to invite my son, they have invited me and Emily, as well. And you must be invited too, right? Or maybe they've even stuck you with hosting the party?' And she sneered.

I held my breath. A warm breeze knocked a few petals on the ground from the oleander bush behind us. I peered at the Msasa trees surrounding the square in the faint light of the metal lamp posts. How did she know?

She put her hand on my knee. 'Clarice, I like you.' It was the first time she used the informal 'you' with me. 'You are different from other women. You pay attention to things that others don't. Things which are not important to other women are important to you. You are just like me, or rather, like me in my younger days.'

The idea that I might be like Mrs. Simonian was the last thing that would ever occur to me and the last thing I might wish for. Why was everyone saying that I reminded them of someone? Nina said I reminded her of Violette, and now...

She lifted her hand from my knee. 'I don't like this city. It's been years since I liked any city I've been in. I put up with it for the sake of Emile and Emily.' She fell silent. I noticed once again that she was talking more informally than usual.

Her eyes were fixed on the water tank. 'Ever since I was old enough to know myself, I have always chosen to put up with things. First for the sake of my father, then for my husband, now for my son and granddaughter. I have never done anything for my own sake.' She seemed to be talking to herself. I stared at the water tank, standing atop its metal legs like a giant bogeyman peering down from on high at us two women.

She sneered again. 'Are you surprised? Like everyone else, you suppose that I have done and had whatever I wanted in life?' She slid off the bench and stood there. 'Come on. I want to show you the rest of the photographs.' And off she went.

I did not think of the children's dinner, nor of Nina, nor of Mother and Alice. I did not want to deal with any of them. I wanted to do something that I wanted to do. I wanted to see the photographs.

The gate of G-4 was open. We crossed the yard. The flowerbed on the right was overgrown with weeds, but the soil in the flowerbed on the left was newly overturned. Did he pull the weeds himself, I wondered? Did he hoe the ground himself?

The house was dark and quiet. Mrs. Simonian headed for the bedrooms. She stopped next to the statue of the elephant with the broken trunk to stroke its head. 'Ganesh is the god of fortune and wealth for the Hindus.' She stroked the broken trunk. 'You see? Even this poor fellow's patience has been broken by me.' She opened her bedroom door. 'Emily is at your house. Emile has gone to fetch her and must have stayed. Is the blond at your house, too? Sit here on the bed.'

I sat on the bed. 'No, she's not.'

She pulled out a heavy album from under the bed. It had a red leather cover etched in gold and embossed in turquoise. I had never seen anything like it. She opened it and muttered, 'She'll show up, no doubt she'll show up,' and then fell silent for a while.

I looked around the dimly lit and sparsely furnished room. It looked as if its occupant had moved in that very day and had not yet had a chance to set out her things, or perhaps the occupant had packed everything up to move out the next day.

Mrs. Simonian handed me a photograph. A young man in a white suit was standing on a broad staircase, one foot on the step above him. The staircase had a stone bannister lined with stone flowerpots full of flowers. The young man was smiling into the camera. His eyes looked to be light in color.

'This was the entrance to our house in Isfahan,' explained Mrs. Simonian. 'The one your mother said it was a pity to sell.' She smirked. 'I hated the entire place: the large garden, the high-ceilinged rooms, the wood floors of the corridors, all the expensive furniture. My father used to say, "What more could you want?" For years I did not know what I wanted, and when I finally figured it out and asked for it, he said no.'

She held out another photo to me, the same young man behind a desk covered with books and papers, staring into the camera, a pen in one hand and his chin resting in the other. He had close-cropped hair and wore a striped coat and vest. I was mentally comparing it to a suit I had seen Mr. Davtian wearing, when my neighbor handed me a third photo. In this one the young man had on a white shirt with a broad, open collar – like a Russian shirt. His hair spilled down to his shoulders and he wore a thin beard. He stood, hand on his waist, next to a high-backed chair, again staring into the camera. A girl was sitting in the chair, her hair gathered atop her head. The girl was wearing a dark buttoned-up blouse and a necklace with several strands of tiny pearls. You could only see her from the knees up. The man's eyes were definitely light.

That girl in the picture, fifty or sixty years on and now sitting in front of me, closed her eyes. 'My father said that a poet was not the kind of person to build a life with. Father said it was only because of my money that he wanted to marry me. No one falls in love with a midget girl, he said. But my husband and my father did fall in love. They fell in love with each other's money. My father said that if I refused to marry him…' She opened her eyes, leaned forward and took the picture from my hands. 'We took this picture without my father's permission, at the photography studio of Thooni Johannes in Julfa. Thooni promised not to tell my father, and he didn't. He was a good man.' She stared at the photo and pressed her lips together, emphasizing the creases around her mouth. The frogs were croaking in the yard.

I was about to ask, 'Then what happened?' when she looked at me and smiled. 'What happened?' She opened the album and flipped to a particular page. There she was with the young man, sitting on a wrought iron bench in front of the Eiffel Tower. In the next picture she was with the young man, riding in a rickshaw pulled by a brown-skinned man wearing a loincloth. Again, she and the young man were in the next picture, sitting at a table in a sidewalk café on a crowded street.

As she talked, I looked at the pictures and listened. 'He followed me everywhere – India, England, France, back to India. When my husband died, I thought I was free, I thought we would finally marry, I thought I was the luckiest woman on Earth.' She ran her hand over the photos, then slowly turned the pages. She came to the last page, which contained a very large photo. It was a grave in a cemetery with large trees. Elmira Simonian was standing next to the grave in a black dress, hat, and veil and holding the hand of a little boy in a black suit and tie. Mrs. Simonian's voice seemed to come from far away. 'A few months later he was gone, too. We were in Paris. I buried him in Père-Lachaise.'

She fell silent, leaned back on the headboard and stared at the ceiling. I felt she was no longer in the room. She might have been at the Eiffel Tower, or in some side street of Bombay, or a coffeehouse in England. Or maybe in the Père-Lachaise cemetery, with its large trees.

I closed the album and picked up the studio photo. The girl in the photo had a cold look. The young man seemed angry and his eyes were green, or maybe blue.

'Did he have blue eyes?'

She drew her hand across her forehead, took the photograph from my hand, stuck it inside the album with the rest of the pictures, and stood up.

We walked together without a word to the end of the yard. The gate was open. She stopped and took hold of my arm. 'I'm sorry. I was feeling sad and nostalgic. Good evening.' As I headed across the street, she called out to me. I turned around. She was the same height as the gate. In the dark I could not see her face, but her voice seemed again to come from far away. 'They were green. The same color as his son's.'

I was left alone in the street. The boxwood hedges and Msasa trees were almost black. Moths were circling the street lamps and you could smell the gas from the refinery.

I opened our door and stepped inside. It was totally quiet. I bent over to pick up a hairband that had fallen near the telephone table. Was it Armineh's or Arsineh's? I couldn't tell. How could anyone tell one sister's hairband from the other's, when even their pencils were sharpened to the same length and had identical bite-marks? Under the telephone table a decorative hairpin sparkled. Whose was that? Not difficult to tell, this one – it belonged to the blond.

I went to the kitchen and wondered when Emile had come to fetch Emily. When had they returned home, and how could I have failed to notice their arrival? Had Nina and Sophie gone? What did the children have for dinner? How long had I been gone? I stared at the sweet peas on the window ledge. My head was still swimming from all the photographs and the talk. The table was filled with dirty cups and dishes. I put on my apron and started washing the dishes. I heard foot-steps behind me, but kept on washing.

Artoush said, 'Were you with Mrs. Simonian?'

I scraped the leavings of a tomato omelette off a plate into the trash. How did he know? He answered my thought. 'Emile went to get you.'

I couldn't see him, but I could picture him, leaning in the doorway, playing with his goatee, with his other hand prob-ably in his pants pocket. When he knew I was upset, that is what he would do while trying to snap me out of it. He would never ask, 'What's wrong?' Not even when, like this evening, my being upset had nothing to do with him. I rubbed some dishwashing powder onto a plate. It was Emile, I thought, and not my husband, who had come looking for me.

I heard the legs of a chair scrape on the floor. 'Your mother and Alice argued again, about what I don't know. They left early. Nina fixed omelettes for the kids. I gave her and Sophie a ride home. The car, confound it, was acting up again. It was a real pain to get it started.'

I held the plate under the water and read on the dishwash-ing canister: 'Norman's Dishwashing Powder. Suitable for cleaning dishes, tiles, bathrooms.' Under the words was a funny picture of Norman Wisdom in his tweed cap. I was about to say, 'Don't read me any bedtime stories, I'm not upset with you. I'm not actually upset with anyone.' Before I could say it, he continued with his recital. 'Armen did not eat. We couldn't find Ishy, and Arsineh cried.' I untied the apron.

Artoush was scooting something across the table from one hand to the other. The sugar shaker, or maybe the salt shaker.

I knew he was searching for something to say next. I guessed he might ask, 'What are you cooking tomorrow?' but when he asked, 'Was Mrs. Simonian alright?' I burst out laughing.

I turned around to look at him, and spoke in measured tones. 'Ishy disappears almost every night. Armen has not been eating for several days because he's fallen in love. I don't feel well, but it has nothing to do with you. Mrs. Simonian was fine, which can't concern you very much.' He looked for a few seconds at the sugar shaker, then at me. He pushed back the chair, got up and left the kitchen. The sugar shaker lay overturned on the table. I was choked up, and turned back to the dishes. Norman Wisdom was still laughing.

29

Armen and Artoush left the house together. Neither of them said goodbye.

In the hallway I tightened the ribbons around the twins' pigtails, one by one, and said goodbye to them. Armineh stuck her recess snack in her satchel and zipped it up. 'Aren't you coming to the door with us?' I kissed her cheek, and shook my head. Arsineh asked, 'Are you tired?' I kissed her cheek and nodded.

Armineh peeked through the lace curtain of the door. 'It's foggy again.' I looked in the yard. The twins were afraid to venture into the yard in thick fog. I never let on that I knew they were scared. I would hold their hands and walk them through the yard, singing 'We're floating through the clouds.'

I straightened up the curtain. 'The two of you can float through the clouds together today, okay?' They looked at each other, then at me. Their eyes looked sad, lacking their usual sparkle.

Through the lace curtain, I watched them walk hand in hand down the path and disappear into the fog. I couldn't see the gate. The swing seat, the willow tree and part of the lawn looked like an impressionist watercolor, wispy and blurred.

I always walked my children to the bus stop. Why, I wondered, not this morning? How could I make them worry like that? So, I'm exhausted and in a bad mood, but what fault is it of the children? My compassionate side offered consolation: 'You're only human. You have the same right as everyone else to be tired now and then. Like everyone else, you...' The telephone rang.

Mrs. Nurollahi asked, 'If you have some time this morning, may I come over?'

As if all the other excitement wasn't enough. I searched for some excuse. 'Aren't you at the office today?'

'My boss has given me some time off. My good-natured boss. I think you know him, no?' She laughed at her own joke.

'Thank God he's good-natured with someone, at least,' I thought to myself. After overturning the sugar shaker, her boss had not spoken a single word to me. I searched for some other excuse. 'I was going to go downtown today...'

'That's great,' she said. 'I have to do some shopping, too. We can meet together at the *Milk Bar* at ten o'clock.' Before I could come up with another excuse, she thanked me with three very long sentences, said goodbye with a single word, then hung up.

There was still some time before ten o'clock. Today was the day to change the sheets. I went to Armen's room.

I tried not to view his room as messy and unkempt. Shoes, socks, books, magazines, 45rpm records, and empty milk glasses which would of course have been impossible for him to return to the kitchen. I picked the balled-up pyjamas and a few books and notebooks off his bed, then pulled the sheets off the mattress. The mattress jiggled slightly, and a piece of paper fell to the ground. I imagined at first it was another of the monthly tests he would hide when the grade was not so good. I found a not inconsiderable number of such papers; he always hid them, like the twins' toys, in what he thought were unlikely hiding places: behind the air-conditioning vent, above the medicine cabinet, under the Persian carpets. I unfolded it and saw from the first line that it was a letter. I told myself I shouldn't read it. It's an invasion of privacy to read other people's letters, even if he is your child. You shouldn't read it. You shouldn't.

And I did. From the scribbled writing and the repetitions and crossed out words, it was obviously only a first draft:

My dear and most beautiful Emily:

I will never forget you as long as I live. I am prepared to folow you to the ends of the earth and save you from your tyrannical grandmother and mersiless father. I too, seek escape from my stupid sisters and my mother who only knows how to criticise and cook and plant flowers and complane, and from my father who only likes to play chess and read the newspaper. Down with all fathers, mothers and grandmothers!

With the letter in my hand, I sat down on the bed and stared out the window at the jujube tree. And there I was, feeling ambushed, as though suddenly thrust in front of a mirror that reflected back an utterly unrecognizable image of myself. I folded the letter and put it back under the mattress, changed the sheets and pillowcase, straightened the bed, and left the room. I could barely read the clock through my tears. It was after nine. I really did not want to go out. I really did not want to see Mrs. Nurollahi, or anyone else. I really wished I was still a child and could put my arms around Father's neck and cry my little heart out.

30

I was the only passenger on the bus. The driver hummed an Arabic song under his breath. I could tell from the soulful way he sang 'Ya habibi' and 'Ya azizi' that it must be a love song. We passed Cinema Taj. It seemed like only yesterday I would take Armen to Cinema Taj. When the twins were small, I would leave them with Mother every Friday and make mortadella sandwiches at home, with diced onions and chopped parsley – he really liked those. He also loved Canada Dry Orange soda, and insisted on going up to the Cinema Taj snack bar to buy it for himself. We would watch the film, eat our sandwiches, and have great fun together. On the way back home, his hand in mine, he would recount the plot two or three times from beginning to end.

The bus stopped in front of the Blue Star store. How long had it been since I held Armen's hand? How long had it been since we went to the movies, just the two of us? Before getting off the bus, I told the driver, 'What a pretty song you were singing.' He laughed – a young man, with three gold teeth.

I stood in front of the Blue Star display window, wondering. What did Mrs. Nurollahi want? Did my boy really hate me? Why hadn't Artoush taken any steps to make up with me? Taped in the window was a square piece of cardboard: 'See our *Easy* model washing machines inside the store. Made in America!'

Several times Artoush had asked me, 'Why don't you buy a washing machine?'

Mother had said, 'Clothes must be washed by hand.'

Alice had said, 'They're quite expensive.'

Artoush said, 'You should definitely buy one.'

I got to the *Milk Bar* and climbed the twisting stairs. Several of the tables against the glass wall were occupied. Young girls and boys, not-so-young women and men. I was uncomfortable. Whenever mention of the *Milk Bar* was made in our house, Alice would arch her eyebrows. 'It's the spot for a morning rendezvous, if you know what I mean.'

I told the waiter I was waiting for a lady friend, emphasizing the word 'lady.' I sat at one of the tables for two and kept a lookout toward the stairs, hoping Mrs. Nurollahi would show up as soon as possible, say what she had to say, and leave. I thought of Armen's letter. Of Artoush and the overturned sugar shaker. Why didn't anyone understand me? I had never before experienced such an unbroken string of unhappy events. I thought about how calm my life had been before Emily and her grandmother turned up in G-4. My critical streak tripped me up: 'So, it was only Emily and her grandmother who overturned the calm life you were leading?' A tall chignon with a polka dot hair ribbon climbing the stairs provided me with a handy pretext for evading that question.

As soon as she was seated, Mrs. Nurollahi asked, 'Are you not feeling well?' I was taken aback. Did it seem so obvious?

Flustered, I explained that things were hectic these days, with constant guests, taking care of the children, the heat and humidity, which all wore me out. And well, children grow up, and their problems grow bigger. And it tires a person out, trying to understand and solve such problems. And sometimes I feel I'm not a good mother, and instead of helping me, the people around me make my burden heavier. And I'm just tired…and I was crying.

Mortified, I wished I could sink under the table. Why was I crying in a strange place? Why was I telling a woman whom I had only met a few times, and was not on intimate terms with, things that I had not told anyone? Mrs. Nurollahi took a tissue out of her purse and put it in my hand. I dabbed my eyes. 'I'm sorry. I just don't know what happened.'

She put her hand on mine. She did not say anything until I raised my head and looked at her. Then she said, 'Your hair is so beautiful. I wish my hair were straight, like yours.' She patted my hand several times and then withdrew her hand. 'They say the café glacé is very good here.'

While she was placing the order for café glacé with the waiter, I turned to the glass wall and looked outside. One of the palm trees on the other side of the atrium was dried out and dying. When I was little, Mother used to say, 'I wish your hair had a little curl in it, like Alice's.'

When the waiter left, we began to talk. 'You Armenian ladies,' Mrs. Nurollahi began, 'are far ahead of us. Muslim women have only now started to fight for some of the things you have had for some time. We are just setting out on the path.'

I should have replied, 'It's not quite the way you think,' but I just nodded my head.

She wanted me to tell her all about the management of the Adab Armenian school, about the Board of Trustees for the Armenian community. I told her that the Armenians had built the school themselves. I do not remember where I had heard this, but the first group of Armenians hired to work for the Anglo-Iranian Oil Company would go after hours to the site of the school, and in essence, built the place brick by brick with their own hands.

Mrs. Nurollahi asked, 'Why did you decide to call the school "Adab", with a Persian, instead of an Armenian name?'

I did not know the answer to that. I talked about the tuition structure. Tuition fees for the pupils were tied to the income of their parents. A sliding scale: the higher the family income, the more the tuition of the children. On the other hand, the lower-income families sometimes paid no tuition, or might even receive financial assistance. I did not tell her that once in a while one of the better-off families would bargain like the dickens in an attempt to lower their tuition. I told her about the annual membership dues that the Board of Trustees had established, also tied to each individual's yearly income. I did not tell her that there were people who would not mind getting out of paying the annual membership dues altogether. I told her about the charity benefits that were held two or three times a year, for which the women baked pastries, and sold the things they had knitted or crafts they had made. The proceeds were given to Armenian families of little means. I did not explain that these bake sales could also become a focus of backbiting, keeping up appearances, and keeping up with the Joneses, with ladies vying with each other about things like their cars, their trips to Europe, and the *Grade* of their husbands in the Oil Company.

She was listening intently. She thanked the waiter when he brought our café glacé and then asked me, 'Do you know Mrs. Emma Khatchatourian?'

'No,' I said, but when she added, 'The cakes she baked were marvelous,' I remembered. Mother, who was not impressed by anyone's baking, used to say, 'You want cake, it has to be baked by Emma!'

Mrs. Nurollahi said, 'When I lived in Tehran, she taught baking classes in the Farah Charitable Society. What wonderful…I forgot the name of the pastry, Nazok?'

'Nazouk,' I said.

'Yes, yes, that's it. What wonderful Nazouks she made.'

Then she talked about their own society and its activities, about the efforts of women to win suffrage, about literacy classes, about how Iranian women were not yet aware of their rights. Now that she was speaking in a relaxed manner, not using those four-dollar words, I was inspired. I told her so, and she laughed. 'I have to talk in a more formal style when giving a public speech, otherwise people will suppose I am not educated enough to be a speaker, or that what I have to say is unimportant.' We drank our café glacés, which were quite tasty.

A young couple, a girl and a boy, went over to the record machine. Word was that the *Milk Bar* had recently shipped it in from Europe; I knew it was called a Juke Box, but had never seen one before. The youthful girl and boy bickered good-naturedly over the song to choose. The boy was tall and thin. The girl wore an orange shift dress, straight and shapeless, with green trim on the hem and sleeves.

Mrs. Nurollahi was looking at her too. 'When I see youngsters laughing and having fun, I really enjoy it. It's the whole reason we've been pulling our hair out. When I think about my own youth...'

The young pair finally picked a record. It was one of the songs Armen often played on his portable Teppaz turntable, dancing *the Twist* to it. I had never been able to make out the words the singer repeated over and over. Sipping my café glacé, I finally figured it out: *Hit the road, Jack*. I had never liked the song until now. Why? It was a nice song.

Mrs. Nurollahi stirred her drink. 'For Armenians, it's no revelation, but for us it's something completely new. My own mother and father, who would be considered educated and progressive, tried to move mountains to get me to marry my cousin. I know that's not a custom among Armenians, but for us Muslims, family marriages are not only not frowned on, they are a kind of good deed, as the old folks say. You must have heard the saying, "The marriage of paternal cousins is made in heaven"?'

I had heard it. I was once again on the verge of telling her that things were not quite as she imagined, that Armenian women have their own problems, but Mrs. Nurollahi did not give me the chance.

She touched the bowtie ribbon in her chignon. Maybe to make sure it was tight in place. 'I dug in my heels against marrying my cousin.' She laughed heartily and two dimples appeared in her fleshy cheeks. 'If you want the truth, I had fallen in love with my cousin's friend, who had come to our house a couple times. Well, we all joined forces – he, my cousin, and I – and kept talking it up to all the mothers and fathers concerned until they finally gave in and consented.'

I was looking at her, my chin propped on my fist. 'You married your cousin's friend?'

She made a ring around her glass with her thumbs and forefingers, looked outside and slowly nodded. There was a faint smile on her lips and in her eyes. 'Almost twenty years ago.'

I wanted to ask, but it was hard to work up the courage. Finally, I said, 'Do you still…?'

She sucked the bottom of the café glacé with her straw. When it made a slurping sound, she pushed the glass back. She blotted her lips with a napkin and laughed. 'I tell the kids not to slurp like that, and here I do it myself. Do I still what? Am I happily married or not?'

I nodded and Mrs. Nurollahi drew a deep breath. 'Do you see this dress? She pinched the collar in her fingers. 'I saw the pattern in a magazine.' The dress had a peter pan collar and six buttons down to the waist. 'I searched all over Tehran to find the cloth for it.' The material was white cotton with large yellow polka dots. 'I went a dozen times to have it fitted and spent a small fortune at the tailor.' She leaned back in the chair and looked at me. I looked back at her, waiting.

She paused as the waiter came to clear the glasses. When he was gone, she leaned forward, elbows on the table. 'After I wore it a few times, it got to be just another dress. Of course, I still love it. I'm careful not to stain it, and each time I wear it, I shake it out and hang it back up in the closet so it won't get wrinkled, but...' She opened her purse and took out a cigarette case. 'Do you smoke?'

I took a cigarette. 'Sometimes.'

She lit a match for me. 'Me too, sometimes.'

I looked at the silver cigarette case, engraved with a tall-stemmed flower. 'What a pretty case.'

She signaled the waiter to bring an ashtray by pantomiming knocking the ashes off a cigarette. Then she looked at the case and smiled. 'It's a present.'

'You were talking about the dress,' I prodded.

She ran her hand over the cigarette box, as if caressing it. She took a puff of the cigarette. 'When I was in Tehran over Norouz, just by accident I found this belt in *General Mode*.' She pushed the chair back a bit for me to see it. 'It's the same color as the polka dots, no?' The belt was indeed precisely the same color as the polka dots, and it had a very large golden buckle.

She pulled her chair forward, looked at her watch and said, 'In short, people have to take care of what they have. It's eleven o'clock. At 11:30 I have a doctor's appointment. There was a whole slew of questions I wanted to ask you.'

She dug into her big yellow purse and pulled out a piece of paper. 'I've noted them all down.' She began reading them off: Laws of marriage and divorce among the Armenians, custody rights after a divorce, history of women's rights in Armenia, literacy percentages among the women. I cut her off and said that I could not provide her with precise answers about all that; she had better speak to the Church and School Society. She nodded and noted down the names of a few people. She wanted to invite Armenian women to attend the meetings of their society. 'The problems of women apply to all women, it's not a Muslim or Armenian issue. Women must join together, arm in arm, and solve their problems. They must teach one another and learn from each other.' Now she sounded like one of her public speeches.

I insisted she let me pay the check, but she would not relent. 'You are the guest of our society.' In the street, as we were saying goodbye, I remembered to ask her if she had come to the 24th of April commemoration. She had come, and when I asked with some surprise what for, she replied, with equal surprise, 'Why wouldn't I? A tragedy is a tragedy, it's not a Muslim or Armenian thing.' That did not sound at all like a public speech.

31

After the cool dim interior of the *Milk Bar*, the bright heat of the street felt good. I was feeling better, lighter. There was a long line at the ticket window as I passed by Cinema Rex. All men, mostly Arab – why weren't they at work at this time of the day? The upcoming feature was *Tom Thumb*. I checked out the film poster and the stills on the wall: Tom Thumb sat on a spool that served as his chair, before an overturned cup that served as a table, and he was drinking water from a thimble. An Arab man was selling dried shrimp from a cart in front of the cinema. I held my nose and passed quickly by. I should bring the twins to see the film, I thought, before they get too old and independent, like Armen.

I bought pants for Armen, the ones he had pointed out a good while before, on the condition that I could exchange them if they did not fit. When I came out of the store, I did not feel like returning home. I felt like walking around and thinking, or maybe walking around and not thinking. I walked and I thought how staying at home all the time, socializing with a fixed circle of people, and grappling with the usual repetitive problems was wearing me out. I had to do something I felt passionate about, like Mrs. Nurollahi. I walked past the Mahtab Bakery and remembered Thursday's upcoming dinner. I turned back, went inside the store and bought pastries and some trail mix.

As I walked out of the store, a box of trail mix, a box of pastries and a wrapped parcel in my hand, I ran straight into Emile Simonian, coming at me head on. Was it my imagination, or did he seem agitated? Before it occurred to me to ask why he wasn't at work at this time of day, he offered, 'I wasn't actually feeling that great, I mean, I didn't have the patience for work, so I took a sick day. I came to the bazaar to buy some gardening gloves and a trowel.'

Before it occurred to me to say that the bazaar was in the other direction, he added, 'If you are not in a hurry, will you come with me? I don't know where to get them.' Why was he so flustered? A voice said, 'Maybe because he ran into you.' I could not tell which side of me was speaking.

'For that kind of thing, we have to drop over to the Gardeners' Club store.' He took the packages out of my hands and asked, 'Where is that?'

We hailed a taxi and I told the driver, 'Alfi Plaza.'

On the sidewalk in front of the Gardeners' Club store there was a peddler selling olives, fresh pickles, and grape leaves. I thought olives and fresh pickles would be good for Thursday night, and bought some. Emile came out of the store with a gardener's trowel and gloves, and a few packets of seeds. 'I bought seeds for sweet peas.' He saw the peddler's cart and said, 'I love grape-leaf dolma. God knows how long it's been since I had some.' I bought grape leaves.

We caught the bus for Bawarda. We talked all the way home and I don't know how many times we repeated, 'How interesting, me too!'

In front of our house he handed me back the packages and said, 'Believe me, I'm not just saying this. I have no one I can talk to like this, on and on.'

It was night time before I finished preparing the dolma stuffing. I asked Artoush, 'Will you take the kids for *fish and chips?*' The kids jumped up and down and Artoush probably thought I was making a peace offering. I put the dolma stuffing in the refrigerator, explaining that I had a lot of work to do for Thursday night. I lingered before closing the refrigerator door so as to avoid looking any of them in the eye.

I opened the door for the twins, who walked out with their hands over their mouths to keep me from seeing the red Kool Aid on their lips. After they passed me I said, 'What pretty lipstick.' They let their hands drop to their sides and laughed. As I was closing the door behind them, I said, 'Take your time.' All four of them turned around in the middle of the path to give me a quizzical look.

I stood in front of the living room window. The lights of G-4 were on and I wondered, 'What is he doing? Maybe talking with his mother or reading a book. Or maybe...'

I quickly closed the drapes, went to the kitchen, put the bowl of grape leaves on the table and got the stuffing out of the fridge.

As I wrapped the first dolma and set it in the pot, the two sides of my mind waged a tug-of-war:

'You're a real fool.'

'Why? Where's the harm in two people sharing common interests?'

'No harm at all, but...'

'So, because one is a woman and the other a man, they shouldn't talk to each other?'

'Are they just talking?'

'Of course they're just talking.'

'...'

'He's the only person who understands what I'm talking about.'

'...'

'I talk to myself so much, it's driving me crazy.'

'...'

'I do things for others so much, it's worn me out.'

'...'

'And here's my answer: My boy thinks I am a critical nag. My husband is not willing to exchange a single word with me. My mother and sister only ridicule me, and Nina, who is supposed to be my friend, only gives me more work to do. Like what I'm doing right now. Yeah, like right now, when I have to make food for people I don't even feel like being around.'

'You don't feel like being around any of them?'

'...'

'Why are you making dolma?'

'...'

'Who are you making it for?'

'...'

'You're a real fool.'

I put the last dolma in the pot and stared at the sweet peas on the ledge.

32

On Thursday night the guests vied with one another to see who could arrive earliest.

The twins and Sophie were out in the yard, sitting on the swing seat, under the willow tree. Every time the swing seat went up, all three of them reached up, laughing and screaming, trying to grab one of the thin green branches. The willow hanging over our swing seat, like all willows, put me in mind of the Armenian poem 'Parvana' by Hovhaness Toumanian, which I had read so often as I child that I had virtually memorized it. I stood facing the kitchen window and the willow tree, chopping cucumbers and tomatoes, and reciting my favorite lines from the poem, practically at the top of my voice:

With a royal clash of cymbals
The lovely young Princess came forth
By her side walked the wizened King –
A daughter bright as the waxing moon,
A father grave as a billowing cloud
Cloud and moon, lovingly arm in arm

A rustle of clothing and the sound of breathing made me look back over my shoulder. The twins and Sophie were standing in the kitchen doorway.

'What a lovely poem, Auntie,' said Sophie.

'Tell it to us from the beginning,' said Armineh.

'Yes, recite the poem!' said Arsineh.

I laughed, 'But I don't remember all of it.'

'Well, then, tell us how the story goes,' said Armineh.

'Please, tell us,' said Arsineh.

I dumped the cucumber rinds in the trash. 'I've read it to you from the book a hundred times.'

'Well, tell it to Sophie,' said Arsineh.

'She probably hasn't heard the story,' added Armineh.

They asked her in tandem, 'Have you heard it?' Sophie shook her head no.

I put the olive oil and the lemon juice on the table and began to mix the salad dressing as I told the story.

At the top of a tall mountain lived a king who had a beautiful daughter. When the daughter was all grown up and it was time for her to wed, from the four corners of the Earth many princes came to ask for her hand. The king gave his daughter a golden apple and said, 'When you have made your choice which prince will be your husband, throw this apple to him.'

The girls were sitting around the table, chins propped on their hands, all looking expectantly at me. For the first time I realized how interesting it was that the girl got to choose her husband, and not the other way around. I wiped my oily hands on my apron. 'The princes vowed to bring the daughter of the king whatever her heart desired. Gold, jewels, even the moon and the stars up in the sky.'

'What a lucky princess!' said Sophie. 'If it were me, I would ask for the moon and for all the jewels and chocolate in the world.' The twins both shushed her.

I stirred the salad dressing. 'The king's daughter said, "What good will gold, jewels, and the moon and the stars up in the sky do me? I only want one thing from my partner in life: the fire of true love."'

The twins looked at Sophie, who was staring at me, slack-jawed.

I shook some salt and pepper into the dressing. 'When the suitors heard the word "Fire," they all imagined she wanted real fire, and without waiting to hear the rest of her request, they galloped off in search of fire. The princess waited for them.'

I slapped Armineh's hand as she snatched a piece of lettuce from the salad bowl. 'And the princess waited years and years. She waited and waited until finally she lost all hope, and with downcast head, she cried and cried. Her tears made a pond that grew deeper and deeper until the whole castle was under water.'

All three of them watched me, rapt, their heads cocked to the side. I set the salad on the counter. 'When you see a willow tree, it's the king's daughter standing there to this very day, head downcast, weeping. And when you see moths at night circling about the lights, it's those princes, seeking fire for their princess.'

A sparrow ran into the window screen, gave a squawk and flew off.

'The poor willow tree,' said Armineh.
'The poor moths,' said Arsineh.
Sophie was still staring at me, mouth agape.

33

Alice sat next to Joop, tittering and batting her Rimmel-extended eyelashes, which fluttered just like Rapunzel's when the children would tip the doll this way and that. Mother, in the chair opposite, might have been watching a ping-pong match, her gaze shifting back and forth between Alice and Joop. Artoush and Emile were playing chess. Emily sat next to her father, feet together, elbows on her knees and chin in her hands, staring at the carpet. Armen, wearing his new pants, stood next to Artoush. On the other side of the room, Violette was flipping through the pages of our wedding album, after insisting on seeing the pictures of me and Artoush getting married. Garnik and Nina spoke now and then with Alice and Joop, now and then with Mother, and most of the time between themselves. Every few minutes they found an excuse to laugh.

Violette asked, 'Why don't you frame one of your wedding pictures and hang it on the wall?' As I was trying to think how to answer that, Emily slapped her cheeks with both hands.

'Oh no! The flower from my shoe is missing!' We all looked down at Emily's jade green shoes. One had a white flower above the toe; the other did not.

Armen stepped forward. 'It must have fallen around here somewhere. Let's look, we'll find it.'

Emily looked at her father, her head cocked to the side.

Emile smiled. 'Go and look. Maybe it will turn up.'

Emily got up slowly, smoothed out her tight black skirt and left the room with Armen. Violette came over, album in hand, to take Emily's place. Artoush told Emile, 'Check! You're not paying attention tonight.' Violette closed the album.

I went to the kitchen on the pretext of fetching the drinks. I was certain that when Emily had come in, both her shoes had a flower. I was quite certain, because I had thought to myself, 'I bought the same shoes a few weeks ago. Did I buy children's shoes, or did this girl buy women's shoes?'

I sallied back and forth between the kitchen and the living room. When was this imposed party going to end? I promised myself that after everyone had gone, and I had washed the dishes and tidied up, I would sit back and relax in the green leather chair and find out what the man in Sardo's story decides in the end.

I reflected on my visit that morning to Mrs. Simonian to invite her once again to come over for the party. This time no one had obliged me to go; I did so because I wanted to.

When she opened the door, I thought she was ill. Her eyes were sunken and she looked pale. She was wearing a loose dress, long and white. We went into the living room and when I asked after her health, she replied, 'I did not sleep well last night.' When I brought up the party, she refused with such vehemence that I did not dare insist. Anyway, the party did not matter that much to me. What I wanted was for her to talk – about the green-eyed man, about Emile, about Emile's wife. I had to know the whole story; having seen the trailer, as it were, I was hooked and had to see the film. But my neighbor seemed in no mood to talk. She stared silently at the Persian carpet on the floor until I felt I should get up to say goodbye. She did not insist I stay. She acted cold, a different woman from the one who had recounted the most personal details of her life for me a few nights before.

I set the food I had cooked for dinner on the stove to warm it up. Rice and Fesenjan, grape-leaf dolma and Ikra, an appetizer that I quite liked myself and which, in anticipation of the presence of Mrs. Simonian, I had made spicier than usual. I was getting the bowl of fresh herbs out of the refrigerator – sweet basil, parsley, radishes, spring onions – and the bowl of pickled vegetable Torshi, when I heard Emile say, 'We've put you to a lot of trouble.'

I turned around. He was standing near the kitchen table. 'No trouble,' I told him, 'As long as you are having fun.' My critical streak chided me: 'Now you've done it!' I quickly added, 'I mean, if everyone is having fun.'

He took the bowls of pickles and herbs from my hands and put them on the tray, next to the salad bowl. 'Clarice. We should talk. When do you have a moment?' His neck chain was spilling out over his shirt. My heart was beating fast.

Nina came in. 'What can I do? Shall I take these and set them on the table?' I only nodded, but my voice would not come out. Nina left the kitchen, tray in hand.

Emile said, 'Monday afternoon?' I began to scoop the rice onto the serving platter and the thought shot through my mind that on Monday the kids would be getting home from school late, because of the rehearsal for the end-of-year ceremonies. And Artoush was going to Khorramshahr that morning, to return late that night. And Alice was on the overnight shift, and Mother was invited somewhere. I nodded yes.

Nina called Emile from the living room and as he left the kitchen, he bumped into Mother and said, 'Pardon me.' They squeezed sideways past one another through the doorway.

Mother did not reply. She came over to the table and said in my ear, 'Well, call us both an ass! We were worried for no reason. You should see how solicitous he is of Alice! It must be destiny. True, he's not Armenian, but so what? Why have you spilled half the rice on the table?'

I carried the platter of rice from the kitchen. 'Kids, dinner!' I called three times before Emily and Armen came to the table. The twins and Sophie wanted to eat their dinner on the swing seat. I was about to say no when Sophie put her arm around my waist. 'Auntie, will you let us eat dinner next to the Princess?'

Nina asked, 'What? Which princess?'

Sophie said, 'The willow tree is the daughter of the king who...'

Nina interrupted her to tell me, 'You sit, please. I'll serve the kids.'

'Looks delicious!' said Garnik, as he heaped rice on his plate, and Violette asked Emile, 'Do you like dolma?'

I looked at the dinner spread to make sure there was nothing missing and wondered, since when do Violette and Emile use the familiar 'you' with each other? I went to turn up the air conditioning. Mother told Alice, who was piling rice onto Joop's plate, 'That's not enough rice, and give him a bigger portion of meat.'

There was no plate for me. Whenever I set the table for a dinner party, I always forgot to count myself. I headed for the kitchen and called out, 'Go ahead and start; I'm coming.' Nobody had waited for this offer; they were all busy eating, except for Emile and Violette, who sat side by side, talking. Nina caught my eye, nodded toward the two of them, and winked at me. As I left the room, I saw Emily staring at Violette with pressed lips. Had she seen Nina wink?

I stopped in the middle of the kitchen. Why was my heart racing? Where was my appetite? Why was I so reluctant to return to the table? When would this night finally be over? I began washing the appetizer plates and glasses. What did Emile want to say to me? And what was he talking about now with Violette? Why was I so exhausted? Why weren't the air conditioners cooling us off?

When I heard the scream, I ran out of the kitchen.

Violette was standing up, looking down at the big green stain on her white dress. Emily, both hands over her mouth, said, 'I'm sorry, it slipped from my hand. I'm so sorry.' The bowl of pickles lay overturned on the floor.

Mother said, 'Quick, pour salt on the stain.' She handed the salt shaker to Artoush to give to Nina, who was dabbing Violette's dress with a Kleenex.

Garnik said, 'It's nothing, folks. A pickle stain comes out with a little water.'

Alice said, 'Lightning never strikes twice.'

Joop asked, 'Two lightnings what?' Alice started to explain for him – no more bad luck would befall them that night.

Emile asked Emily, 'You don't even like pickle, why did you take the bowl?' He was not scolding her, just wondering. Emily looked like she was on the verge of tears.

'Her hand slipped,' said Nina. 'It was an accident.'

I looked at Emily. Was it an accident?

I went with Violette to the bathroom and got her a fresh washcloth to clean the stain. She snatched the washcloth from my hand and rapidly wiped her dress, grumbling under her breath, 'Stupid child. She's ruined my precious dress. It was a souvenir gift from London. I just loved it.' She threw the washcloth on the floor, straightened her hair in the mirror, and venomously announced, as though I was not even in the room, 'Evil girl! Just wait. I'll give you a pretty little lesson you won't soon forget.'

We returned to the table. Emile stood up and did not sit back down until Violette had. Then he told Emily, standing beside him, 'Apologize.'

Emily said loudly, 'I'm really sorry that I stained your pretty dress.'

Violette smiled and caressed Emily's cheek. 'It's not important at all, my dear. Actually, I don't really like this dress.' Emily backed up and left the room. Violette looked at me and smiled. 'What wonderful cooking!' I looked at Emile's plate. He had served himself some salad and a little Ikra. I leaned over to pick up the platter of dolma and offer some to him, when Sophie and the twins ran in squealing.

'A frog as big as a turtle jumped on the swing seat,' shouted Armineh.

'A frog big as a turtle!' emphasized Arsineh.

Sophie turned to me, 'It was jealous of the moths, Auntie.' She burst out laughing.

'What?' asked Nina. Sophie started to tell the story of Parvana. Nina took the plate from Sophie's hands and said, 'Yeah, yeah. Run along now. It's no time for stories.'

Sophie said, 'You never tell me stories. Aunt Clarice did. And it was a very nice story.'

I brushed the bangs out of Sophie's face and sent her outside with the twins. 'Go see what the princess and the frog are doing.'

Garnik asked, 'Did you hear about the incident between Pegov and Shamkhal?'

'Who?' asked Nina. 'Chamkhal?'

'Not Chamkhal,' said Garnik. 'Shamkhal. The head of Public Relations for the Oil Company.'

Nina said, 'Oh, so you mean Chamkhal.' She laughed heartily and turned to me. 'The Ikra turned out delicious!'

Mother said, 'It's too spicy. And if the eggplant had grilled a bit longer, it would be better.'

Garnik asked Artoush, 'Did you know that Shamkhal used to be the Crown Prince of Daghestan?'

Artoush took some dolma. 'I heard something or other.' I looked at Emile's plate. He had yet to try the dolma.

Garnik held his plate out to Nina. 'Will you give me some Fesenjan? When Clarice makes it, I can never get enough… Just think of it. The son of the former Shah of Daghestan is now the host of the Soviet Ambassador!'

Nina asked, 'Where is Daghestan, anyway? Mrs. Voskanian, shall I pour some Pepsi for you, or Canada Dry?'

Joop gave a little cough and said, 'With your permission, let me explain.' He gave a detailed explanation of Daghestan, or Dagestan as he pronounced it, a mountainous country between the Caspian Sea and Georgia. It is called Daghestan because 'dagh' means mountain in Turkish, and until the Russian Revolution, it had a king, or shah. After the communists took power, it became one of the Soviet Republics. The erstwhile shah fled to Europe, and now his son is the Chief of Public Relations for the Oil Company in Abadan.

For a few seconds everyone was still and quiet, staring at Joop, until Alice began to clap and said, '*Bravo!* What an encyclopedic explanation!'

Joop blushed. 'I take a considerable interest in history and geography.'

Garnik turned back to me and Nina and whispered, 'Unless I miss my guess, he's gotta be a spy or something.'

He giggled and Nina scolded, 'You and your tasteless jokes.'

Garnik said for all to hear, 'In short…at the appointed time for Pegov's visit to the Refinery, Shamkhal goes with a deputation of the department chiefs to welcome him. The former Crown Prince and the Soviet Ambassador first look each other over, head to toe.' Garnik got up, his spoon and fork in hand, to mimic their demeanor as they sized each other up.

'Everyone around them is afraid they might get in a fight.' With the spoon and fork he pantomimed a sword fight. 'Then the zealous communist and the deposed royal shake hands and exchange a friendly hello, probably in Russian, and everyone breathes a sigh of relief.'

As Nina handed back his plate full of Fesenjan, she said, 'Hey, watch out there, Mr. Burt Lancaster. You almost stabbed me in the eye with your fork!'

Garnik sat back down and when he had stopped laughing, he said, 'I saw Shamkhal a couple times. He's a very humorous and pleasant fellow. Extremely learned. He knows five or six languages… Kudos to the chef for the marvelous Fesenjan!' He served himself salad and added, 'It's a crazy world we live in these days. They just pick up an eraser and wipe whole countries off the map.'

Artoush said, 'Isn't it about time we removed this-istan and that-istan from the map and made them all equal?'

Garnik reached out for the herb platter. 'Yeah, and we can all speak Russian and read Maxim Gorky.'

Together, Nina and I said, 'Now don't the two of you get into it again.' For a few seconds everyone was quiet, except for Mother and Alice, who were explaining to Joop how to make Fesenjan. Emile said something in Violette's ear, and the two of them chuckled. Nina said to Garnik, 'So it's Chamkhal, is it?'

Garnik pinched her cheek affectionately and said, 'Cutie.'

Joop was explaining something to Alice, and Emile and Violette were whispering again. Before I could think what they might be talking about, Alice said, 'Listen to this, everyone. Go ahead, tell them,' she said to Joop, who blushed and shook his head. Alice turned to us. 'Listen. Who knows what Braim and Bawarda mean?' And she turned around to face Joop. 'How did you learn all this?' Joop blushed again and Alice turned back to us. 'Well? Anyone know? Braim is the name of a kind of date. Before the English bought the land for Abadan, the whole area of Braim was a date palm orchard, producing this particular kind of date.'

Garnik said, 'Kudos for the dolma! Of course, dates are very tasty, too.'

It was one of the few times that Artoush listened carefully to what my sister was saying.

Alice set her fork and spoon on her plate and leaned forward. 'Now listen to the rest of it. Can you guess where "Bawarda" comes from? Don't know, do you? This whole area belonged to an Arab man who had a very very beautiful daughter, called Warda. Warda means "rose" in Arabic.' She turned back to Joop. 'Did I get it right?' Joop nodded and Alice continued. 'They called this Arab, according to the custom in Arabic, "Bu Warda," meaning Father of Warda. So the English buy the land and they call the neighborhood after its former owner. After a while, Bu Warda contracts to Bawarda.' She cocked her head to the right. 'North Bawarda,' and then to the left, 'south Bawarda.'

Artoush said, 'That's very interesting.'

Garnik muttered under his breath, 'Like I said, a spy or something...' Nina elbowed him to be quiet.

Alice looked at Joop, and said, 'How interesting! We have to keep you around.' Joop blushed again and laughed.

Mother offered the herb platter around. I thought, if Joop's story is true, the father of Warda must be one of the few Arab men who was called after his daughter rather than his son.

Joop and Artoush were talking to each other. Joop said, 'A myth it may be, of course.'

Artoush said, 'Fact or myth, it was interesting.'

I was clearing the table and thinking no one had noticed that I had not eaten dinner, when Emile said, 'The dolma was outstanding, though how could you know, since you did not touch a single bite all night?' He began helping me.

Mother came up and told him, 'Please have a seat. Clearing the table is no job for a man.' Emile headed toward Nina, who was calling to him, and Mother grumbled under her breath, 'I detest men who tie on the apron strings. Did you hear what Joop told Alice at dinner? He said…'

I stacked the dirty plates, picked them up and headed toward the kitchen, saying to myself, 'I did not hear and I don't want to hear. Leave me be.'

When everyone was leaving, Nina whispered in my ear, 'I think it's a match.'

Violette only said, 'Thank you.'

Mother said, 'Remember to store the leftover Fesenjan in a porcelain dish.'

Joop took fifteen minutes to say thanks and goodbye. I closed the door behind them all.

While I was washing the dishes, Artoush came into the kitchen, leaned over the sink and said, 'The girls want a story.' He laughed. From the beginning of the evening he had been laughing constantly.

'I don't feel like telling a story,' I said.

He looked at me. 'Why not?'

I did not look at him. 'I'm tired.' He started playing with his goatee. I turned my head back and looked at him for a few seconds. 'Why don't you shave your beard?' I asked.

34

I was in a huge house, with a maze of rooms and corridors. There were many people coming and going, none of whom I knew. I took the twins by the hand and tried to leave the house, but could find no way out. A tall priest came forward and said that I did not have permission to leave until I solved the riddle. Then he pulled the twins by the hand and dragged them away with him. I ran after them.

I was in a huge courtyard, with rooms on all sides. In the middle of the courtyard was an empty round pool. I was crying and calling out to the twins. A young woman carrying a child came in through the door. She wore a long red skirt that trailed on the ground. I was calling out to the twins and crying, and the woman in the red skirt was laughing, dancing around the pool, tossing the child up in the air over and over.

I woke up. My heart was racing and I was drenched in sweat. Artoush was asleep. I threw off the covers, put a thin sweater on over my nightgown, slid my feet into my house slippers and walked out into the yard. It was barely dawn. The scent of red clover was in the air, and there were some new buds on the rose bush.

I paced up and down the front path, from the door to the gate and back a few times, thinking about my dream.

I sat on the swing seat, which was wet from the overnight dew. The branches of the willow did not quite hang down to the back of the swing seat. The house in my dream was not familiar. I did not recognize the priest, nor could I recall the riddle. The yard and the round pool were, however, things I had really seen. The moisture on the swing seat was irritating.

I got up and walked into the backyard. The twins had dug a little pit under the hose faucet. One of the games they played involved filling the pit with water, mixing in some stones and weeds and dirt, and stirring it with a couple sticks to 'make soup.'

Mother had said, 'It is not more than two hours from Isfahan to Namagerd.' But I was ten years old, and the trip seemed to take much longer than that.

Alice whined all the way. 'When will we get there?'

Mother had said, 'We're going to Namagerd to buy suet.' Father loved the dishes mother made with suet.

I walked hand in hand with Father through the narrow alleyways of the village and watched the dirty, scrawny children who were pressed up against the cob walls for shade, or stared out of their crooked, crumbling window frames at the travelers from the city.

Alice whined non-stop. 'I'm choking on the dust and dirt.' But I was not concerned with the heat and dust and dirt. I watched the women of the village, who were dressed in the local costume. The younger women veiled their mouths with the trails of their long colorful headscarves. Mother was listless from the heat and dust and the steady warm wind blowing in our faces. When I asked her why they veiled their mouths, Mother said that young brides were not supposed to talk, especially in front of their in-laws. The long red and yellow and green headscarves were the only colorful objects to be seen in the village. Everything else was the color of dust.

We stepped into a courtyard. Alice was pulling Mother's hand, pleading, 'Let's go back.' In the middle of the courtyard was an empty round pool, and all around the yard were rooms with wooden doors and glass transoms covered in dust. In a corner of the courtyard a few young women were sitting around a small brick oven making bread. An old woman kept criticizing them and complaining about the way they were going about it. Father was talking to the owner of the house, a man with bulging eyes, much chubbier than Father. Alice nagged the whole time. I looked silently around, feeling as if I was about to burst into tears.

A woman entered the yard through the open door of the house. She was tall and very thin, barefoot, with long unkempt hair, full of straw. A scrawny, mangy dog followed her. When the woman saw us she laughed. Alice fell silent and we both stared at the woman, who was by then singing and dancing around the empty pool. The dog sat at the side of the courtyard near the door, howling. For a few minutes the only sounds were the woman singing, the wind rushing and the dog howling. Then the owner picked up a stick from the ground and shook it at the woman, shouting, 'Go! Get out! Have some shame.' The young women laughed through their long headscarves and the old woman told us, 'Don't be afraid. She is crazy, but harmless.' Then she picked up a pebble near the foot of the oven and tossed it at the mad woman. 'Have some shame.' The woman covered her face with both hands and began crying. Then she began to sing again and danced out of the courtyard along with the dog.

On the way back to Isfahan, Mother explained that in Julfa, if someone goes mad, his relatives take him to Namagerd. There are families in Namagerd that will, for a monthly fee, look after the insane. I cried all the way to Isfahan and Alice asked me several times, 'Why are you crying? There's no more dust and dirt, and it's cooler now.'

I circled around the jujube tree and the herb bed. I bent over to pull out the weeds growing among the herbs. Some blackened, dried-up jujube fruits were scattered under the tree. I picked up a few of them and sat on the ground, leaning back against the tree trunk and juggling the jujubes from one hand to the other.

I tilted my head back to look at the jujube branches. Was it Youma who had said – or had I read it somewhere – that the jujube tree is another name for the lotus tree, the leaves of which are used to make shampoo powder? It got me to wondering how many trees had a different name from their fruit. The fruit of the lotus is a jujube, the fruit of the palm tree is a date. I could not think of any others. How interesting that both these trees were found in Abadan. I got up, tossed the blackened, dried-up jujubes among the herbs and went back to the bedroom. I got dressed in silence, put a note on the telephone table and left the house.

35

The church was dark and smelled of frankincense.

The caretaker woman talked about her child's illness as she opened the door of the church for me. I put some money in her hand and told her it was not necessary to put on the lights, and that I would not need any frankincense. I closed the door of the church behind her.

I took a small lace scarf from the table near the door and covered my head. I crossed myself, walked across the red carpet and went up to the altar. I sat in the first pew and gazed for some time at the image of the Christ child in the arms of his mother, until the morning light shone through the stained glass windows, brightening the church a little.

My eyes drank in the altar table and its candle sticks, the large silver vases with their plastic flowers, the chalice of holy wine and the priest's gold-embroidered stole next to the chalice. I had seen all of these things so many times before, but now I was noticing them as if for the first time.

The painting of Christ looked like Armen as a baby. I remembered Nina had said, 'Every time I see this painting, it reminds me of Tigran as a baby.' The image of Christ also looked like the twins when they were babies, I reflected. Maybe, I thought, all children look like this image of Christ when they are infants.

I drew a deep breath, crossed myself, closed my eyes and prayed. *Our Father, who art in heaven, hallowed be thy name.* When did I first recite this prayer? *Thy kingdom come. Thy will be done on Earth, as it is in Heaven.* When was the last time? *Give us this day our daily bread and forgive us our debts as we forgive our debtors.* It felt like I was reciting it for the first time. *And lead us not into temptation, but deliver us from evil.* I finished the prayer: *For thine is the kingdom and the power and glory forever.* I opened my eyes. *Amen.* I crossed myself, looking again at Christ and Mary. Mary wore a blue shawl over her head and shoulders and cradled in her arms the infant Christ, swaddled in a yellow cloth.

My feet were asleep. I got up and went over to the votive table, put some money in the little wooden box and, as always, took out seven candles – six of them for the children and Artoush and Alice and Mother, and the seventh candle for my father. I lit the seventh candle and said softly, 'Help me.'

I walked around the church, past the choir alcove, past the old organ, and the little plaques on the wall that people had donated after regaining health or achieving a wish. I had been to this church so many times over the years, but had never paid much attention to the plaques. Most of them were in Armenian, a few in English, and one small marble stone was inscribed in Persian:

VIRGIN MARY, MOURNFUL MOTHER
I DID ADJURE THEE BY THE WOUNDS OF THY SON
AND THOU DIDST RESTORE TO ME MY CHILD

I ran my hand over the little marble plaque. 'Poor woman,' I thought. I circled around to the door of the church, wondering, 'How do you know it was the mother of the sick child who gave the plaque, and not the father?' I turned around to face the altar, crossed myself, and backed out of the church.

I headed for home. The heat felt good. How long had it been since I enjoyed hot weather? Before reaching Cinema Taj, I turned my head to the right to look down a cul-de-sac at the end of which was a big blue door, always closed, and always with a sentry standing guard. I had heard there was a compound like the Kuwaiti Bazaar behind this blue door, with coffee houses, stores, vendors, and houses. The women who lived behind the blue door did not set foot outside their compound except maybe once a year. I had always wanted to see what was behind the blue door, but knew it was impossible.

An Arab man was walking along the sidewalk, driving five or six goats along in front of him. He was talking with another Arab man riding a bicycle alongside him. The bicyclist was trying to ride slowly, at the same pace as his conversation partner. The front wheel of the bike kept swerving, now left, now right. The smell of gas from the Refinery was in the air, but there was not a cloud in the sky.

I followed the street, with its scattered palm trees and clumps of wild grass, until I reached Cinema Taj. I had been in Abadan for many years, but was always shocked by the contrast between the Oil Company's section of town and the rest of the city. It was like stepping from a waterless desert wasteland into a lush garden.

The identical houses on either side of the wide boulevard with their uniformly trimmed boxwood hedges looked like children just back from the barber, all lined up and waiting for the school headmaster to come tell them, 'Excellent! What clean and orderly children.'

I turned onto our street. The only sound was the chirping of crickets and an occasional ribbeting of frogs. I looked around and thought, 'I do like this hot, green, quiet city.' I opened the gate and stepped into the yard.

Artoush was in the kitchen with the children. The twins gave me an anxious, worried look, but when they saw my smile, they jumped into my arms. Armen came over to me and did not draw back when I kissed his cheek. Artoush asked, 'Shall I make coffee?'

It was the children's decision not to go to the Club for lunch.

Armineh said, 'We have to study.'

Arsineh said, 'It's almost final exam time.'

I warmed up last night's leftovers.

Artoush had dolma with plain rice. 'Don't tell your mother, but dolma with plain rice is quite tasty.' He had laughed at my mother many times whenever she asserted that the Armenians in Julfa eat dolma with plain rice. As he got up from the table, he said, 'The food last night was spectacular. Especially the dolma – perfect!'

36

Ashkhen was dusting the dressers in the bedrooms and talking non-stop.

'Mrs. Clarice, hon, I would do anything for you, but I'm sorry, I don't wanna work in Mrs. Simonian's house. First off, she insists I have to come on Fridays. I usually have guests over on Fridays, since it's not a workday, and I need to help my husband with his bath, and there are a thousand chores to take care of. And then, she constantly criticizes what I do: "Why do you wash like that? Why do you iron like this?" And then, she's arguing the whole time with her son and granddaughter. Her son's a gentleman, through and through – doesn't say a single word of reproach or reprisal. But the granddaughter – oh lord! That one is a little monster. She's sassier than sassafras and has quite a potty mouth, too. She throws things and tears into stuff with the scissors, cutting them to bits...' She set the dust rag on the ground. 'I heard her on the phone telling someone, "If you love me you have to slap Mr. Vazgen in the face." You know him, don't you, Mrs. Clarice, dear? The principal...'

I told Ashkhen, who had forgotten all about dusting, that I did know Mr. Vazgen and that after she finished dusting the bedrooms, she should go brush the dust off the living room furniture.

I came out of the bedroom wondering, 'Who was the girl talking to on the phone? Armen? Armen had better not slap...' The phone rang and I went to get it. Maybe I should have a talk with Armen. I picked up the receiver.

Emile's voice was calm, as usual. 'I wanted to thank you for the dinner Thursday night. You went to a lot of trouble. By the way, I found a book last night that I thought you might like, and set it aside to bring for you on Monday. You haven't forgotten our appointment for Monday?'

One half of me was shouting, 'Tell him you are busy on Monday! Say you don't have time. Say something has come up. Say...' I answered abruptly that it hadn't been any trouble, thanked him for the book, and said I had not forgotten the appointment. I put the phone down. My inner selves were locked in mortal combat.

I leaned over the telephone table and tried to think of something else. What pretext could I use to start a conversation with Armen? Ashkhen was calling me again – what does she want, now? It's a quarter after four, why aren't the kids back?

I raised my head, and through the lace curtain I saw them coming, the twins hop-scotching half-way up the path, and Armen walking behind, hands in his pockets. Ashkhen called to me again, 'Mrs. Clarice, hon!' I opened the door.

'Hello,' said Armineh. 'One A+ and two As!'

'Hello,' said Arsineh. 'Two As and an A+!'

I harbored my suspicions about the twins' identical grades, and sometimes fretted that they might be making similar mistakes on purpose, so as to wind up with the same grades. But how would that even be possible? Still, I had arranged with their teachers to have them sit on different benches, far apart from each other.

Armen closed the door and waited for the twins to stop jumping up and down. His habit of late had been to go straight to his room and close the door, so what was he waiting for? When I looked at him, he said, 'Will you call Miss Judy? We should postpone the piano classes for a couple weeks until the exams are finished.' The twins nodded in affirmation of their brother's observation. He took me by surprise with his sudden interest in studying for the exams, only to further ratchet up my astonishment by asking, 'Will you quiz me on my history? I have a practice test tomorrow.'

Ashkhen came into the hallway. 'Mrs. Clarice, hon.'

I elbowed the twins to be polite and greet her.

Ashkhen raised her voice an octave and warmly greeted the twins, affectionately fussing over them: 'Hello my lovely and hello my pet! One sweetness, the other light. One milk, the other honey! No, no, no. You couldn't possibly be the culprits.'

Armineh and Arsineh said at the same time, 'We didn't do anything!'

Ashkhen tightened the knot of her kerchief at the back of her head, and gestured toward the living room. 'The easy chair?'

We all went to the living room. The furniture cushions were sorted in piles on the floor. Ashkhen pointed to one of the easy chairs, and we went over to it. On the chair frame, under the cushion, there was a hole. It looked like someone had taken a knife or some kind of sharp tool and punctured it. I looked at Armen, who was looking back at me, stupefied. 'I swear to God...' he said, and ran out of the room. The twins looked at me, then at Ashkhen, then back at me.

'Armen did not do it.'

'I swear Armen did not do it.'

Before I even posed the question, 'Then who did?' they chimed, 'We don't know who did it, but...'

'...but it wasn't Armen.'

Ashkhen, her hands folded over her sizeable tummy, shook her head. 'Tsk, tsk, tsk.'

I told the twins their snack was on the kitchen table and asked Ashkhen to cover the tear with the cushion for the time being.

I paid Ashkhen in cash and she tightened the knot of her headscarf, this time tying it under her chin (when she tied it in the back, it meant time to get to work, and when tied under the chin, it meant her job was done). She zipped up her wallet, slung the bundles of clothes and the bags of food I gave her to take home under her arm, thanked me and left. I closed the door behind her and watched her for a few seconds through the lace curtain. She went down the path to the gate, huffing and puffing with the bags and bundles in hand. 'Poor woman,' I thought. 'She has got nothing but hard labor out of life.' I untied my apron and tossed it in the dirty clothes hamper. I had worked side by side with Ashkhen all day long, and I had a dirty apron to show for it.

I went to Armen's room, determined not to say one word about the tear in the easy chair. I had something more important to tell him. As he put his history book in my hands, I asked him, 'What's new with Mr. Vazgen?'

He sat down on the bed. 'He's not bad. Why?'

I opened the book. 'Just asking.'

He got up and opened his satchel, searching for something. 'As it happens, today I went to the front office. Mr. Vazgen was there, too.'

I closed the history book. 'Why did you go to the principal's office?' Armen was not usually summoned to the principal's office except to reprimand him for mischief or misbehavior. I certainly hope he had the sense not to slap the principal!

He gave me a slip of paper. 'For this.' My heart dropped; I would probably be summoned to the school. He must have been punished again. He must have...I read the slip: 'Commendation for Armen Ayvazian for his effort and determination in math.' I jumped up and hugged him, showering him with kisses. He laughed out loud and said, 'You're squishing me.'

When the excitement abated, I said, 'If you want to know the truth, I have been very worried about you lately.'

I was trying to think how I could work the topic of Emily into the conversation, when he told me, 'I know why you were worried. But don't be. You never need to worry about me. Your son is no dunce. Now quiz me on history.' He bent over, picked up the text book off the floor, and handed it to me. How could I have forgotten that my son was a master at taking me by surprise?

Over the weekend I had finished reading Vazgen's manuscript. I made Maash Polow for Artoush, with the eggplant casserole he liked so much. I made almond cake for the kids. I did not nag Armen about keeping his room tidy, and I took the twins to see *Tom Thumb*. Armen said, 'That's for kids,' and did not come with us. The next night, as soon as he mentioned that the Naft Club was showing *Tarzan*, I said, 'Okay, I'll take you, as long as you promise not to whine when it's time to wake up tomorrow morning.' The twins were astonished and also delighted that I was willing to take them to the movies two nights in a row. When Artoush complained, 'I don't feel like driving,' the twins said, 'We'll take a taxi.'

It was something to see the look on the faces of all four of them when I said, 'It's not far to the Naft Club, and the streets are not busy at this time of the evening, so...let Armen drive us.'

In the open-air theater of the Naft Club, the kids and I really enjoyed Tarzan's heroics and laughed at Cheetah's antics. In the still warm evening air, you could smell the river on one side and Kebab on the other, from the Naft Club restaurant. I was happy seeing my children happy.

37

Monday morning the sky was cloudy and the wind was blowing hard.

I was getting the kids ready for school when Armineh asked, 'What if there's a storm?'

Arsineh said, 'Miss Manya will probably cancel the rehearsal.'

Armen grabbed his satchel and set out, exclaiming, 'So much the better!'

I told the twins, 'Don't forget to give the novel and the translation to Miss Manya or Mr. Vazgen.'

Armineh said, 'You promised to read it to us.'

'Mr. Vazgen is in a hurry,' I said. 'Once it's published, we'll read it together.'

With an 'okay' they offered me their round cheeks, and we exchanged kisses and together walked down to the gate.

If the rehearsal got cancelled, the children would get back home sooner. Did I want them home sooner, or not? Should I pray for the storm, or for calm weather? Emily was standing in front of her house, wearing her school uniform – navy blue smock, lace collar and white bobby socks. When the bus arrived, Armen stood by the door, waiting for Emily to get on first.

In the garage, Artoush was sitting behind the wheel of the Chevy. I held my breath. The engine started on the second try, and I breathed a sigh of relief. Artoush smiled and headed out. The brake lights came on in the driveway and he popped his head out the window to say, 'I'm coming back late today, remember?' I smiled and nodded. As the Chevy and the bus faded into the distance, I closed the gate and headed inside. In the yard, the wind buffeted about a couple of bougainvillea blossoms in the air.

I had not yet closed the front door when I heard the metal gate squeak. Through the lace curtain, I saw her coming, dressed in a skirt and blouse, both black, with flats, and a white shawl over her shoulders. For the first time, I was genuinely happy to see her.

She sat at the kitchen table and asked for coffee instead of tea with milk. While I was fixing the coffee she did not speak, except to say, 'There's a storm brewing. When we were in India, weather like this meant the monsoons were coming.' She had her hair gathered behind her head and wore only a single piece of jewelry, a pair of pearl earrings. I set the coffee down on the table with a plate of Nice cookies, and sat down opposite her. She looked silently at her cup for a moment. The wind outside seemed to be churning up all the desert sand throughout the length and breadth of Khuzestan province. The sweet peas on the ledge were trembling.

'Are you feeling better?' I asked, and not just for the sake of conversation. I was genuinely concerned about her, although she no longer looked pale, and had put on peach-colored lipstick.

She took a sip of coffee and raised her head. Her eyes were like black marbles. She coughed once. 'I don't know why I prattled on that night. It's not my habit to share my troubles with others. I have never talked to anyone about myself before. Maybe because I always thought no one would understand. What made me think that you would understand, I don't know.'

She fell silent. The wind whooshed by and the flower box tipped over on the ledge.

She took off one of her earrings, rubbed her earlobe and fastened it back on. She spoke softly, as though she did not want anyone to overhear. 'The only thing Emile inherited from his father was the color of his eyes and his love of books. In contrast to his father, who was able to distinguish between poetry and real life, Emile lives in poems and stories. He's always falling in love, ever since he was a child. He thought he was in love with Emily's mother. The girl was from a poor family – her father was an alcoholic and beat her. Emile appeared in the role of savior figure and, well...the girl was beautiful. At first, I opposed their marriage, but then, when it was too late to stop it, I gave in. Before two months had gone by, he realized it was a mistake. It was God's will that the girl died a few years later.'

The wind whooshed by again and the flower box full of sweet peas fell off the ledge. I heard it break. A feeling of sadness suddenly overwhelmed me. Was it because of the flower box breaking, or because someone could talk so lightly about death?

She said, 'He's always made the wrong choices. Always fails to think things through. I've moved from one city to the next and from country to country to keep him from doing anything that might hurt himself, or me, or Emily. It doesn't matter so much for me anymore, but Emily could not bear it. I'm afraid she would do something rash. Her mother was not psychologically…'

She did not finish the sentence, but shook her head, took the last sip of coffee and set the cup down in the saucer. For conversation's sake, I pointed to the cup and asked, 'Shall I read your fortune?' What kind of nonsense was that! I neither believed in fortune-telling, nor did I know how to do it. I only said it to make conversation.

As though just waking from sleep, she suddenly shoved backed her chair and stood up. She ran her hand over her hair, adjusted the shawl around her shoulders and said, 'I don't want to take up your time. Fortune?' She looked at the coffee cup and sneered. 'My fortune was determined ages ago.' She closed her eyes and opened them again, gazing at the silhouette of Sayat Nova. 'He loved Sayat Nova's poems. They are true to the heart, he said. He himself always wrote from the heart, as well. No one understood him.'

I walked with her to the door.

At the door she turned around, put her hand on my arm and smiled faintly. 'Emile quickly loses his heart.' She wrapped the shawl up around her chin. 'Help him out. It's not a good decision. Give him good advice.'

She started down the path. The wind twisted the shawl around her shoulders. Pink bougainvillea blossoms were scattered all over the pathway. The willow tree looked distraught and downtrodden, like a woman in mourning, pulling out her hair in sorrow. The drops of rain turned to steam the instant they touched the ground, and the sky was as red as could be.

38

I went through all the rooms, moving stuff from one place to another that was fine right where it was. I stood in front of each window and looked outside. The leaves of the tomato plants were shuddering non-stop, and the flowers were bowing and then straightening up again. Armineh and Arsineh's trees had surrendered all their blossoms to the wind. Emily's tree still held a few flowers. The willow tree plucked her hair. Only the lotus tree seemed unperturbed by the storm.

I drew all the curtains. I should go pick up the broken flower box under the window ledge, I thought. But I did not. My favorite flowers were smashed, and it all seemed strangely unimportant. When the Oil Company siren signalled the end of the working day, I went into the bedroom. I thought of Mr. Morteza. Whenever the siren sounded, he would pronounce the word 'Feydus' like a sacred mantra, pack up his things and go home. It took a long time before I worked up the nerve to ask him what Feydus meant. Mr. Morteza laughed. 'It means "Quitting Siren."'

My critical side sneered. 'Are you thinking about Mr. Morteza to keep me from asking you why you're putting on lipstick? Or why you are brushing your hair? Why so meticulous with the hand cream?' I set the brush down on the dressing table.

What does he want to say? If he says it, what do I say? What should I say? His mother said, 'It's not a good decision.' I smoothed out my skirt. My compassionate side offered some advice: 'Say that we are friends. Good friends.' I dried the sweat under my arms and when the doorbell rang, I blotted the excess lipstick with a Kleenex. In the hallway I wondered why it was so dark.

As I turned the door handle, the door blew open with a strong gust of wind. Emile came in, accompanied by a whirl of dust, earth, leaves, and grass that spilled all over the floor. Among the debris were khaki-colored things that looked like locusts. Together we managed to push the door closed, then leaned up against it to recover. Emile was out of breath, his hair and face dusty. 'What's going on?' I asked.

He brushed off his head and shook out his shirt. 'Locusts.'

'What?' I looked down at the floor. What had looked like locusts really were locusts, ten or twenty of them, dead or just barely alive. I probably turned pale and was surely shivering, because he grabbed me by the arms and asked, 'Why are you shaking? Don't you know about locusts?'

I looked back at him, confused. 'Don't know what?'

He brushed off his pants. 'Sometimes, when locusts migrate…You don't look well. Here, have a seat.' I looked at his face again, still confused, then let him lead me to the kitchen, which was as dark as could be. He sat me down on a chair, turned on the light, opened the fridge, and poured me some water. As he put the glass in my hand, I exclaimed, 'The children!'

He pulled up another chair, set it down facing mine, and sat leaning forward toward me. 'Don't worry. I phoned the school before I came over. They'll keep them there until things die down. You don't have any windows open? All the air conditioners are off?' I looked mutely at him in a way that must have told him not to wait for an answer. He got up swiftly and ran through the house.

I drank a gulp of water. Or did I? I got up and went to the window. The ledge was covered with locusts, dead and half alive. I wished I had gathered up the toppled flower box. The sky was dark, and the sound unlike anything I had ever heard before. Behind me, Emile said, 'It's the sound of locusts' wings.'

We stood side by side, mesmerized by the view in the yard. Locusts were raining from the sky and as they hit the ground, they sounded like a ton of crinkling, crumpling paper. I was still shaking, or must have looked pale, because he asked me, 'Don't you think you'd better sit down?'

We sat down on the two facing chairs. 'You've never heard of it before?' When I shook my head, he continued. 'Locusts swarm and migrate.' His face was right in front of mine. 'Sometimes they fly kilometer after kilometer.' There was a little cut on his chin. 'When they can go no further, the swarm splits into two layers. One group forms a base layer and the upper layer rests atop them, to regain their strength.' The cut was barely visible. 'The bottom layer dies from exhaustion and falls to the ground.' He looked out the window; it was still dark. 'The swarm usually separates into layers as they pass over the sea or the ocean, but it also sometimes happens as they pass over cities.'

The racket outside was unrelenting. It now sounded like a squadron of propeller aircraft passing directly overhead. I may have still been shivering, because he said, 'Relax. It will be over in a minute.'

All at once, I remembered. 'Your mother!'

He looked to the darkened window. 'She took a sleeping pill and is lying down. She is not feeling well. Once in a while she feels quite ill.'

We sat quietly, while the sound of airplanes and crinkling, crumpling paper gradually diminished. It got brighter and brighter outside. It seemed like it had all been a dream.

When the phone rang, I jumped up, put my hand to my cheek and pressed it hard, perhaps to make sure I was not in a dream. The phone rattled out a third ring. I told Mother I was fine, that it was great that Alice had phoned from the hospital, and how wonderful that Joop had phoned to check on Alice. No, Artoush had not phoned from Khorramshahr. The children were at school, and yes, it was the most terrifying thing...

When she asked, 'So you are all alone?' I said, 'I'll call you back,' and hung up the phone.

I had only taken two steps away from the phone when it rang again. I told Nina, 'Yeah, yeah, it was terrifying... Good thing Garnik was home... Violette just laughed? How brave of her... Artoush went to Khorramshahr... Yeah, I was going to phone the school, too.'

When she asked me, 'So you were all alone in this chaos?' I said, 'I'll phone you later.' I hung up the phone and returned to the kitchen.

He was still sitting there on the chair, legs slightly apart, upper body leaning toward the facing chair, looking out of the window.

I leaned on the doorframe and ran my hand over my hair. My hand felt as if it were caked in dirt, like after changing the soil of a flowerpot, or gardening. I sneezed twice in succession.

'Are you better?' he asked.

I nodded and said under my breath, 'Dust gives me hay fever.' I pulled my chair back a little and sat down. I was sweating. For a few seconds we sat in silence, the smell of dust hanging in the air.

He looked at me. 'Listen, Clarice. I know you have never experienced it before, but...'

Hurry up and say it, I thought to myself.

He drew a deep breath. 'The yard is not such a pretty sight now. I know you don't like locusts, but...'

Now I had to press both cheeks with my fingertips to make sure I was not dreaming. The yard not a pretty sight? I don't like locusts?

I got up and he got up. We went into the hall. He opened the door and I looked at the yard. I must have been dreaming. Surely, this could not really be happening?

The lawn, the trees, the hedges, and the path – everywhere and everything was khaki, the dusty color of locusts. It took me a few seconds to realize that it was not just dust, but actual locusts. Locusts were everywhere. It made me dizzy. He put his hand on my shoulder. 'It doesn't matter. We'll clean them up.' I don't remember how we got back to the kitchen or sat back down.

Emile made coffee and I stared, light-headed, at the vase on the table. I had picked the two red roses in the front yard that very morning, after his mother had left. How is it there are no locusts on them, I wondered.

We drank the coffee and Emile talked about the different kinds of locusts: desert locusts, red locusts, Moroccan locusts. He said that in one species, only the males had wings, and they were not even for flying; by rubbing his wings together, the male attracted the female's attention. Whenever the population in a particular colony grows too large, their shape and behavior changes. They change color, from brown to pink or yellow, and they form locust swarms. In the Old Testament, the Jewish prophet Joel warns the people to repent of their sins if they wish to be spared from the plague of locusts.

The sound of the school bus pulling up made me jump.

I reached the twins in the middle of the path. There were traces of long crying in their faces, and when they saw me they immediately burst into tears again. Armen was walking behind them, trying to look nonchalant, but his pale face and sweaty forehead gave him away. I hugged and kissed the twins and told them several times, 'It's over now, it's over. Yes, it was terrible.'

Then I turned to Armen. He put his hand on my shoulder and asked, 'Weren't you afraid all alone?'

On the verge of tears, I kissed him and whispered, 'I was not all alone.'

The twins clung to either side of my skirt and we walked across the locusts and made our way inside. With the instep of their shoes, Emile and Armen swept out the locusts that had fallen over the floor in the entryway. I took the twins to the bathroom to wash their hands and faces. When I came back, Emile was talking to Armen by the door. Armen looked at me. 'If you need me, call me,' he said, and went to his room. I drew my hand over my face. I was nauseous, swooning, my stomach cramped. I leaned on the telephone table.

Emile looked at Armen's closed door and then at me. 'I wanted to talk, but it didn't work out.' His head dropped. 'Later, maybe.' He headed for the door. 'Emily must be home. She might be afraid.' He turned back to look at me, and smiled. 'Though she is more fearless than her grandmother.' He reached for the door handle and stood motionless for a second or two. Then he let go and turned back to me. 'But I really must tell you. You are my only friend. I am sure you will understand. I've decided to marry Violette.'

39

I was emptying the ashtray into the garbage pail when Artoush walked into the kitchen. 'Didn't sleep well last night?'

I looked everywhere except into his eyes. 'I couldn't fall asleep. I read.'

He put his hand on my shoulder. 'Probably all the excitement of yesterday. You look pale. Try to rest today. Let me call Company Services.' He went into the hallway. All the excitement of yesterday? He must mean the attack of the locusts. My shoulder, where he had touched me, was hot.

I closed the kitchen curtains to block the view of the yard and started setting the breakfast table. There were two voices slogging it out in my head:

'How many times in these seventeen years has he worried about you? How many times did he show it or say it?'

'Very rarely.'

'So today, out of the blue, just happens to be one of those rare occasions?'

'Why wouldn't it be?'

'For the simple reason that...'

Armen came into the kitchen and said something. I looked at him and mumbled, 'For the simple reason that...'

Armen looked at me. 'Did you say something?'

'What's that?' I asked.

'I said, don't worry. I'm going to tie my shoelaces in just a second. Why do you look so pale?'

I looked at his shoes. *For the simple reason that...*

The twins ran in.

'Good morning!'

'Good morning!'

Armineh said, 'Last night I dreamt we went to the pool with Emily.'

Arsineh counted off on her fingers all the people in the dream: 'Emily and Sophie. And Auntie Violette. And Uncle Emile.'

Armineh sat down at the table. 'There were not that many people.'

Arsineh, with her hand on the back of the chair, said, 'There were, too.'

'No there weren't.'

Arsineh stomped on the floor. 'There were so.'

I could not remember the twins contradicting each other before. This day of all days would have to be the day for them to start arguing. 'Enough!' I shouted.

They were quiet for a while. Then Armineh whispered to her sister, 'Did I have the dream, or did you?'

Arsineh pouted. 'I was in the dream, too, wasn't I?'

Armineh thought for a moment. 'You were there.'

'Well then,' said Arsineh, 'Sophie and Auntie Violette and Uncle Emile were, too.'

Armineh gave in. 'Fine, they were. Milk, please, Mom.'

Arsineh's frowning face burst into a sunny smile and she sat down at the table. 'Yesterday, when the locust rain started, the school janitor said the end of time is nigh. What does it mean?'

Armen explained. At some other time, I would have been surprised about Armen's more or less correct knowledge of theology. It was not some other time.

Armineh whined. 'The yard is full of locusts. How are we supposed to get to the bus and...'

Arsineh put her milk down on the table. 'Yeah, how are we supposed to get to the bus?'

Armen said, 'I'll carry you one by one and set you down by the bus. Okay?'

The twins laughed heartily. 'Oh, goody! We'll get a piggy back ride!'

I watched Armen laugh with the twins. How changed he is – all grown up, I thought, as he poured milk for Arsineh. I wanted to cry. Why, I didn't know. Well, I did know and I didn't know.

Artoush stepped into the kitchen, hand on his goatee. 'The Company employee seemed to think it was a big joke. I asked them to send someone to clean the yard and he laughed out loud. "It will be clean before noon," he said, and hung up. When I get to the office I'm going to go complain to the Chief of Services...'

The doorbell rang. Who could it be, so early in the morning? It was Youma, and behind her stood four boys with suntanned faces and crew cuts, all in a row. All five of them, smiling ear to ear, had a sack, a bag and a cardboard box in hand. I had not seen the boys before that day and it was the first time I had seen Youma smile. She had four gold teeth and her large red headscarf, printed with large green flowers, hung all the way to her waist.

'What has happened, Youma? Have you been invited to a wedding so early in the morning?'

The boys all chuckled and Youma laughed out loud. 'Mrs. Doc, this day be no less than a wedding! I told the boys we first'll go over to Mrs. Doc's place. She'll do right by us and won't charge us poor unfortunate folks much. Right, kids?' She turned around to face the boys, who nodded and giggled again. Their teeth shone brilliant white in their bronzed faces.

I was staring at Youma, confused, when Artoush came up behind me to ask, 'What's happened?' Armineh and Arsineh were clinging to either side of my skirt. Armen asked, 'What's going on?' As we all stood face to face, our five-man crew stared back at their five-man crew for a few seconds.

Youma figured out the problem before anyone else. She turned around and said something in Arabic to the boys, who all cracked up laughing. Then she explained that they had come to buy the locusts, that the Arabs in Khuzestan roast them and eat them. 'S'like sunflower seeds, ya know, Mrs. Doc? Like roasted seeds. Like so.' She held her thumb and hennaed forefinger in front of her mouth, pantomiming the cracking open of a sunflower seed in the front teeth.

The twins both said 'Yuck!' but Youma did not hear. She continued her explanation. 'Sometime we boil 'em. In a pot.'

Armen broke out laughing. Youma laughed too and the boys looked at each other and, probably because everyone else was laughing, they laughed as well.

I told Youma to start by gathering up the locusts on the path before going on to the rest of the yard. When I told her I did not want any money, she raised her two bony arms up to the sky, with ten or twenty bangles on each wrist, and said, 'You are a great lady, God keep you, God give you everything you want, God give you...' She was still saying prayers for me when I closed the door.

Armen called the twins into his room. 'I have three new pictures of Tarzan and Cheetah.'

Artoush put an accordion file down on the telephone table and rifled through some letters and papers. 'How poor does a person have to be to eat locusts?'

The carpet in the hallway was crooked. I bent over to straighten it. 'They eat locusts in lots of places. They've been doing it for eons.'

Artoush looked at me and said nothing. The twins came into the hallway. They pushed the lace curtain aside, craned their necks to see into the yard and shouted in unison, 'It's cleared up to the gate!' Seeing Armen stand at the mirror in the hallway, combing his hair, they knitted their eyebrows.

Arsineh complained, 'You mean we don't get a piggy back ride?'

Armineh said, 'We don't get a piggy back ride.' They went out the door grumbling.

Artoush, on his way out the door, said, 'So the Company Services employee wasn't kidding at all!' I went out with him.

Youma and the boys were hard at work. Within ten minutes there were three sacks full of locusts sitting next to the gate.

I had never seen our street so crowded as on that day. Men, women, and children, dripping with sweat, were rushing around shaking the trees and hedges. The locusts fell from the branches into the sacks and bags, or whatever else they had brought to cart them off in. There was bickering over whose tree this was, and how far that house's hedgerow extended. Was this same scene, I wondered, being repeated all throughout the city?

The school bus had yet to arrive. I saw Armen crossing to the other side of the street. Emily was standing by the gate of G-4.

Arsineh tugged at my sleeve. 'Look at the hedges!'

Armineh shouted, 'Look at the trees!'

Artoush said, 'Look at that!'

Two Arab men were shaking out the hedge of the house to the left of us. As the locusts fell off the bushes, there was nothing left but the wooden branches. I stared dumbfounded at all the hedges and trees. There was not a single leaf left anywhere. I had never seen Abadan without its luscious greenery.

Armineh started, 'It's like they've all gone to the barber and...'

Arsineh finished, 'And shaved off all their hair.'

I waited outside longer than on any other morning, and waved goodbye to the school bus and to Artoush's Chevy.

When I stepped back into the yard, Youma was shaking out the willow tree. The only thing left of Hovhaness

Toumanian's Princess were long, naked branches, like a skeleton. I turned to look at the lawn. One spot was still covered in locusts, but where Youma's boys had already gathered them up, there was nothing but bare dirt. You would never guess that only yesterday in our yard we had a lush green lawn and so many beautiful flowers. Everything was the color of dust, and now it really was just dust.

40

There were not enough chairs for everyone at the table.

'Wouldn't we be more comfortable in the living room?' I asked several times, but with everyone talking at the same time, no one heard me. I sent Armen to bring the chairs from his room and the twins' room, and finally we all sat down.

Artoush was telling the story of his phone call to Company Services to a guffawing Garnik. Armen stood behind Artoush, leaning back on the kitchen counter. The twins and Sophie were talking about the rehearsal for the end-of-year performance, and Mother was making bread and cheese bites. Alice was putting on lipstick in the mirror of her compact case, and Nina was recounting the attack of the locusts: 'As if the locusts – the devil take them – were not enough, sounding like a jet about to take off right over our heads, we also have Garnik running around the room shouting non-stop, "Don't be afraid. Don't move. Don't talk." I finally poured water in a glass and shouted at him, "Keep your cool, man! You're more scared than the rest of us." And I force-fed him the water.' She gave a boisterous laugh and put her arm around Garnik's neck.

Garnik was scratching his head. 'Yep, so help me Jesus. Big bear that I am, I lost my courage, but for my wife and for this one, it was like nothing out of the ordinary was going on.' He gestured toward Violette, who was the only one other than me neither laughing nor talking. She was turning her coffee cup round and round in its saucer.

Mother split an apple into quarters and gave one piece each to the twins and to Sophie, and held the fourth out to Armen. When Armen said 'I don't want it,' she bit into it herself.

'I was not in the least bit afraid, either. I was only worried about Clarice and the children. Mostly I was worried about Clarice, being all alone.'

I got up from the table and quickly began collecting the dessert plates. 'Those are not used yet, Auntie,' said Sophie. 'Why are you clearing them away?'

Armineh asked, 'More apple, Nana.'

Arsineh said, 'Nana, apple!'

Mother said, 'Hold your horses, just a second,' and took another apple from the fruit bowl.

Alice was saying, 'I kept telling Joop, "Honestly, I'm not afraid," but he said, "Come hell or high water, I'm going to get myself to the hospital, right now." I managed to convince him not to come. There was no need for him to be there, anyway – I'm not a child.'

Garnik reached over to Nina's plate and took a few grapes, popping them one by one into his mouth. ''Scuse me, Alice dear. Do the Dutch know how to say "hell or high water" in English?' And he cracked up laughing. The twins and Sophie were in stitches, too.

Mother said crossly, 'No laughing with your mouths full. It will get stuck in your throat.'

Alice put her lipstick and compact case back in her purse and glowered at Garnik.

Nina slapped the back of Garnik's hand. 'Stealing from my plate, again?' Then she turned to Alice. 'Forget about him, you know how he is – just waiting for some excuse to talk rubbish. Don't you have a date tonight?'

Alice looked at her nails, turned the ring on her finger and pursed her lips. 'Joop is busy tonight. He has to write a letter to his mother and his aunt.'

Garnik cracked up again, and after a good laugh, he said, 'Couldn't be busier than that!' He winked at the twins and Sophie, who had caught the giggles from his infectious laughter.

Alice announced, 'I'll have to take a couple of days off work, soon.'

Nina elbowed Garnik and said to the still tittering children, 'What are you standing around here for? Go on, skedaddle!'

Mother was fanning herself and Artoush was spinning the fruit knife on the table.

Armen was leaning over my shoulder trying to reach the plate of sweets. I gave him two cookies and looked at Violette, who had not said a word since she arrived. What's wrong with her, I wondered?

Sophie said, 'We want to play house with the dolls.'

Armineh said, 'We want to get out the dolls...'

Arsineh said, '...and we want to play house.'

Armen said, 'I'm going to ride my bike.'

Alice said, 'I have no choice but to take some days off work.'

Violette got up and went to the window. 'Did the locusts eat the flowers?'

I looked at her. She had her hair in a ponytail and was wearing white flats. She swiped her finger on the window, leaving a smudge. 'Poor things,' she said. Was it my imagination, or did she have a faint smile on her lips?

This time Alice said it very loud. 'I have to go to Tehran to...'

'Tehran?' asked Nina. 'What for?'

With her back to us, Violette said, 'When they migrate they fly for kilometers. Each locust eats its own weight in foliage every day. In Cambodia, cooked locusts are considered a delicacy.' I did not need to guess where she had heard that.

'To renew my passport,' Alice replied. 'Joop said we'll go to Holland together in September to see his mother and aunt. We'll get married there. Of course, we may have a small wedding party here first.'

Me, Mother, Artoush, Nina, and Garnik all turned to Alice.

Violette turned to us. 'Poor things.'

We all looked at Violette, who was looking back at us. 'I meant the locusts.' Then she turned to Alice and laughed. 'How marvelous! Congratulations.'

Alice smiled a little. 'Thank you, Violette. At least one person has sense enough to congratulate me.' She slid her chair back and stood up, turning her big round head toward

Mother, who was still staring at her open-mouthed. 'I'm going. Are you coming with me, or staying?'

Mother jumped up and tugged hard at her purse strap, slung over the back of the chair. The strap broke. Mother tucked the purse under her arm with its broken strap and walked out of the kitchen after Alice. Her chair tottered back and forth a few times before falling over. We all stared at the toppled chair.

I do not know how much time passed before Violette, to shake us all out of our trance, jokingly recited the line from the children's game: 'Red light, green light, freeze! Nobody move...' Then she stepped forward, set the chair upright and sat down on it.

Now all eyes were on Violette, picking out a pair of cherries connected at the stem from the fruit bowl. She looked them over. 'How pretty!' She hung them over her ear as if they were an earring and glanced at each of us in turn. She arched her thick eyebrows. 'Well, why are you all speechless? Marriage is not such bad news, is it? After all, I'm going to get married, too.'

At that moment both the twins and Sophie ran in, out of breath. They each lifted a finger in the air, imitating a pupil asking the teacher for permission. 'May we ride our bikes, sir?'

Violette turned her profile to the children, tilting her head left and right. 'Isn't my earring pretty?' The two cherries were swinging back and forth, making the children laugh. Violette laughed as well. 'Girls, would you like to be bridesmaids at my wedding?'

Armineh, Arsineh, and Sophie jumped up and down, clapping. 'Super, super! What color dresses will we wear?'

'Pink for me,' said Armineh.

'Blue for me,' said Sophie.

'Pink for me,' said Arsineh. Artoush looked at me, Garnik at Nina, and Nina at Violette. The girls were dancing around in a ring, calling out, 'Wedding, wedding!'

Violette took the cherries off her ear, plucked out their twin stems, and ate them both.

Garnik asked Nina, 'What did she say?'

Nina asked Violette, 'What did you say?'

Violette got up, tossed the two pits in the dessert plate and said, 'Kids, come on. Let's decide who will wear what color. I will wear white, of course, because I am the bride. You all...' And she stepped out of the kitchen with the kids.

Nina stood up. 'She's off her rocker.' She told Garnik, 'Get up. Get up, let's go see what in the world's gotten into your niece; it's obvious she's even nuttier than I am.'

I stayed in the kitchen with Artoush, who was scooting the sugar shaker back and forth from one hand to the other. Kshsh...Kshsh...Kshsh...Kshsh. I held my tongue...Held my tongue...Held my tongue. In the end, I shouted, 'Stop it!'

41

I was uneasy in the green leather chair, tucking up my legs, stretching them out, sitting up straight, slouching to the side. I dangled my arms over the armrests, then folded them across my chest. I leaned all the way back, closed my eyes, then opened them again. I picked up Sardo's novel from the bookcase, read two or three lines from the spot I had bookmarked, then closed the book. I didn't care any more whether the man in the story would choose love or responsibility. I hated the hero of the story for being so stupid, and the heroine for not seeing the hero's stupidity. I got up and went to the kitchen, chiding myself, 'You are the stupidest of them all.'

A glance at the kitchen clock showed that the children would be back before too long. I opened the refrigerator. We had no milk, not much cheese, and the butter was missing. I was sure we had had butter that morning. Glancing around the kitchen, I spied the butter dish. It had been left out on the counter since morning and the butter was by now almost completely melted. The unwashed dishes from breakfast were piled up in the sink.

How many times over the past seventeen years had the breakfast dishes sat unwashed in the sink until the end of the day? Maybe only once or twice, and that in the final months I was pregnant with the twins. My eyes settled on the silhouette of Sayat Nova. Two of the thumbtacks were missing, and the head of the poet was sagging away from the wall. I went closer. My, it was ugly! How come I had always thought of it as pretty? Maybe because Artoush's niece had sent it to us from Armenia? But it did not matter where it came from. It was ugly and, stupid me, up until that very moment I had fancied it was pretty.

I tore down the silhouette and crumpled it up. And then I crumpled it some more, balling it up until it fitted in the palm of one hand. I juggled the balled-up paper from hand to hand a few times, turned toward the garbage pail and took a shot. Sayat Nova hit the rim of the pail and fell to the floor. I picked up my purse and left the house.

The gate of G-4 was half open. I walked all the way to the water tank in the neighborhood square. I passed by the benches and the leafless trees and the deflowered oleander bushes. I tried not to look around me as I walked along. I had never seen Abadan the color of dust; the city looked tired and listless. Like myself, very tired and very listless.

At Adib's store, a sign hanging on the door said: CLOSED. I had never come at this hour of the day to buy anything, and so had never seen this sign before. And I never came at that hour, knowing the store was closed from one to three o'clock.

I looked at my watch. It was five minutes to three and the children would be home in another hour. We had no butter and not much cheese, and the children would be left snack-less. How could I have forgotten we were out of cheese and milk, and that the store closed for a long lunch? Instead of tending to the duties of the house that morning, I had squirmed around in the leather chair, resenting the heroine of the story and her stupidity, and the hero's stupidity, and...

I took a deep breath and rapped on the glass door with my wedding ring, right in the center of the letter 'O.'

I exhaled when Mr. Adib opened the door. 'Oh, it's you, Mrs. Doc? You've never come around at this time before!'

The store was hot and dark. Mr. Adib chatted as he weighed out the butter and the cheese. 'Ever seen such hot weather? They say it's 'cause of the locusts. After a locus' attack, the weather heats up. For sure, the kids'll jump in the Shatt. And God knows how many of 'em the sharks'll get. What're the poor things to do? The heat makes 'em reckless. I for one have never seen such hot weather.'

I was looking at Mr. Adib's scale, rusted in places and the pans warped or dented here and there. I did not have the patience to tell Mr. Adib, 'You have seen even hotter weather than this. Me, too. Tonight and tomorrow night and the next night, the kids of the Arab quarter, of Ahmadabad, and of neighborhoods I've never been to and don't even know the names of, will jump in the Shatt for the umpteenth time, and if the sharks don't take their life, they'll take their arm or their leg, and we'll hear from Alice that "they brought seven shark-bite victims to the hospital yesterday, eight today, ten last night." Me and Artoush and Mother will say "tsk tsk" and after a shorter or longer spate of silence – whatever seems appropriate for a death or the loss of a limb – we'll concentrate on our own children, who will be asking, "What are we having for our after-school snack? What are we having for dinner? The heat is killing us! Why don't you turn up the air conditioner?"'

'I just got a shipment of some first-class Halva,' said Mr. Adib. 'Shall I get you some?'

At our house no one liked Halva but me. 'A few ounces, please,' I said.

With the bag in hand, I headed for home. Our street was empty and the sun was hot. Even the frogs were quiet. The door of G-4 was closed.

As I entered our yard, I saw him standing by the door of our house. I passed by the dusty flowerbeds and the denuded trees and bushes.

'Barev, Clarice.' His green eyes were the only speck of green to be seen.

'Barev,' I said, and opened the front door. 'I bought some butter. Before it melts, let me put it in the fridge.' He followed behind me into the kitchen. I put the butter, cheese, and Halva in the refrigerator and started to wash the dishes. Behind me I heard no footsteps and no chair dragging across the tiles. So he was not sitting down, but must still be standing in the doorway.

My polite side whispered, 'It's bad manners, ask him to sit down.' I turned my head around. He was staring at the empty space where Sayat Nova had been.

'Won't you sit down?' I said.

He sat down and got straight to the heart of the matter. From the first day he saw Violette in our house something told him, she is the woman you have been searching for all these years. The next day, as he was leaving the Company, he sees Violette again, who happened to be passing by. They go together to the *Milk Bar* for coffee, and they talk. They arrange a few further meetings on the banks of the Shatt.

The clean dishes were in the dish rack. As I sat listening to him, I remembered: Artoush had said, 'Violette asked me and Emile all kinds of questions about which division of the Company we work in and what we do. I couldn't imagine these things would be of interest to her.'

Nina had remarked: 'Violette is still upset about the divorce. At sunset she walks alone along the banks of the Shatt.'

And Violette herself had told the kids: 'One day soon I'll take you to the *Milk Bar* for ice cream.'

And when Garnik asked her, 'How do you know about the *Milk Bar*, you little imp?' she just smiled.

Emile was worn out. He kept running his hands through his hair, putting them in his pocket, pushing back his chair, pulling it forward, talking. 'My mother never approves of anything I do. She always thinks I am making a mistake. She doesn't believe I can reason things through to the end. She has always done things by the book. She doesn't believe in love. But the meaning of life is love, no? Surely, you agree with me?'

He was quiet for a while, looking at me with anticipation.

I put out my cigarette in the ashtray, and sat quietly, thinking. I don't want to know what decision the man in Sardo's story takes. I don't like Sardo's writing. I lit another cigarette.

He said, 'I didn't know you smoke.' And then he began to talk about Violette again, about how guileless she is, how kind, how humble. How much she likes poetry and music. He talked just like a Sardo novel.

When we heard the voices of the children coming up the path, Emile got up. 'Will you talk to my mother? I don't wish to offend her, but if she will not agree, I will have no choice…' He said goodbye, and then looked doubtfully at me. Then he took me by the arm and said, 'Please.' And then he left.

I gave the kids their snack and tried to concentrate on what they were saying.

'The math test was very easy.'

'We have two weeks to go before the end-of-year celebration.'

'We were practicing the poem "Four Seasons" today.'

'Emily is Cinderella in the play.'

'The Prince will be played by a classmate of…'

Armen gathered up his sandwich and his milk, and slid his chair back. 'I have a geography test tomorrow.'

The twins watched Armen go to his room and close the door. Then they lowered their voices. Armineh said, 'After the rehearsal, Armen slapped his classmate, the one playing the prince.'

Arsineh added, 'But before they could fight, the principal came by.'

'What did Emily do?' I asked.

They answered in tandem. 'She laughed.'

42

It was late in the afternoon and the sun was no longer so intense. But our old Chevrolet was parked on the street, and the garage was wide open to welcome the green Cadillac. The twins were leaning on their elbows over the kitchen table, flipping through the monthly issue of *Lusaber*. I took the magazine. 'You have an exam tomorrow.'

Armineh pouted, her lower lip protruding. 'We just got it today.'

Arsineh's lower lip followed suit. 'At least let us flip through it to the end.'

I tossed the magazine on the counter. 'Before bed. For now, revise your history, and I'll quiz you.' They looked at one another and left the kitchen without another word. For the last couple of weeks they had not been stubbornly insisting on things. I wondered why. Was it because the children sensed I had no patience?

Artoush said, 'They're not big coffee drinkers, they'll have tea.' I filled up the kettle and set it on the stove. Half an hour later I took the tea tray to the living room. The guests said thank you under their breath. Artoush smiled and closed the door behind me.

I went to the bedroom and stretched out on the bed, staring at the ceiling fan while I had a little talk with myself: How come you only notice the stupidity of others? Why don't you listen properly to what people are saying? Why do you criticize Alice? You are worse than she is.

I got up and went to the window. It was sunset and the branches of the lotus tree looked greyish in the fading light. I should be doing something, anything to occupy my mind and keep it from ruminating. Shall I straighten the drawers? I had done that only last week. Read? The books were all in the living room and I did not want to disturb Artoush and his guests. Even that was just an excuse, as I did not feel much like reading. And dinner was already prepared. I could go to the garage – for some time I had been meaning to sort through the junk piling up in the garage and toss some of the stuff out.

As I stepped out the front door I heard a noise. It sounded as if someone was sneaking through the boxwood hedge into the garage. Who could that be? Artoush's guests were still in the living room and the children were studying. The door to our garage was now closed. So was Mr. Rahimi's. Armen had better not be messing about! He might scratch the Cadillac or something. Stupid me – here I thought my boy was all grown up. I opened our garage door.

I don't know who was more scared, me or the young man bent over the open trunk of the Cadillac. I screamed. The man turned around with an armful of papers and as I screamed a second time, his foot caught on the bumper and he fell to the ground. He cried out in pain on the garage floor, his flyers scattered all about.

Artoush was sitting at the kitchen table. 'How many times are you going to ask me? I said I did not know. I was not aware of it. They decided this on their own.' He was pushing the sugar shaker back and forth on the table.

I was shaking and shouting and I did not care a whit if I was yelling. 'You didn't know? Your precious friend deliberately parks his Cadillac in our garage to…'

'He's not my friend.'

'Whatever. Your precious enemy. Of course he's not your friend! A friend would not treat a friend like this. He drinks our tea and coffee, spinning his ridiculous plans, and meanwhile orders his minion to come and collect seditious flyers from our garage? What if they were following him? What if they broke into our house? If you were, and still are, so hellbent on being a political activist, you should never have married. You should never have had children. If SAVAK broke in here, what would happen to me and the children? You don't think of anyone but yourself!'

On and on, I held nothing back. Artoush just took it. Then he picked up the sugar shaker from the table. I was still yelling: 'Thoughtless, selfish.' He was playing with the cap of the sugar shaker.

'I slave day and night for you and the children, and for what? So you can do just exactly as you please. So you can play chess, devote yourself to your supposedly important political projects, and play at being a hero, while the children suck the life out of me and leave me with no time to do anything for myself, and no one even once stops to ask me, "Are you tired?" And…' I put a tissue to my eyes and began sobbing out loud. Artoush was twisting the sugar shaker open and closed.

It was the first time that he had not walked out in the middle of an argument.

'I dance to every tune you play. Living in Braim is bourgeois, fine. What do we need a high-end model car for, fine. I have guests coming, fine. I like chess, fine. I'm going to Shahandeh's, fine. And…now things have come to the point where they're distributing dangerous political flyers from my house and his highness, the master of the house, says, "I was not aware of it. They decided this on their own." If you are so stupid that you don't know what happens in your own house, then…'

I did not finish my sentence, but stared in shock as Artoush unscrewed the top of the sugar shaker and without a single word, poured sugar all over the table, the chairs, and the kitchen floor, as though he were watering the flowers. Then he screwed the cap back on the sugar shaker, set it down on the table and left the kitchen.

43

At the kitchen table I was mending the twins' school uniforms, torn again at the pockets.

The kitchen had been swept several times after the argument with Artoush, both by myself and by Ashkhen. But each morning a long line of ants marching this way or that told me that traces of sugar were left in spots. I had not spoken a single word to Artoush since that day. Instead I had been waging an internal struggle about who was in the right, me or him. The twins were out in the yard, on the swing seat, singing a song:

We had a lovely dog,
We loved that dog to pieces...

The gate squeaked, followed by laughter and shouting from the twins.

'Thank you, Sophie!'
'Thank you, Uncle Garnik.'
'Both of them green!

'How pretty!'

'Just like Sophie's!'

'Thank you, thank you!'

I had a pot of kidney beans on the stove. I turned off the burner and went to open the door. The twins were jumping up and down, each holding a hula-hoop.

From the front step, smiling, I called out, 'So you had to go out and do it, in the end?'

Garnik looked in my direction, waved and came up to me. 'A man and his word! I told them I would get one for them, so I did.'

I cleared the table and set the uniforms and the sewing basket on one of the chairs. 'Every month some new toy is all the rage. If we bought them all, we'd go broke and the children would be spoiled. Not that they're not already spoiled. Will you have coffee or sherbet?'

Garnik sat down and took a large handkerchief out of his pocket. He wiped his neck and forehead. 'First water, then coffee, then sherbet! They only love toys while they are children, and they're only children for a few years. Blink a couple of times and they're all grown up, swimming in a sea of troubles, like us. And no one's gone broke yet buying toys. Where's Artoush?'

I took out the pitcher from the fridge and a glass from the cupboard, poured the water, set the glass on the table and got the coffee pot. I measured out the coffee. 'Sweet or medium? Where's Nina?'

Garnik drank the water in one go and put the empty glass down on the table. 'She went to the bazaar with Violette to buy American sheets. Now that's what's going to make us go broke! Sweet, please. Artoush isn't back yet?'

I stood by the coffee pot to make sure it did not boil over. 'I have to buy sheets, too.' I poured the coffee into a cup and sat down with him at the table. 'Shall I cut some Gata for you?'

He drew the coffee cup toward him. 'Did you have a fight?'

The kids were counting loudly in the yard. 'Forty-five, forty-six, forty-seven...'

Garnik sipped his coffee and asked, 'Want to know how I knew, huh?' He looked at me and laughed. 'First of all, you've made coffee for me a hundred times and you know I like it sweet. Second, I asked you twice where Artoush is, and each time you changed the subject. What happened?'

Should I tell him? Shouldn't I tell him? I told him. 'I'm at my wit's end with Artoush playing politics.'

In the yard, Sophie said, 'Whoever gets to a hundred spins first is the winner.'

Garnik watched me for a moment and played with his coffee cup, sliding it back and forth a few times. Then he looked out the window. 'Well, everyone's got to believe in something.'

On more than one occasion, Artoush had said, 'ARF supporters can't see beyond the end of their nose.' Each time Garnik had replied, 'Doesn't the end of our own nose take priority over the noses of other folks?'

I got up and stirred the kidney beans. 'It's not a question of belief. It's a question of selfishness. We women have to slave sun-up to sundown to get everything ready for you men, while you go on imagining you are building a better world. Meanwhile you have no consideration for your wives and no consideration for your children.'

I went on lecturing about 'we women' and 'you men' for five minutes while Garnik listened quietly. The problem was that what I was saying did not seem entirely fair, even to me. I must have left something out. I was sure that I was somehow in the right, but I did not know how to say it without coming off like a nagging wife, whining and complaining after a quarrel with her husband.

Garnik got up and went over to the stove. He lifted the lid off the pan and inhaled. 'Mmm, smells delicious! Here's what I'm thinking: if we selfish men, as you call us, don't try to build, as you say, a better world, what would you have to cook in this pan? That is, if we still had pots and pans?' Still holding the lid, he looked over at me. Then he cocked his head and smiled.

In the yard the girls were shouting, 'Ninety-eight, nighty-nine, one hundred, hooray!' I was sure there must be a good answer to Garnik's question. I was sure of it, but nothing came to mind. I asked, 'Want some beans?'

44

Joop said, 'I do hope, good sir, that you will, like myself and Alice, be happy and content with this decision. I have sent a correspondence to my mother and aunt in Holland. They too are happy and content. If you, good sir, be content and happy, Alice and I, too, are happy and content.' Artoush loosened the knot of his tie and shifted position in the easy chair.

The day before, Alice had said, 'Tell Artoush to put on a tie. You dress up nice, too. With lipstick. Send the kids over to Nina's, or, I don't know, anywhere. Just so long as they don't disturb us.' It did not even occur to me to ask why she could not hold this little courtship dinner at her own house.

To keep myself busy, I got up and offered sweets to everyone. Joop took one of the cream puffs that Alice had bought and did not touch the pastries I had made from scratch. 'I like creamy puff. *Shad-shad* thanks.' He looked at Alice and smiled.

Alice laughed and turned to me. 'I'm teaching him Armenian.' Then she pushed the dish of homemade sweets away. 'He only likes cream puffs.' She cocked her head and smiled at Joop.

Mother, with a smile that looked pasted onto her face, said '*Shad-shad lav*,' nodded, and peered into the narrow space separating Joop and Alice.

Armen was in his room and the twins had gone bike-riding. I gave them money to buy bread from the *Dairy* and 'whatever they felt like' from the *Store*. Their eyes lit up.

Joop was explaining in great detail the water-heating system in his house in Holland for Artoush. Artoush was listening carefully, whether to occupy the time, or because he was really interested, I could not tell.

Looking up at the ceiling, Alice said, 'I hear Emile and Violette are getting married.' Ever since her marriage to Joop was semi-officially announced, Alice no longer looked in my face when speaking to me. At least it seemed like she was looking down at me, and since she was shorter than me, that took some doing. 'Poor Violette, with that nutty mother-in-law. She probably imagines that the instant they marry, the lady midget is going to hand over all her jewels to her daughter-in-law on a silver platter.'

Mother helped me set the dinner table and she talked non-stop as we walked back and forth between the kitchen and the dining room.

'I always hoped Alice would get married in our church here in Abadan. God bless the cross in that altar! It has granted each and every favor I prayed for and every vow I made. For the safe delivery of your babies, for the setting of Armen's broken arm; for the quick recovery of the twins when their tonsils were removed. And now, for this. You've made a ton of salad again? No one here eats that much salad.

Still, it's a good thing you did. These days Alice eats nothing but salad.'

Armen and the twins were playing Chutes and Ladders on the kitchen table.

'It was a four.'

'Nuh-uh, it was a three.'

'It was four, wasn't it, Arsineh?'

'It was four. No cheating, Armen!'

'One, two, three, four. Swoop, up I go! Your turn, Arsineh.'

Mother poured dressing on the salad. 'I would hate Joop to think I am one of those mother-in-laws who butts into everything. If they want to marry in Holland, well, so be it. There's no difference from one church to another.'

Armineh said, 'Nana, when you said church, it reminded me of a joke one of the sixth graders told today. Shall we tell them, Arsineh?'

'Let's tell them,' said Arsineh. Then she warned Armen. 'Your piece is right here, in this square. Above this big chute, here. No cheating, now! Go ahead, Armineh. Mommy, Nana, listen.' And they began telling the joke, each jumping in amid the other's words.

'A naughty boy kept knocking on the church door.'

'As soon as the priest opened the door, the boy would run away.'

'Finally, the priest hides behind the door.'

'As soon as the kid knocks...'

'The priest jumps up and opens the door.'

'The naughty boy is caught off guard, but asks...'

'Pardon me, is Jesus home?'

The twins both cracked up laughing. Armen said, 'That's an old one.' Mother tried not to laugh. 'We don't joke about Jesus and the Church. It's a sin.'

I told the kids to put the game away, and I set the dish of rice on the table. Mother began inspecting the platter of herbs. 'I told Joop that they have to hold a party here in Abadan.' I was hoping the platter would make its way to the dinner table before Mother had thrown half of the herbs into the garbage because she considered them 'wilted.'

'My girl's no foundling that I would send her off to her husband's home without a proper celebration. Hand me the platter, I'll take it to the table. It's a shame the Tahdig turned out soggy.'

I ladled the Ghormeh-sabzi into two bowls and muttered to myself, 'Just let Alice get married – in the church, outside the church, with a party, without a party. Just let her be married.'

Mother came back laughing. 'Did you hear what Joop said? He said…'

I cut her off. 'Take the casseroles while I arrange the Parinj on the serving dish.'

Mother removed the cloth I'd wrapped around the pot lid to absorb the excess moisture from the Parinj. 'Well, if we can't have a wedding party, we'll just have to do without. Why should we spend all that money just to feed people, anyway? Mmm, the Parinj is fantastic! Here, give me the dish. You're tired, I'll serve it.'

I passed her the dish and leaned back on the counter to drink the Vimto fruit cordial I had fixed for myself. Suggesting I was tired was just a pretext. Mother believed that only the

Armenians of Julfa knew how to make authentic Parinj. She would have some hard-to-find parinj grain sent to her every year all the way from Isfahan. Since Mother had prepared it especially for this evening, she naturally wanted to be the one to arrange it on the platter, lest I wreck the presentation of this delicacy.

The ice had melted in my glass and the Vimto was luke-warm. I could not be bothered to get myself more ice, but then remembered we would need ice for the dinner table, so went over to the refrigerator.

Mother carefully laid out the chunks of meat on top of the Parinj. 'It's up to them. If they want to hold a celebration here, fine. If not, well, that's fine too. Who are we to interfere?'

I poured the ice into a crystal bowl. Mother tilted her head to the left and then to the right, assessing the arrangement of Parinj on the platter. 'Let's see if our dear son-in-law likes Parinj or not.' She picked up the dish and headed for the door. 'But I do wish they would have a little party.' The twins ran in.

'Mommy!'

'Mommy!'

'Look what he's brought!'

'See what he brought?'

Joop had brought gifts for the twins – a boy doll and a girl doll. I picked up the ice bowl and went with the kids and their dolls to the living room. 'Please have a seat at the table, everyone,' I announced. I thanked Joop for the dolls and signaled the children to do likewise.

Armineh went up to Joop, offered him her cheek to kiss, and said, 'Thanks.'

Alice said, 'Say "Thank you, Uncle Joop."'

Arsineh offered her cheek and said, 'Thank you, Uncle Joop.'

Joop kissed them both and Artoush asked them, 'What have you named the dolls?'

The twins looked at each other and announced at the same time, 'We have to think about it.'

Armen came into the room holding a brand new shiny tape recorder; everyone said, almost in unison, 'Wow, fabulous!' Joop blushed and Armen went over to shake his hand and thank him. Joop said, 'You welcome, you welcome,' several times in reply.

Joop complimented the Parinj over dinner, and Mother replied in Armenian, '*Anoush, anoush.*'

Alice translated for him: 'It means "May it nourish your soul."'

Then Mother explained, with Alice's help, that Parinj is made from a grain like cracked wheat or barley, that we first sauté and then cook with meat and plenty of sautéed onions and turmeric until it makes something like a pilaf. While it steams, it has to be constantly stirred to keep from sticking to the pan. Alice, who was by now tired of translating Mother's recipe, said, 'Okay, enough already! No one is going to enter a cooking contest tomorrow.'

When it came time to say goodbye Joop kissed the twins, and Armineh announced, 'We have chosen a name for the dolls.'

Arsineh whispered in my ear, 'What was Uncle Joop's last name? Don't say it out loud.' I told her and she ran over to Armineh and whispered in her ear.

Arsineh held the boy doll out to us. 'Mr. Joop Hansen.'

Armineh held the girl doll out to us. 'Mrs. Alice Hansen.' It was Alice who laughed the loudest of us all.

When Joop offered his hand, instead of shaking it, I stepped closer, gave him a hug, kissed both of his cheeks and congratulated him. Artoush and my mother were certainly surprised. And Alice? God only knows what she thought, but I did not care. All I knew was that I was very much obliged to Mr. Joop Hansen.

That night I told the twins a story about a girl who had done something bad and then dreamt she was turned into a frog. She was very frightened and, in the morning when she got up and saw she was not a frog, she was so happy she decided not to do bad things anymore.

Armineh yawned and said, 'That was a strange story.'

Arsineh said, 'But it was a bit silly. Wasn't it, Armineh?' Armineh had fallen asleep.

I read 'Three Apples Fell from the Sky' with Arsineh and then turned out their light. I came out into the hallway, thinking, 'Arsineh is right; it was a silly story.' I headed for the living room.

After the guests had gone, Artoush rubbed his stomach and laughed. 'I ate so much Parinj that I'm going to burst. I'm off to bed.' And off he went to the bedroom.

So I sat on the sofa, in front of a blank television screen, and stretched out my feet on the coffee table. My hand found its way to my hair and began to twirl. I was not tired, I felt good. Why? Was it because I'd washed all the dishes and dusted the living room, and because the rooms were, as Mother would say, spick and span? Or was it because Alice was finally getting married, and Joop really seemed – contrary to Mother's and my first impressions – like a good, kind man? Maybe it was also because Artoush had come home earlier than usual the day before with a flower box full of pink and white sweet peas. At first I stared for a moment at the flowers. Then I went up to him, and when he hugged me, I burst into tears.

I turned out the living room light and told myself, 'Maybe it's because you woke up this morning and saw you were not a frog.'

45

It was ten in the morning.

Nina was on the phone. 'You see how Miss Clever Wiles had everything under control the whole time? Clueless me! I thought she didn't know how to go about things and was going to need my help. The only thing left now is for us to formally meet the future mother-in-law. Day after tomorrow is the kids' end-of-year celebration. I was thinking about inviting them the Thursday after that. You and Artoush have to be there! Alice and your mother will be back from Tehran by Thursday, won't they?'

I confirmed they would.

'Then give me the number of the Simonians so I can invite them.'

'Don't you remember your old phone number?'

'What?'

'The phone number of G-4. Have you forgotten it?'

She laughed so loud that I had to hold the receiver away from my ear. 'As your mother says, "Call me an ass!" I was never so on the ball that I can now afford...' Finally, she said goodbye.

I put the receiver down and went to the living room. The sewing machine was set out on the dining table. I was making the twins' costumes for the end-of-year celebration. I had bought pink silk for spring, red cotton for summer, orange taffeta for fall, and white calico for winter. I sewed strips of rabbit fur to the sleeves and hem of winter's dress. One of Artoush's relatives from Tabriz had brought us the rabbit fur years ago. I remembered how Alice and I had laughed about that. 'What sane person would bring fur as a souvenir to Abadan?'

'Hang on to it,' Mother urged. 'You never know when it may come in handy.'

I made a crown of wheat spikes for fall. Youma had brought me the wheat spikes after I gave her a detailed description of what it was I was looking for.

The house was cool and quiet, filled with the smell of the almond cake I was baking in the oven. I glued the spikes together and wondered why I had failed to mention to Nina that I had had no contact with the Simonians lately. I knew that Emily had been absent from school for a few days. When the twins asked, 'Maybe she's sick – may we go look in on her?' I said no. And when Artoush mentioned that 'Emile hasn't been to work for a few days – don't you want to look in on them?' I said no. The twins frowned and Artoush just raised his eyebrows and left it at that.

I sewed blue and pink artificial flowers on a wide ribbon that Armineh was supposed to tie around her head to go with the dress for spring. Why didn't I want to go over to the Simonians? Maybe I did not want to get caught up in their predicament. If I went over and got sucked into the argument, whose side would I take? The mother's or the son's? I glued together the two ends of the tall crown of cotton balls I had made to go with winter's dress, and looked out the window.

The Simonians had come to seem surreal to me. For several days now, this family of three seemed so remote from me, or maybe it was I who was distant from them. I felt the whole adventure had been like a movie, a movie I saw long, long ago and had no particular desire to see again. There was a breeze blowing outside, and through the branches of the Msasa trees, you could catch a wavering glimpse of the living room window of G-4.

I had not yet figured out what to do for summer's headband. If I glued flowers on it, it would look the same as spring. Besides flowers, what would make for a good summer symbol? I couldn't think of anything. 'I'll decide what to do about it later.'

No, I don't feel like going over to the Simonians. It's better if I don't intervene. As I looked down at the dresses, an idea hit me – a crown of boxwood for summer.

46

The school yard was all decorated, small colored lights hanging from the trees, children's paintings covering the walls. The stage with its green velvet curtain was set up at the end of the yard, and rows of chairs were neatly lined up from the foot of the stage nearly to the gate. Armen was one of the ushers, whose job was to guide parents and guests to their seats and staff the buffet table.

I had just sat down and was busy greeting acquaintances when Artoush tapped my shoulder and gestured toward the stairs leading up to the stage. 'Manya.' Manya was waving to me from the top step to come over.

I told Artoush to save my place and went backstage. The choir girls in their uniform white blouses and navy blue skirts, and the choir boys in their white shirts and navy blue pants, were talking non-stop, raising a racket. Mr. Zhora, the music teacher, kept saying 'Quiiiii-et,' to no avail.

As usual, Manya was a bag of nerves but very excited. She tightened the ribbon in the hair of a little red-headed girl and said, 'Off you go, stand in your spot and don't fidget so much.

Your ribbon comes undone minute by minute.' Then she turned round to me. 'Any news from Emily Simonian?'

A few days before, Armineh and Arsineh had been constantly talking about her: 'Emily didn't come to school today.'

'Miss Manya said that if Emily doesn't come tomorrow, we'll have to find another Cinderella.'

'One of the seventh graders will be Cinderella.'

'We thought Emily made a prettier Cinderella.'

'No, I've no news,' I said. 'I heard you substituted one of the seventh graders for her?'

Manya grabbed the arm of a little girl who was holding the stage curtain open, waving to the crowd. 'Hey, you naughty creature! Who told you to come up here? Run along to the dressing room until it's your turn to go on.' She gave the girl an affectionate pinch on the cheek and the girl, decked in a colorful regional costume with layered skirt, ran off laughing. Manya looked around her. 'Yep, I found a new Cinderella,' and she pointed out a girl in a long green skirt standing by the dressing room door and tying on her bandana at a jaunty angle. 'She's pretty, isn't she?' I looked at the girl, who looked up at me and smiled.

Manya explained, 'I was so busy this week I didn't get a chance to telephone the Simonians.' Then she shouted to the new Cinderella, 'Jasmine, dear. We don't tie our bandana at an angle. Cinderella was not so coquettish before she went to the Prince's palace.' Then she turned to me. 'My problem now is not Cinderella. My calamity for the evening is the Prince. The mother of the Prince has just phoned to say her son has come down with the measles. Now I'm pulling my hair out trying to figure out what to do.'

'Surely you don't want to saddle me with the role of the Prince?' You never could tell with Manya.

She chuckled. 'Not a bad idea, at that. You're tall and charming enough.' Then she turned serious. 'Listen. Armen came to all the rehearsals, especially the scenes with Cinderella and the Prince. Sometimes he would prompt the kids when they muffed their lines. I can't think of anyone better for the job than Armen. I sent for the costume from the measles' victim, and it will fit Armen – they're about the same size. By the time the chorus and the poetry reading and the dancing are finished...' She was looking at her watch. 'Then we have the student prizes to give out and...the way I figure, we have a little bit over an hour. We might even be able to rehearse it through once. It's not a bad idea, is it?'

I stepped aside to avoid getting hit by a microphone making its way to center stage and said, 'It's not a bad idea at all. If only Armen would agree.'

Manya laughed and put her hand on my back. 'You go find him and send him up here. Leave the rest to me.'

I walked down the centre aisle between the rows of chairs, which were now almost full, thinking that she might have a chance getting him to agree, at that. Even though Armen was a marvel of unwavering stubbornness when he did not want to do something, Manya was a miracle-worker when it came to getting what she wanted done. I remembered how she had cajoled our grouchy Church priest into playing the role of the Bishop for the New Year's play a few years before.

I looked for Armen. He was arranging bottles of Pepsi and Canada Dry in the ice chest at the buffet table. I told him to go see Miss Manya backstage, and when I returned to my seat, Nina was sitting there, next to Artoush. She picked up her purse from the adjacent seat. 'Here, I saved you a spot. Okay, so tell me what's happening.'

I asked her, 'Where's Garnik?'

To which she swiftly replied, 'He's away in Ahvaz on business for a few days. Why isn't anyone answering the Simonians' phone?'

I looked around. Violette wasn't there.

Nina pulled my sleeve. 'Yoo hoo…! As I was saying, they don't answer their phone. Violette's whimpering like a whipped puppy. I tried everything to get her to come tonight, but she stayed at home, waiting for Emile to call.'

The spotlights lit up the stage and Nina, along with the rest of the crowd, had to be quiet. The curtain opened and Manya came to the microphone to welcome everyone. Watching Manya, I worried why the Simonians were not answering their phone. Maybe something serious had happened to them. Maybe they were really ill? I should have looked in on them. Why hadn't they called us up themselves?

The welcome speech was over and everyone clapped. Vazgen Hairapetian came to the microphone and presented the annual school report. Why should the Simonians have called us? The chorus sang all the usual songs that were performed every year: 'The Majestic Mountains of My Homeland,' 'Farewell Alma Mater,' and a short aria from *Anoush*. Was I upset at my own foolishness, or at Emile and his mother? Armineh and Arsineh turned with the seasons, spring, fall, summer, winter, and recited the poem without any mistakes. I forgot to tell the school photographer to take their pictures! Why should I be upset with Emile? Or with his mother? One boy, as he came up to the microphone, tripped over the cable and almost fell over. The crowd, me included, first held its breath, and then burst out laughing when the little boy, from up there on the stage, turned to his mother and father and called out to them, 'It wasn't my fault!' When he finished reciting his poem, he got the most applause of all.

A fifteen-minute intermission was announced and Nina started up again. 'Violette was right. That lady midget was the one who fanned the flames of destruction. She was jealous. Of Violette – how pretty she is, how young, how Emile fell in love with her. What should we do now? You have to help. Go talk to his mother. You have to...'

I was about to shout, 'Leave me out of it!' when Artoush lifted me by the arm. 'Come here, I need you to do something.'

We went to the buffet. Artoush bought a drink from a girl wearing one of the red usherette armbands and gave it to me. The drink was sweet, and it made me feel better.

The girl said, 'Hello, Mrs. Ayvazian. Did you see Armen dressed as the Prince?'

I looked at her and remembered she had come to our house a couple of times with the twins. Armen called her Roubina, the rotund. I smiled. 'How are you, Roubina?'

She closed her eyes and said, 'He's just like a real prince.' Then she opened her eyes, blinked a few times and went over to help a man who had by now asked her twice, 'Two mortadella sandwiches, please.'

I turned round to Artoush. 'What did you need me for?'

He shook hands with one of the teachers and exchanged greetings. Then he told me, 'Nothing. I just wanted to rescue you from Nina.'

Vazgen Hairapetian gave out the prizes to the star pupils. Armineh and Arsineh both got one and, together, ran up to us. Arsineh sat next to me and Armineh sat next to Artoush to show off their prizes. They received books – for Armineh, an Armenian translation of *Gulliver's Travels*; for Arsineh, *Little Lord Fauntleroy*. Nina was fidgeting in her chair, hoping to talk more, but she did not get the chance. The lights in the schoolyard went dark, the curtain lifted and the play began.

Armen and the girl Manya had pointed out to me – she had mentioned her name, but I could not recall it – played the role of the Prince and Cinderella so well that they got three ovations and numerous bravos from the crowd. Armen, wearing black tights and a waistcoat lavishly adorned with gold brocade, strutted up and down the stage so convincingly that he looked as if he was in a real castle. When he bowed to Cinderella and they danced together, I marveled. 'How did he learn to do that?' Then I thought, 'Is this my "poor little baby"?' And then I wondered, 'Where did all the years go?'

When the Chevy started up on the first try, Armen and the twins said, 'Long live dear ole Chevy!'

Artoush gleefully announced, 'Now we'll have dinner at the Club to celebrate my girls coming top of their class and my son becoming a first-class actor.' The kids said, 'Goody, goody!' We laughed along with them and I forgot I had promised Nina to drop in on the Simonians as soon as I got home.

From the school all the way to the Golestan Club the twins talked non-stop about the ceremonies and everything that had happened behind the scenes or in the dressing room. When they praised their brother's acting, Armen said, 'It wasn't so hard.'

We got to the Club, and on our way through the door, Armineh turned to me. 'Did you tell the photographer to take pictures of us?'

'Lots and lots of pictures?' asked Arsineh.

Mortified, I was fumbling for some way to explain when Artoush piped up, 'I told him.' He walked into the dining room, the twins holding his hands and jumping up and down on either side of him. For a few seconds I stood stock still, watching him from behind.

The dining hall was not crowded. We were sitting at our table reading the menu when a high-pitched voice cried out, 'Good evening!' The bow in Mrs. Nurollahi's hair was light blue with tiny brown flowers.

Artoush stood up and offered her a chair. Mrs. Nurollahi asked, 'I'm not disturbing you, am I? I saw you come in, and I thought I'd come over and say hello. I was on my way to see Mr. Saadat about the arrangements for next Friday's talk.'

She stroked the twins' hair and smiled at Armen. Artoush, out of politeness I imagine, asked about the topic of her talk. 'The History of Women's Rights,' Mrs. Nurollahi answered, and looked at me. 'You probably don't have time, but I would be delighted and honored if you could come.' With a final pat on the twins' heads, she said goodbye and left.

As we ordered our food, Armineh asked, 'Mommy, what does "women's rights" mean?'

Arsineh repeated the question, 'What are "women's rights"?'

I handed the menu back to the waiter and told them, 'You'll understand when you're older.'

I looked over at Mrs. Nurollahi, who was by the door of the dining hall talking to Mr. Saadat. I remembered that I had a blouse and skirt of the same material as Mrs. Nurollahi's dress. Artoush said something and the children laughed.

Armen asked, 'Did you hear that, Mom?'

I said, 'I'll be back in a sec,' and got up.

Mrs. Nurollahi was not at all surprised to see me again, in fact she almost seemed to expect it. When I asked her how I could help her with the work of their society, she looked at me and smiled. 'There's a lot you could do. We'll talk about it on Friday.'

'We'll talk on Friday,' I said and went back to our table.

As Artoush pulled up by our front gate to let us out of the car, the twins and I shot a glance across the street. Artoush parked the car in the garage and Armen collected the Four Seasons dresses from the trunk. The gate to G-4 was wide open.

Armineh asked softly, 'Mom, can we look in on Emily tomorrow?'

Arsineh pleaded, 'Please, please, let us look in on her?'

I ran my hands through their curly hair. 'Sure, we will look in on them tomorrow.'

47

When I woke up, the sun's rays were reflecting off the mirror on the vanity table. I remembered Artoush whispering in my ear as he left for work, 'Sleep. The kids have no school today.' I put my hands behind my head and watched the play of light and shadow in the mirror. The sparrows in the yard were chirping. 'Today I got up later than you,' I told them out loud, and laughed to myself.

Was it the chirping sparrows, the light show in the mirror, or the coolness of the room that made me feel so wonderful? Whatever it was, it was nice. I felt good. I threw off the sheets and got up.

I opened the wardrobe and looked through my clothes – the ones I usually wore at home, then the ones I hardly ever wore. I took out a flower-print spaghetti-strap dress I had worn only a couple of times, because Mother and Alice had told me, 'It's too revealing.' I brushed my hair in front of the mirror and rubbed my hands together. There was no dryness or chapping.

I headed for the kitchen, repeating a couple of lines from the Cinderella play that Armen had delivered with such grand gestures and regal bearing, 'Who is this vision of loveliness coming hither? Ahhh, the girl of my dreams!' I laughed out loud and peeked into the girls' room. Their beds were empty. I went to Armen's room, and his bed was empty. On the kitchen table stood three half-empty glasses of milk. I cleared the glasses and just as I was wondering where they had disappeared to, the three of them turned up together.

Armineh said, 'There's no one in G-4!'

Arsineh said, 'Neither Emily, nor her father, nor her grandmother!'

Armen said, 'I think they have moved out.'

One of the glasses fell from my hands onto the tile floor. The twins shrieked, 'Oh no!' and jumped back.

Armen came to me, 'Are you okay?'

'I'm fine,' I said. 'You all be careful.' I got the broom and dustpan from the corner. Where had they gone? Why had they gone? When?

The twins were jumping in one another's sentences: 'Emily must have been very sick, and they took her to the hospital in Tehran.'

'But then where's the furniture?'

'Maybe the grandmother is sick.'

'But then where's the furniture?'

'They must have moved out yesterday while we were gone.'

Armen picked up two shards of glass and tossed them in the garbage pail, telling the twins, 'You two jabber too much. Out of the kitchen, before you cut yourselves.'

* * *

When Artoush came home that evening, he knew no more than this: Emile had resigned. No one knew why he had resigned or where he had gone.

We were eating dinner when the phone rang. Armen jumped up. 'I'll get it.' The twins looked at each other and smirked, and when I asked them, 'What is it now?' they both grew serious and replied in unison, 'Nothing.'

Armen returned to the kitchen to say, 'Aunt Nina for you.'

Nina did not sound like her usual happy self and her voice was not ringing. 'What a disaster! Have you heard? The jerk just upped and left without a word and since then, Violette has been pacing round the house, crying and cursing and shaking her fist at heaven and earth. Thank God Garnik won't be back until the day after tomorrow. But when he comes back, what then?! If this girl does something awful to herself, how will I answer her mother? I just don't know what to do!'

I tried to calm her down and asked, 'Were things really as serious as that?' Immediately I regretted saying it. If things had not been that serious, Mrs. Simonian would not have just packed up and left town. Nina recounted in detail what Emile had said to Violette and what Violette had said to him. All the while I was wondering how many times the mother had moved by now because of her son. Would it always happen so suddenly? Maybe not. Had she done the right thing, or not? Maybe if Emile married Violette, things would not turn out all that bad. Or maybe they would. Still, she should not have intervened. But maybe she knew her son quite well and had no choice but to intervene? Nina's voice freed me from the grip of all the shoulds and maybes.

'Can Sophie stay with you for a few days? I have to go with Violette to Tehran.'

Of course Sophie could stay with us, I said. And if I could do anything else, she should let me know. Distracted, Nina thanked me and said goodbye. I put the receiver down.

As I hung up, Artoush and Armen were leaving the kitchen. Armen said, 'Dear ole Chevy is sick again. We're taking the doctor to look him over.' He went with Artoush to the garage. I leaned on the telephone table, thinking of the Simonians. How swiftly they had come, and how swiftly they were gone. Like the rain in Abadan – as soon as you notice it might be raining, the rain stops. It would be better if Mother and Alice did not get wind of this, I thought. I had no patience for Alice's opinions on the matter, or Mother's I-knew-from-the-very-beginnings. I heard the twins talking in the kitchen.

'Do you remember how she told us to throw tomatoes at Mr. Zhora?'

'Yeah. Good thing we didn't listen to her.'

'But she threw one! And she blamed it on one of the eighth graders.'

'Yeah. And she pulled the chair out from under Roubina in the lunch room. Then she claimed, "I didn't do it on purpose." But she did do it on purpose, didn't she?'

'Yeah, she did it on purpose. She also poked that hole in the arm chair, didn't she?'

'Yeah. The reason she made friends with us in the first place was on account of Armen. And she didn't even like Rapunzel one teeny bit.'

'It's terrible how she cut up Rapunzel's red dress. Why did you let her?'

'Because she said it wasn't pretty.'

'She cut up her own blouse, too, the white one with the puffy sleeves.'

'She got us to taunt Marguerita in the school yard: "Marguerita, like a cheetah."'

'That was not a nice thing we did.'

'No, it was not a nice thing we did.'

48

The kids had gone to the pool with Sophie, and Armen was at a friend's house. I was waiting for Mother and Alice, who had come back late the night before from Tehran.

The phone rang. I picked up the receiver and glanced at myself in the hall mirror. Was it my imagination, or had I put on some weight? I said, 'Hello? Yes? Who is it?' But there was no answer. I put down the receiver and opened the door for Mother and Alice. Mother kissed my cheek and Alice gave me a big hug.

'You're looking very pretty,' she said. 'Seems like you put on a few pounds, no? In exchange, I've lost a few. See?' She twirled all the way around for me, there in the hallway. She was right, she had lost some weight. I didn't know whether to be more surprised by her slimmer figure, or by the warm greeting with a hug and kiss.

We went to the kitchen and Mother and Alice set the boxes of Peroks and Gata they brought from Tehran on the table. Alice could not keep still. She took the coffee pot from me. 'I'll fix it.' She fixed coffee and filled me in about the trip. 'We decided to get married right here. I gave the order for the wedding invitations to a friend of Mr. Davtian who owns a printshop. Oh, and Davtian sends his warm regards. What a nice man! If he hadn't put in the order himself, the invitations would not have been ready on time. I'll order the cake from Mahtab. Now try and guess what I bought in Tehran.'

She took the coffee pot off the stove, set it on the counter, and turned around. She opened her arms, cocked her head, and smiled. 'A wedding dress!'

Mother broke out laughing and I joined in with a good heartfelt laugh as well.

This time it was me who went up to my sister, hugged her and gave her a kiss. 'Congratulations, congratulations! And blessings.' The morning passed by making the arrangements for the wedding party and writing down the list of people to invite.

The twins and Sophie came back for lunch. Alice hugged all three of them and told them they must be her bridesmaids, in blue and pink dresses.

Armineh said, 'Auntie, are you getting married first, or Auntie Violette?' And she stood there, with Arsineh and Sophie, looking straight at Alice. Alice and Mother looked at me.

I hemmed and hawed. 'Aunt Violette's wedding has been delayed. I mean...'

Sophie made things worse. 'So that's why Aunt Violette was crying all day yesterday and the day before.'

Arsineh and Armineh asked simultaneously, 'She was crying?'

Sophie looked at me, unsure whether she should tell or not, but eventually she did. 'She was crying and she kept repeating, "It's the old crone's fault."'

Armineh asked, 'What's a crone?'

Arsineh said, 'It means midget.'

Alice got up from the table and put some sweets on a plate for the children. 'Crone does not mean midget,' she said. 'And it's not nice to say either one of those words. Run along now; take your sweets and go have a tea party with your dolls.'

As they were leaving the kitchen, Arsineh threw her arm around Sophie's shoulder. 'It's not that bad. There will be a wedding anyway, and we'll get to wear bridesmaids dresses, and you can stay over at our place, with us. Right, Armineh?'

Armineh said, 'Yeah. Gosh, I hope that Auntie Nina doesn't come back too soon.' And they left the room, all three laughing.

Mother looked at me. 'Well, what happened?' Alice was leaning over the table.

I told them. When I had finished, Mother said, 'Didn't I tell you from day one that that woman is crazy? Didn't I tell you her son is crazy, just like her? If I'm lying, go right ahead and say so.'

Alice was playing with the twine on the box of Gata. 'Don't accuse people without cause. We don't know what happened. Anyway, it's none of our business. But...poor Violette.'

I looked at Alice as if seeing her for the first time. As long as I could remember, my sister had been flinging accusations left and right, night and day. And she had her opinions about the smallest details of everybody's business and would determine for them just exactly what they should do. And now... *don't accuse people without cause. It's none of our business. Poor Violette?* I knew then that I really, really liked Joop.

The phone rang and Armen, who I hadn't even realised was home, shot out of his room like an arrow. 'I've got it.' Shortly, he came to the kitchen to say, 'The Dutch gentleman for Aunt Alice.'

Alice put her arm around Armen's shoulder and kissed his cheek. 'First of all, has the cat got your tongue? You forgot to say hello to me! Second, what's with this "Dutch gentleman" business? From now on, call him Uncle Joop.'

Laughing, she went to the hallway to get the phone. Armen repeated 'Uncle Joop' several times, laughed, and greeted his grandmother with a kiss. My mother caressed her grandson's cheek.

'I hope I live to see your wedding day, too.'

49

Nina helped every step of the way with Alice's wedding. My fear that she would talk endlessly about Violette proved baseless. After returning from Tehran, Nina did not breathe a word about her.

The night before the wedding, Artoush and Garnik took the children to the Annex for fish and chips. I stayed home, sitting at the kitchen table with Nina, making little packets of candied almonds as wedding favors for the guests. We poured the colorful almonds in little square nets that Mother had embroidered with flowers, and then tied them up with a little satin ribbon. On one end of the ribbons was printed, 'Joop and Alice,' and on the other end, the date of the wedding.

Alice had gone home. 'I should go to bed early tonight so I will be bright and fresh for tomorrow. If I can sleep!' And Mother was supposed to sew, as Joop put it, a 'Red-and-Green.'

Joop found all the little customs of the wedding ceremony fascinating. One of the wedding customs of the Julfa Armenians is to drape two broad satin sashes over the shoulders of the bride and groom, one red and one green. When the priest recites the benediction, the best man shifts the placement of the sashes back and forth a couple of times. The green sash symbolizes good fortune and wealth, while the red symbolizes love. Artoush agreed with nary a grumble to act as best man at Alice and Joop's wedding.

Nina was drinking sour cherry sherbet and faintly humming a song.

I couldn't stand it any longer. 'How is Violette doing?'

She poofed loudly and shrugged. She tightened the string on a wedding favor and put the packet in the basket, which was decorated all the way around with artificial flowers. She drained the sherbet and stirred the ice at the bottom of the glass. 'The longer you live, the more you learn. As usual, I raised a big hullabaloo and fretted over nothing.' She put the glass down on the table and picked up another square net. 'When we got to Tehran, she spilled tears for three days and busted up her poor mother's good china. That is, until she saw the upstairs neighbor's brother. When this fellow entered the picture, she calmed back down and turned into the same old Violette that everyone knew as "poor girl, how sweet and innocent." And, by the way, I sent Tigran to the university dorm. The environment at the aunt's place was far more dangerous. Pass me a ribbon.'

As I handed her a ribbon, Nina said, 'Do you remember when I said that Violette reminded me a little of you? As your mother says, "Call me an ass!"' And she burst out laughing.

I put a packet of almonds in the basket and thought, 'No, call me the ass.'

Nina knotted a ribbon around the net she was holding and stared out the window. She was no longer laughing. The sweet peas were not easily visible from where we were sitting. She said, 'Speaking of Mother, have you thought about what to do after Alice leaves…'

I looked out the window. These past few weeks I had been trying not to think about the living arrangements for Mother after Alice leaves. I played with the bow of the packet I was holding. 'I don't know.'

Nina put her packet of almonds into the basket. 'You haven't spoken with Mother about it?'

I put my packet of almonds in the basket. 'Not yet.'

She looked at the sweet peas again. 'Well, maybe after the wedding, huh?'

I looked at the basket of wedding favors and nodded. 'After the wedding.'

50

It was a few days after Alice and Joop's wedding and they had already left for Holland.

We had seen them off at the airport. Joop kissed me on the cheek and said, 'Clarice, I thank you for all your troubles. Rest assured I will make Alice happy. My mother and my aunt have asked me to make Alice happy.' On the day of the wedding, it was Joop's mother and aunt who sent the largest bouquet of flowers – red and white Dutch tulips. Artoush marveled, 'How did they get these all the way to Abadan from their little hamlet?'

I was sitting on the swing seat with Nina. Armen was fiddling with his bicycle near the front gate. The twins and Sophie were playing hide-and-go-seek. 'Who will be It?' asked Sophie. 'Let's draw lots.' The three of them stood in a circle, and Sophie tapped everyone on the chest in turn. 'Eenie...meenie...miny...mo...catcha...tiger...'

Nina said, 'I've never understood what it's supposed to mean, this counting rhyme.' Then she gestured toward the kitchen. 'So, you've spoken to Mother, have you?' Mother's white hair was visible through the kitchen window.

'Yeah,' I said.

The girls ran around to the backyard. Nina pushed off with her foot, and the swing rocked backwards. 'Artoush didn't complain?'

I looked at the third ornamental tree – either Judas or Persian Turpentine or Ash – which had remained nameless for a while. After the locust attack, it sprouted again and had really flourished; now it was giving more blossoms than the Armineh and Arsineh trees.

I pushed off, and the swing seat rocked. 'Not only did he not complain, he was the one who suggested it.'

Nina leaned sideways toward me. 'You're kidding!'

The night before the wedding, when I was about to broach the topic of Mother being left all on her own after Alice left, Artoush asked, as he hung up his pants in the wardrobe, 'So when will Mother be moving in with us?'

Nina cracked up laughing. 'I, for one, can't figure out that husband of yours the least little bit! One minute a grouchy, grumpy crab, and the next minute, kinder than...' Garnik drove up and honked. Nina finished her sentence. 'But with your Mother's fussiness and her nagging, God help you.' Then she yelled, 'Sophie, come on. Your father's here.' She stood up and limped a few steps. 'Ouch, my foot's asleep.' She turned toward the kitchen window. 'Goodbye, Mrs. Voskanian.' Then she turned back to me and whispered. 'Maybe a teaspoonful of fussing and nagging may not be so bad for you, huh?'

I got up from the swing seat and walked her to the gate, thinking, 'One teaspoon or a bucketful?'

Mother poked her head out the window. 'Nina, where are you going? Stay for dinner. I made Red Pilaf.'

The twins and Sophie, dripping with sweat, ran up from the backyard and stood in front of us, jumping up and down.

They pleaded, 'Let Sophie stay with us!'

'Aunt Nina, please, pretty please, let Sophie stay with us.'

Sophie pleaded, 'Gee, I like Red Pilaf!'

Nina looked at the kids, then at me. 'Go ahead and take care of your shopping,' I ventured.

Nina looked at the kids again. 'What am I going to do with you little wiggle worms? You've been together for the last two nights; haven't you had enough?' Then she looked at Mother. 'I have a lot of souvenirs to buy to take to Tehran, and besides, your Red Pilaf is *perrr*fect.' Mother's Istanbuli Polow, or as Armenians called it, Red Pilaf, really was perfect.

I stood at the gate and waved to Garnik. Armen was still working on his bike. 'Still not fixed?' I inquired.

He shook his head. 'Bikes from the stone age can't be fixed in a jiffy.'

I pressed him on the point, 'You mean the stone age was last year?'

He looked at me and laughed. 'Last year was the stone age.' His hair was spilling over his forehead.

As I walked back through the yard, the twins came running out of the house. Armineh had a book in her hand. 'Mommy, will you read the last part of it for us?'

Arsineh reminded, 'You promised us you would read it!'

Sophie added, 'You promised yesterday, Auntie. A woman and her word!' They all laughed and the four of us squeezed onto the swing seat.

When I read the last page of *Little Lord Fauntleroy* and closed the book, Sophie said, 'That poor little boy!!'

'Why poor?' asked Arsineh.

Armineh reasoned, 'It all turns out well for him in the end.'

'Yes,' said Sophie, 'but he was very miserable at the beginning.'

The phone was ringing in the hallway. The twins and Sophie looked at Armen, and when they saw that he could not hear it, Armineh jumped up and ran into the house. Sophie said, 'Wait up,' and ran after Armineh. Arsineh, looking down at the cover of the book, said, 'I wish all stories could turn out well in the end.'

Armineh shouted from the front door, 'Armen, telephone! It's Jasmine.'

Sophie echoed her. 'Armen, telephone. Jasmine.'

Armen dropped his bike, ran up the path and disappeared inside.

I turned around to Arsineh. 'Jasmine?'

Arsineh pushed off with her foot, and the swing seat jerked back. She looked at me and laughed. 'Don't you remember? Cinderella!' Then she picked up the book, jumped down off the swing seat and ran after Armineh and Sophie, who were beckoning to her from the doorway.

Mother was calling after them in the hallway, 'Running in the house again with muddy shoes?!' Now from the outside, through the screen door, I saw her frail silhouette, with its white hair and black dress, sweeping the entryway. Having Mother live with us would surely be a big help. A big help, yes, but...

Mother brought out the little Persian carpet from the entryway and shook off the dust.

A gentle breeze was blowing, unusual for Abadan at that time of the year. I pushed off with my foot, and the swing seat rocked back. I was thinking about what clothes to bring and what souvenirs to take for our summer stay in Tehran, when a butterfly passed right in front of my face. A white one, with brown polka dots. As I was remarking how pretty it was, I saw another, and then another. Seven or eight of them in all alighted on the red rose bush.

'Butterflies migrate, too,' he had said.

I looked at the sky. It was blue. Not even a spot of cloud.

GLOSSARY

Places and proper names of people and foods that Anglophone readers would not generally find familiar are given in the text with capital letters, and briefly explained below. Most of the italicized words in the text are English words (or book and film titles), borrowed as such into Persian or Armenian, especially by people in Abadan working for the National Iranian Oil Company, which was British-run until 1951, and especially influenced by the English language.

Abadan, a city planned and built up around the oil refinery, which opened in 1913, after the British discovered oil at Masjed-Soleiman. The oil industry and the huge refinery dominated the economy, making Abadan into a company town. Abadan city was divided into neighborhoods or districts, with the factory workers generally living in a neighborhood just southeast of the refinery. Pirouzabad, on the northeast side of the airport, was for labor personnel. See also Bawarda and Braim, the neighborhoods that mostly appear in the story. The city, which is right across from the border with Iraq, and about twenty miles from Basra, suffered immense destruction during the Iran–Iraq war in the 1980s.

Adab School in Abadan was a private school, elementary through high school, for Armenians. The curriculum was partly in Persian and partly in Armenian, the Armenians being one of the few linguistic minorities in Iran (where Persian is the national language but Arabs, Azeris, Baluchis, Kurds, etc., speak a different mother tongue), allowed to run schools in their own language.

Ahmadabad, a neighborhood in Abadan to the northeast of Bawarda, largely for the poorer inhabitants.

Anoush, a 1912 opera by Armen Tigranian, inspired by Armenian folk music and based on the poem 'Anoush' (1892, by Hovhaness Toumanian, on whom see below). It is a central work in the Armenian musical repertoire, recounting the story of a village girl, Anoush, who falls in love with the shepherd, Saro. Anoush's brother, who has been humiliated in a wrestling match with Saro, kills him, leading Anoush to throw herself from a cliff. Quite apart from the character of the opera, in conversation the word *anoush* (said in response to a compliment to the chef or hostess), means, may the food nourish your soul.

April 24th Ceremonies, a day of mourning observed in commemoration of the victims of the Armenian genocide, the beginning of which is dated to 'Red Sunday' on 24 April 1915, when the Ottoman government in Istanbul rounded up and later executed some two to three hundred prominent

Armenians. This day is observed in Armenia, and by Armenians in diaspora, as Genocide Remembrance Day (estimates of the number of Armenians killed in Ottoman territory during 1915–1918 run anywhere from half a million to 1.5 million).

Armenian Revolutionary Federation, or ARF (Dashnaktsutyun) was an International Socialist Party formed in 1890 in Tiflis with the goals of national self-determination for the Armenian people (then subject to Ottoman rule), democracy, and social justice. It helped to establish the first Armenian Republic in 1918, but in 1920 it was disbanded by the Soviet Union and its leaders exiled, many of them coming to Iran. It continued to fight for Armenian independence.

Barev, Armenian for 'hello.' Armenians in Iran live in a bi-lingual, sometimes tri-lingual environment, with Persian being the standard language of wider communication, Armenian being the language of communication between Armenians in Iran, and English being a medium understood to some extent by many of the employees of the National Iranian Oil Company in Abadan.

Bawarda, a district or neighborhood of Abadan, where Clarice and Artoush live. It is the older central and southern part of Abadan. See also Braim.

Boupacha, Djamila. A young activist for the Armée de Libération Nationale in the Algerian war for independence against the French, who was arrested in 1960 and accused by the French of planting a bomb. She was tortured and brutally raped in detention. Simone de Beauvoir and other French intellectuals formed a committee to defend her and Djamila became a cause célèbre of French liberal opinion against the Algerian war.

Braim, a newer, chic neighborhood of Abadan, to the northwest of the refinery, and southeast of the airport. It was the part of the city where the English employees of the Anglo-Iranian Oil Company lived, before it was nationalized under Mossadegh in 1951, becoming the National Iranian Oil Company (N.I.O.C.). Braim was itself subdivided into Sehgoush Braim, Braim Village, Braim Estates, and the inhabitants of these various neighborhoods were segregated by their job 'Grade' and standing in the National Iranian Oil Company. Through the 1950s, employee housing was rented, and only for the duration of employment. But plans were made in 1959 so that employees could purchase homes from the Oil Company and continue to live in them after retirement.

Chelow Kebab, the traditional Persian grilled meat dish, usually lamb, served with white rice. In older culinary tradition, a raw egg yolk was served on top of the rice.

Cinema Rex was one of the larger cinemas in Abadan. In 1978, many years after the events of the novel, it was set on fire and burned to the ground, killing over 400 people, in one of the seminal events of the Iranian revolution.

Cinema Taj, one of the larger, modern and more fashionable cinemas in Abadan, between the city center and Bawarda. In the early 1960s, this cinema showed dubbed foreign films, American and European, almost exclusively.

Delon, Alain. The great French heart-throb actor of the 1960s and 70s, who enjoyed great popularity in Iran, as well. See also Schneider, Romy.

Döner Kebab, or 'Turkish Kebab' as it is known in Iran, thin slices of spit-roasted meat, usually lamb, similar to Gyros or Shawarma.

Ejmiatsin, a town to the west of Yerevan in Armenia (also spelled Echmiadzin), home to the Mother Cathedral of Holy Ejmiatsin, a church built circa 303 c.e. that remains the central seat of the Armenian Apostolic Church and the Chief Catholicos of all Armenians, who is the chief bishop, or pope, of the Armenian Church.

Farah Charitable Society (Anjoman-e khayriyye-ye Farah), a charitable organization dedicated to pre-school education of Iranian children and assistance to orphans. It was established by Farah Diba in 1960 after becoming queen consort of Mohammad-Reza Shah (it was his third marriage) in 1959, at the age of twenty. Many charities run by her office empha-sized bettering the situation of Iranian women.

Fesenjan, a tart Persian casserole dish made with ground walnuts and pomegranate paste, and nuggets of meat or poultry. Like other casseroles (*khoresht*, sometimes called 'stews'), it is usually served with rice/pilaf.

Gata, a kind of Armenian puff pastry; some are made with a sweet filling, whereas others are unsweetened, or 'salted.'

General Mode, a well-known department store in Tehran.

Ghormeh-sabzi, a traditional Iranian casserole, eaten with rice pilaf, containing sautéed chopped parsley and fenugreek, leeks, dehydrated lemons, kidney beans, and usually lamb. It is considered a dish for special occasions, often served to honored guests.

Golestan Club, a large club in Braim for Senior and Junior Grade employees of the National Iranian Oil Company.

Halva, a confection popular from the southern Mediterranean to South Asia. The name derives from Arabic. It comes in two forms: a semolina flour-based paste made with oil and sugar, saffron and sometimes with rosewater. A second type, made from tahini or nut butter and sugar, forms a crumbly loaf.

Ikra, Russian eggplant 'caviar,' a kind of dip or spread made out of pureed vegetables, using either eggplant or squash, along with onions, carrots, tomatoes, vegetable oil, and cayenne pepper.

Iran–Soviet Society, see VOKS.

Istanbuli Polow, or Estamboli Polow as pronounced in Persian, is a rice pilaf made with cubes of red meat, potatoes, tomato paste, and onions. In Armenian it is called 'Red Pilaf.'

Julfa, or New Julfa, a section or neighborhood of Isfahan where Armenians have lived in large numbers since the early

1600s. The Safavid Shah Abbas forcibly relocated them to his capital at Isfahan, having turned them into laborers as the result of an Iranian military victory in Armenia. There are many pre-modern Armenian churches still in use in this neighborhood.

Kebab, see Chelow Kebab and Döner Kebab, above.

Khorramshahr, a major port city about ten kilometers north of Abadan, at the confluence of the Shatt al-Arab (through which the Tigris and Euphrates empty into the Persian Gulf) and the Karun rivers. Formerly called Mohammereh, a diversionary channel of the Karun river was dug here a millennium ago, creating the Bahmanshir and the man-made Haffar branches of the Karun, between which sits the island of Abadan, and Abadan city.

Lavash, a flat, thin unleavened bread made of flour, water and salt, and traditionally slapped on the wall of a clay oven to bake. It is popular in Iran, Turkey, Armenia, and Georgia, and can be stored by rolling, when moist. When dried it has the consistency of a thin cracker.

Lubia Polow, a traditional Persian pilaf dish of rice mixed with green beans, often with red meat, flavoured with a tomato sauce with onions, cinnamon, and saffron.

Lusaber (Armenian for 'Light-bringer'), the name of a monthly Armenian-language children's magazine published for the Armenians in Iran.

Maash Polow, a mung bean pilaf, with tomatoes, onions, saffron, and other subtle spices.

Majles, the Parliament, established by the first Iranian revolution of 1906–1911 as a constitutional check on the power of the Qajar Monarch. In 1963 the Majles approved a law granting Iranian women the right to vote (see the Six Reform Bills).

Masjed-Soleiman, city northeast of Abadan in the province of Khuzestan. The British first discovered oil in this ancient Iranian city in 1913.

Mashhad, a large city in the northeast of Iran and a center of pilgrimage for Shiite Muslims as the shrine and burial place of Imam Reza, the eighth Imam of Twelver Shiism.

Naft Club, a club with an open-air cinema, located near the Annex Restaurant, north of the city center of Abadan.

Namagerd is one of the rural Armenian farming villages in Peria (Fereydan), to the west of Isfahan, a district where in the seventeenth century Georgian and Armenian farmers were forcibly relocated to help revive the Safavid agrarian economy.

Nazouk, an Armenian butter pastry.

Norouz is the Persian new year, a big national and largely secular holiday occurring at the Spring Equinox.

Oil Company, the National Iranian Oil Company (N.I.O.C) dominated the city of Abadan, the refinery of which was one of the world's largest. The company was established by the British in 1908 as the Anglo-Persian Oil Company, rechristened Anglo-Iranian Oil Company (it is now British Petroleum), before it was nationalized in the early 1950s under Prime Minister Mohammad Mossadegh (deposed by an American and British covert operation in 1953) as the National Iranian Oil Company. After nationalization, N.I.O.C. subcontracted to American and European companies to help refine the oil.

Parinj, explained in the text in Chapter 44.

Perok, an Armenian fruit glaze pastry.

Piroshki, a deep-fried bun with a meat, vegetable, or sweet filling, popular in Iran through the influence of Russian cuisine (similar to a donut).

Pirouzabad, see Abadan.

Polow, pilaf (the English word comes from the Persian, via British India) a general term for Persian rice dishes, either cooked together with vegetables or other ingredients and eaten as a main entrée, or eaten plain with a casserole (khoresht), or curry.

Red Pilaf, see 'Istanbuli Polow,' above.

SAVAK, Iran's secret police, the National Intelligence and Security Organization, established with the help of the CIA in 1957 and widely feared for its torture of political dissidents and activists.

Sayat Nova, the eighteenth-century national poet-singer (*ashik*) of Armenia, who composed in Azeri Turkish, Armenian, and other languages, using the Georgian alphabet.

Schneider, Romy, the Austrian actress. She married Alain Delon in 1959, only to part ways, amicably, in 1963.

Senior Grade, an English term borrowed into Persian by the Iranian National Oil Company, which hired engineers and doctors at *Senior Grade*, and other educated employees at the lesser rank of *Junior Grade*. Ordinary workers ranked below both these '*Grades*.'

Shatt al-Arab, a waterway formed by the confluence of the Tigris and Euphrates rivers before they flow into the Persian Gulf. In the twentieth century, it became the international border separating Iran, specifically the province of Khuzestan, from Iraq.

Sherbet, a cold refreshing sweet drink made from fruit juice or fruit syrup, similar to lemonade, but made in various flavors, such as rosewater, sour cherry, plum, etc.

Shad-shad lav, Armenian for 'very well, very good.'

Six Reform Bills were a series of initiatives introduced to the Majles (Iranian Parliament) by Mohammad-Reza Shah Pahlavi as part of his 'White Revolution.' The first six reforms were submitted to a popular referendum and approved in January 1963 (the novel takes place in the spring of 1962). These included expropriation of lands from feudal lords to make them available to sharecroppers for purchase below market value, thus enabling sharecroppers to become small landowners; nationalization of forests and pasturelands; privatization of government-owned factories; awarding factory workers a 20 percent share in profits; formation of a national literacy corps; and women's suffrage.

Tabriz, a large city in the northwest of Iran, in the province of Iranian Azerbaijan, that has had a sizeable Armenian enclave since the Mongol invasions.

Tahdig, literally 'bottom of the pot' in Persian, a thin layer of bread or potatoes cooked to a crisp at the bottom of a pot of rice, and considered the most delectable portion of the rice.

Torshi, an Iranian condiment (literally sour stuff) of assorted pickled vegetables, usually eaten with rice pilaf or sometimes with bread, as an appetizer.

Toumanian, Hovhaness, poet from the Lori region of Armenia (1869–1923), known as 'the Poet of All Armenians' (on the paradigm of Catholicos of All Armenians).

Van, a city in Anatolia, present-day Turkey, where Armenians have lived since antiquity. During the genocide, the Armenians of Van, then a part of the Ottoman Empire, organized armed resistance against the Ottoman army after Armenians had been slaughtered in other cities of the Ottoman Empire.

Vigen (Vigen Derderian, 1929–2003), a widely popular Iranian singer of Armenian background. He introduced original pop songs along western lines into the Persian language, and also starred in several movies in the 1950s and 1960s. His tall good looks and his career as an actor and singer earned him the title of the Sultan of Pop, and 'the Elvis Presley of Iran.'

VOKS, the Russian acronym for the Society for Cultural Relations with Foreign Countries, an organization created by the government of the Soviet Union to promote cultural exchange, and, it was sometime alleged, communist propaganda.